ON THE

SEVENTH

DAY

BY

MARK WILSON

Copyright

This book is a work of fiction. Names, characters, places and incidents are either the product of the author's imagination or are used fictitiously. Any resemblance to real persons, alive or dead, is coincidental and not intended by the author.

First print, 2015

ISBN-13: 978-1517457648

ISBN-10: 1517457645

www.facebook.com/markwilsonbooks

www.markwilsonbooks.com

Follow on Twitter: @bellshillwilson

Dedication

For Mum, who brought me into the world and saved me from its darkest part.

Acknowledgements

My editor/proof-reader, Stephanie Dagg. Steph is a wonder and I wouldn't print a book without her input.

Thanks to my test-readers Derek Graham, Louise MacDonald, Tracy Stewart, Barbara Wilkie, Tom Bater, Phil Jones, Chris King, Zoe Greenan and Allie McKellar.

Very special thanks to Jayne Doherty and Gayle Karabelen for their continued support of my writing career and to Michelle Ruedin for her insights and enthusiasm for the project.

Special thanks also to Ryan Bracha whose support, as well as his consistently brilliant writing, pushes me to develop and to never want a comfort zone.

Thanks also to Frank Turner and BMG/ Chrysalis Ltd for kindly allowing me to quote lyrics from the track *The Next Storm*, taken from Frank's wonderfully emotive album, *Positive songs for Negative People*.

Finally, a massive thanks to Chris Pillans and Garry Crawford for trusting me with their names.

A huge thank you, as always, to my wife Natalie Wilson for unwavering encouragement and support. I wouldn't have written a word without your belief in me.

Foreword

On the Seventh Day is intended as a satire, as entertainment and as a social commentary.

No offence is intended to anyone of any religion. I fully respect the rights of every person to believe whatever they wish to without judgement.

Please enjoy the following novel in the spirit in which it was written.

Mark Wilson

September 28th, 2015

PS: God thinks you're a cunt.

"We lost faith in the omens,
We lost faith in the gods,
We just ended up clutching at the empty rituals
Like gamblers clutching long odds.
And I don't care what the weather man is saying,
Because the last time that I saw him he was on his knees, he was praying.
The preachers and the scientists got soaked just the same,
And we wondered if they'd ever get dry again."

Lyrics from *The Next Storm*, by Frank Turner. Taken from the album, *Positive Songs for Negative People,* published by BMG / Chrysalis Ltd. Reprinted with permission.

"Oh, but I wouldn't want to. I wouldn't want to get in on His terms. They're wrong."

- **Stephen Fry, speaking to Gay Byrne**

Saturday

1

Nick

NICK TOOK IN THE ROOM, his top lip curling into a sneer. It was just *his* kind of place, all thin veneer, expensive wines and whiskeys, and coke in the bathrooms. Ordering a gin and tonic for himself and a double Auchentoshan for Stewart, Nick slipped his smartphone from his pocket and reminded himself of a few key details in his notes.

Ten years at Level Two.

Four years at Level Three.

Further education programme complete.

Dedicated and enthusiastic approach demonstrated consistently by the candidate.

All phases of training complete.

Recommend promotion to Level One.

Nick didn't really need to read the notes as he had committed the candidate's details to memory, but it comforted him to read the words, settled his nerves. The gin helped also. She was ready, no doubt about it, but Stewart had the final say, and he'd take some convincing despite the candidate's exemplary performance. He always did need convincing, but particularly when the candidate was a woman.

Spotting Stewart passing the restaurant window Nick took a belt from his gin and relaxed his face into business mode, ridding it of any signs of anxiousness or enthusiasm. Stewart was best approached calmly.

Never one to make an understated entrance, Stewart crashed through the doors, barking loudly at the Maître D who'd rushed to greet him, reaching for his jacket.

"Get tae fuck, son. Make yourself useful and bring me a double Macallan '39."

Stewart strode around the bar to the rear left corner of the room. Hair, long, curled, blond and mulleted, dressed in denims, expensive cowboy boots, leather jacket — unzipped to show the art of his T-shirt, a nun fingering herself and the legend *Jesus is a cunt* — Stewart looked like an expensively-dressed redneck. His accent was all Lanarkshire.

That fucking accent.

He yanked the seat back and snorted loudly, into his nose. The gurgling, crackling movement of thick phlegm being dragged from his nostrils into his mouth threatened to break Nick's composure before a word had passed between them.

Grabbing the back of his heavy, leather-padded chair, Stewart screeched it a few feet away from the table. Nick watched as his boss flicked his eyes up to drill into his own. As Stewart's eyes danced with cruel amusement, he let a long tail of yellow-green gunge slide from his lips into the glass of Auchentoshan on the table.

Watching the deposit bob and eddy around for a second, he took his chair, shoving the glass over to Nick.

"Get that shite off the table, Nick. Fuck sake."

The Maître D arrived with Stewart's Macallan swirling in a heavy-bottomed glass and an ice bucket on a silver tray.

Unacknowledged he silently slid the drink and the ice within reach of Stewart, who snatched the glass up and drained its contents.

Stewart slammed the glass onto the table-top.

"Keep them coming," he said.

Nick nodded at the Auchentoshan-nasal deposit mixture, which the Maître D scooped up. "I'd have drunk that, Stewart."

"Fuck all stopping ye, son," Stewart said, fishing his lighter and cigarettes from his jacket pocket. He scanned Nick's face, waiting for a come-back. None came.

Nick watched as Stewart went through the little series of gestures and rituals he performed when having a cigarette. Tap the end on the table, smooth the filter and rotate it on moist lips for a second. He caught sight of the upside-down *lucky fag* in the packet as Stewart tapped and licked his chosen tab.

"No smoking in here, Stewart."

"What they gonnae dae?" he asked, touching the petrol flame to the end of his cigarette.

Nick sighed. "Do we have to do this again?"

Stewart's eyebrow lifted as he considered whether or not he could be bothered winding the cunt up. Finally, he cocked his head a little to the side in acquiescence.

"Look, Nick. These cunts in here won't say a word, I guarantee it."

Nick gave him a nod.

"Fine," he said, happy that his boss would take care of the smoking issue discreetly for once.

Taking a long drag on his first Regal King-Size, Stewart regarded Nick, amusement dragging the corners of his mouth into a tight, snide grin.

"Where is this cow, then?" Stewart asked, enjoying Nick's discomfort.

Very quickly, Nick's face shifted from discomfort to flushed anger.

"Christ sake, Stewart. Give her a chance." Sick of the same old shit, the tired routine, he spat the words across the table.

Stewart blew a cloud of swirling, blue-hazed smoke out of the side of his mouth, face rigid with anger of his own.

"Who the fuck are you talking to, Nicholas?"

Nick knew that he should back down. When Stewart got like this, there was little chance of shifting his mind on something. They'd worked together for more years than Nick could recall. Nick training the candidates, tutoring them to develop the skills and mind-set needed to be promoted, to earn a place upstairs with Stewart's team. Stewart taking the credit when presenting a new *graduate* to his staff.

Christ, it was gruelling and thankless, but without Nick and his department, Stewart would take only those he considered the very best. The people of a certain station and type. He'd always been an elitist prick, but Stewart had got worse, more prejudiced with age. His expectations and list of demands for the attributes a successful candidate must possess had become almost impossible to fulfil. Still, that was the point: Stewart wanted Nick's department fucked, once and for all, leaving him free to decide for himself the criteria for promotion.

Given his own way, Stewart would pass over so many candidates who'd never have the opportunity to work, develop or improve themselves to the required level.

This was the reason for Nick's department and the reason he took so much shit from Stewart. If not him, then who? Nobody else could take working in effective opposition to Stewart. It helped that they were best friends and had been their whole lives... out of office hours, at any rate.

Nick's stomach lurched as Stewart glared across the table at him. His apology forming in his vocal cords, Nick pushed it back and listened to the wee part of himself that had won him his department in the first place.

"I'm talking to you, Stewart. Back the fuck off."

Stewart's eyebrows creased in the centre; his scowl brought ice to Nick's heart. *Fuck. Wrong choice.*

Standing, Stewart's eyes widened in fury. His eyes tore the air between them, smoke shooting through his nostrils.

"You remember who I am and who the fuck you are." Stewart stabbed at Nick's chest, his strong finger digging deep into the flesh. "You're a fucking cog, son. A bureaucrat. By fuck, you're practically my damned secretary. You should be under this table with your overactive lips on my cock. It's about all you're good for."

Shocked into silence, Nick assessed his options for a moment as Stewart glared over the table at him. Relaxing his shoulders, Nick decided to push his luck.

"Yes, well you'd know better than I the qualities in possession of a skilled oralist."

A beat passed. Stewart's expression melted.

"Aye, you're right there, Nick." He laughed, all anger gone.

Stewart nodded over at the waiter who was making his way to the table.

"Might make that one give me a blowy just now."

Nick peered across the room, assessing the man.

"He's a bit lardy for your tastes, is he not?"

Stewart shrugged.

"Aye, but he's a good height. Big laddies like that have always a grand big boaby on them. Who gives a fuck if he's carrying a bit ay timber round the waist?"

Exasperated, Nick shook his head. Stewart had been having a *gay phase* for years now, which was fine, but recently he'd been a bit too obsessed with girth and length. *Pushing ma boundaries, son,* he'd said. Nick reckoned that acting the size queen was beneath his boss, but figured that his temporary obsession with big dicks was an improvement from the *heroin phase* Stewart had thrown himself into some years earlier. The boss got Catholic as fuck on the smack; he was more balanced on the cock.

Stewart could have this coked-up big laddie on his knees under the table, his balls resting on the waiter's chin in two minutes... easy. Such was the power of his persuasion, wealth and status. Just last week he'd had a six-foot-nine England International gobbling him as he ate at the Twickenham Social Club, interviewing another candidate. The poor bastard left the restaurant, Stewart's spunk still to hit his stomach, wondering how the fuck he'd ended up noshing the old man in full view of the entire restaurant as Stewart sucked back oysters, muttering the odd instruction as he consigned the candidate in front of him to another stint on Level Two.

If Stewart decided he wanted something, it happened. Simple as that.

"Leave him, Stewart. We've better things to do," Nick said, nodding at the woman making her way to their table.

Stewart grunted non-committedly, assessed the waiter for a full, uncomfortable second, and then waved the lad away.

"Just more drinks, son. We'll order in half an hour," he said.

The red-haired woman, impeccable suit, hair tight in a bun, heels like stilts, walked elegantly towards them. She had dressed perfectly and displayed all the physical cues and mannerisms Nick had spent so many hours teaching her. *A good start.*

∞∞∞

Taking the blond man's hand, I smile at him broadly and look deep into his eyes. Nick warned me of the effect his eyes and voice would have on me, and he's right. The eyes are lagoon-blue; warm and hard at once, they search your soul and pull you into his influence which seems to fill the room. His voice is seductively brutal as he welcomes me gruffly. I feel my pulse race and I remind myself of Nick's words. *Everything depends on this man's decision. You'll have perhaps five minutes, maybe ten maximum.* I steel myself.

I take a moment to flip through the various buzzwords and phrases we've practiced. Despite *him, his* presence and the overwhelming desire to flee, the nerves aren't showing. The burns from the ligatures on my wrists and ankles and the gouges in my thigh sharpen my focus and keep me in the moment.

I almost feel proud of myself, but catch the stray thought. No pride. He hates pride and arrogance. Nick pulls a chair for me. I look to *him* for permission. Without looking at me, he makes an offhand gesture that I should sit and lights his next cigarette from the smouldering butt of the last.

Pulling myself towards the table, I remind myself to sit straight, to look him directly in the eye at all times and to never, ever forget that *he* will decide what future I'll have.

∞∞∞

She was doing well so far, remembering all the little mannerisms he'd taught her. She'd displayed contrition, enthusiasm, respect and confidence, all in the first thirty seconds of meeting Stewart. She'd dressed well, blue-grey business suit, not too prissy, not too slutty. She carried herself well, in control, professional but hungry to work. A poppy-seed-sized speck of hope began to germinate. The last seven had been total failures, sent back downstairs within three minutes of meeting the boss. It had been a prolonged bad run, one that would fuel Stewart's justification for having Nick's department buried. He needed a win here tonight. So far Stewart seemed to have decided to consider the girl.

Stewart took a long draw on a Regal, eyeballing her as he inhaled. Nick clenched his arse cheeks, recognising Stewart's *let's bury this bitch* face.

"Mary. How do expect to make it to Level One when you're such a fucking heartless little bitch?"

Stewart's voice was gentle, kind even. He genuinely wanted to know.

To her credit, Mary didn't flinch.

"Sir, I know the mistakes I've made and I've work..."

"Piiiiiish!" Stewart bellowed at the top of his voice. The waiter looked over, but checked away instantly not wishing to offend the spending customer.

Stewart jabbed a finger at Mary. "That's a load ay pish, hen, and ye fuckin' know it."

Softening his face, the kindly uncle-figure emerged and he placed a hand gently on Mary's, which rested on the table.

"Look, Mary hen. Work isn't an excuse to leave yer weans in a fucking nursery all day. Or impose upon your poor fuckin' parents. Sixty-eight years old and worked every day of their miserable lives, just at the point where they can fuck off tae a tiny villa on the coast of whichever slightly sunny shitehole they can still afford after spunking their money on you and your siblings over thirty years. And you? You have the fuckin' cruelty in you to land them with a screaming, shitey-arsed infant so you can develop your career?" Stewart makes quote marks with his fingers in the air. "That's cold as fuck, hen."

Nick barely manages to keep his expression neutral. He's certain that Mary will snap and give the usual justifications.

Providing for my child.

Working every hour spare to have a better future.

My parents support me, they raised an educated woman for a reason.

Single mothers working hard enough for two parents.

Stewart would tear through that bullshit in the blink of a Jap's eye. She was fucked if she bit back.

Mary nodded respectfully at Stewart. "You're absolutely right, sir. I made far too many mistakes. I really believed with all of my heart that my son would benefit from a strong mother, who provided for him and gave him a hard-working, determined and courageous role-model. I truly believed that."

Mary bowed her head in a genuinely contemplative, penitent gesture.

"My son did well for himself; he's a lawyer, pro-bono. He helps so many people. We... we were close, but he lives so far away now. I guess we just sort of got used to being separate."

Stewart nodded along as she spoke.

"My kid, I'm so proud of him. He's a great father, never puts anything before his kids."

Stewart leaned back, tugging hard on his cig. Blowing the smoke across the table, he winked at Nick.

"You don't deserve this chance. You're a selfish little bitch whose only contribution to life has been a nice pair of heels, punctuality and a fucking clean house. Your kid has learned how *not* to be a parent from you, Mary. That's the fuckin' truth of it."

All pretence of nonchalance was gone from Nick's face and his body language. This was the fatal blow that Stewart delivered to propel each candidate to anger. Make them feel hard done by. Reveal any lingering pride or false justifications they hid behind and force them to show their true colours.

Nick was unashamedly desperate for Mary to take the hit, to accept that Stewart was an unmatched cunt of epic proportions, but that he was the gateway. And that ultimately the cunt was right.

She needed to forgive herself and swallow back on any injustice she felt. She needed desperately to forgive herself for something she considered to be a good choice when she'd made it. She needed to forgive *him* for dragging her painfully over the sword she'd forged in her own lifetime.

Mary closed her eyes taking the long seconds she needed to compose herself. Nick sagged in his seat, waiting for the usual outburst. The rant, the litany of excuses and justifications and outrages that candidates resorted to. Stewart sipped on his Macallan and fought to hide a grin.

Mary... Mary simply opened her eyes and spoke softly. Her voice was small but strong, firm but respectful. Like an Angel's. All of Nick's lessons were meaningless in this moment.

"I know. I don't deserve the glory of your Kingdom, my Lord. But I forgive myself for the mistakes I've made. I accept who I am and I see you for the absent parent of a Creator that you are and forgive you for that also. All mistakes are my own. All pain, deserved. Do with me as you will."

Nick's heart sang.

Stewart downed a double Macallan and scowled. Mary simply bowed her head, closed her eyes and spread her arms in acceptance of His judgement.

Mary vanished in a startling cacophony of light, her entire being swept and propelled upwards, bathed in heavenly radiance and warmth.

"You're a fucking jammy cunt, Nick," Stewart spat across the table.

Nick's mouth hung open in disbelief but only for a beat.

"Yes, well. Even our heavenly Creator has a bad day every once in a while, Stewart."

Business mode vanished and Stewart's face stretched into a wide, self-satisfied grin.

"Where'd you find her? How'd you pull that off, ya snidey basturd?"

Nick shrugged.

"You know how it goes. They come to me down in Sheol, angry, disillusioned, indignant and in disbelief of a God who could be so cruel. So heartless. I torture and burn and brutalise them. I force them to relive each and every cruelty. I teach them to forgive you for being an uncaring God. An almighty deity who allows suffering and persecution and hate and disease to run rampant through the human race."

Stewart glared at his adversary and best friend.

"You magnify my glory by sending me pure souls, more able to embrace the grand experiment I've set in motion."

Nick regarded his Creator. The being who'd created him, and set him as his adversary after he'd argued that the humans had the capacity to long, strive and reach for Heaven. After he'd convinced the Almighty that humankind were out of nature, capable of attaining the spiritual heights of the very Angels *He* had fashioned in His own image.

Stewart's face began to shine with the radiance that all of His Angels, even the fallen ones, craved... required to sustain themselves.

"Light-Bringer... Nick. You were the most diligent of my Angels, my most trusted friend... and then you fell in love with the humans. What a fuckin' wasted career you've had, son."

Nick regarded the drink in his hand for several moments, then leaned across the table. Taking his best friend's hand he whispered quietly.

"My Lord, I will be your opponent until the legions of souls in Hell are elevated to Heaven. Until I can teach each of the souls who come to me that the path to glory is forgiveness. Forgiveness of your callous disregard of their spirituality and capacity for greatness. Forgiveness for the rape, torture, genocide and hate that you allow to proliferate because you think the humans beasts, like each of those you created to prowl and slither and scutter across the earth.

"They are not. They have transcended you and the need for the idea of you. Each and every soul I send to you magnifies your greatness. I will send a torrent of eligible souls to you. I will empty Hell and increase your glory."

Stewart lit another Regal King-Size and eyed his eternal adversary and best friend.

"Fancy the calamari, Nicky?" He asked.

Nick grinned. "I do, chief. I do."

∞∞∞

Nick sat back into the padded leather armchair set in the lounge of the gentlemen's club they'd moved to after eating. He hated this sort of place, so archaic, but Stewart favoured the range of whiskeys they stocked in the bar. Despite the earlier interview and Nick's little victory, they'd had a cracking night. It'd been centuries since they'd laughed so easily in each other's company. It felt like old times, back before Nick had taken on his current role.

Despite the moment, Nick scanned his friend's face and decided to break the spell.

"When will it end, Stewart?" he asked.

"What?"

"Your petty need to deny that humans are out of nature. That they *are* spiritual entities."

"For fuck sake, Nick. Again?" Stewart asked.

"Always," Nick replied.

Stewart bit back on his growing anger, leaned across the little table between them and asked simply, "You've given yourself over to serving them for eternity, old friend. Why do you love them so much?"

"Why *don't* you?" Nick asked.

"They're just animals, Nick. They have their place in this world, in nature, not with us."

"I've disproved that many times."

"No, you haven't," Stewart snapped. "You've sent me a fraction of *souls* from all the humans who've ever existed. These are simply rare abhorrents amongst the species. They are what I created them to be."

"I'll never accept that, Stewart." Nick drained his glass.

"Just look at how they behave, how they treat each other and the planet I gave them. They're pushing their luck, Nick," Stewart said.

Screeching his heavy chair back, Nick stood.

"Fuck this. I'm done with this tonight."

Nick left without looking back at his friend, boss and Creator who had begun to work himself up into a fury and was making His way towards the unfortunate barman who would bear the brunt of His anger.

Nick stepped out into the street, changed his mind about heading home and went in search of a late-night bar. He didn't have to walk far: you never did in these northern towns. Nick paused at the doorway of the first pub he encountered, made a decision, then entered. He felt his shoes attach to the tacky floor as he crossed to the bar.

The barmaid wiped the rim of a glass with a filthy towel and smiled. "What you after?" she asked.

Nick nodded at a tap. "Pint of Carling and a double Bushmills please, love."

Fetching a glass, she pulled on the lever he'd indicated, sending foaming, amber liquid swirling into the glass.

"Tough day?"

Nick grinned humourlessly. "Tough eternity, darlin'," he replied. She looked at him quizzically for a moment, before fetching his whiskey.

An urge to unburden himself and vent to this stranger came over him. This often happened to him in bars. Nick looked around the place. Aside from a semi-conscious drunk, the place was dead. The barmaid plonked his pint and short on a sodden beermat next to his hand.

"Take one for yourself, love, and come join me," he told her. "I'll tell you all about it."

She smiled at him and looked around the empty room.

"So long as you're paying, I'm listening," she said.

Nick smiled sadly. "Might take a while..."

"Beth," she said.

Nick nodded. "I'm Nick. Might take a while, Beth."

Regarding him, Beth took in his appearance, decided that he looked interesting enough or perhaps that he had deep pockets, judging by his expensive suit, and reached for a bottle of Grey Goose. Placing it onto the counter she leaned onto the wooden surface and clinked the ice and vodka around the glass.

"Fire away, Nick."

2

Jay and Mo

MO TOOK A LONG DRAG ON THE joint then passed it to Jay without missing a beat of the game flickering on the screen in front of them. As Jay's eyes flicked between the handover and the screen, Mo pressed his trigger, yelling, "Fuck take it," at the screen.

Jay mishandled the joint, allowing it to slip through his fingers and sizzle onto his right leg.

"Fuck sake, Mo," he squealed, rushing to his feet, patting at his leg. Snatching the joint up before it scorched the carpet, Jay shot a look at his best friend.

"Dick move," he said, jutting his chin at the screen which showed an image of his character facing the camera with a bullet hole in his forehead.

Mo shrugged. "So what? Should've seen it coming, dude."

"Fuckin' good trousers on here an' all," Jay whined.

Mo hissed through his teeth in derision. "No loss there, Jay. Those combat trousers are fuckin' tragic, son." His braying laughter brought a scowl to Jay's face, replacing the indignation.

"Aye, very good," Jay replied, "says the man sitting there in a shitty Hebrew robe and sandals."

Mo shrugged again and motioned for Jay to pass him the joint. "They're comfy, mate," he said.

Jay tossed the joint at his chest, laughing as his friend swatted at it, sending embers scattering across the carpet.

"Fuck sake. My mum made this for me, you prick."

"Should've binned it years ago, Mo. It's rancid."

Mo eyed his friend for a moment before waving him away with a backhand gesture.

"Yeah, well, doesn't change the fact that you're seven kills behind, lad," Mo said.

Jay nodded, conceding.

"That fucking music is putting me off." Jay poked a finger at the large speaker present in their office — in every office and corridor, as it happened. Paolo Nutini singing 'Caledonia' on repeat… for eternity.

Mo laughed. "Fuck off, you should be used to that shit by now. Your old man has been piping that through here for three years now."

Jay nodded. "Better than the previous ten years of Del-a-fuckin-Mitri."

Mo shivered at the memory.

""Nother game?" he asked.

Taking a long drag on the butt of the joint, Mo grinned.

Yeah, mate…"

The follow-up insult didn't come. Instead, Mo's eyes widened and his face froze as he looked past Jay out into the corridor.

Jay's eyes closed and his heart lurched in his chest.

Fuck.

Only one person could elicit the look of fear currently painted on Mo's face.

Turning to meet the storm sweeping along the corridor, Jay took in His appearance.

Scowling.

Belligerent.

Determined.

Drunk.

The man in charge strode towards them, barking at a middle manager to get the fuck out His way.

Entering the room, He radiated rage. Pure malice was His cloak. He swept His furious blue eyes around their office, taking in the empty Stella cans, Dorito packets and roach-filled ashtray. His eyes bore into Mo: he'd never liked Mo much, not after that Sinai thing.

Jay stepped between them and attempted a friendly smile.

"Hi, Dad. How was dinner with Ni—"

"Fuck off, arsehole," Stewart spat.

Shoving his son roughly aside he poked a stubby middle finger at Mo.

"You. Hipster-cuntface."

You will insist on keeping the beard, Mo, Jay thought, wincing.

"Yessir?" Mo whimpered.

"Get me a fuckin' joint rolled."

Mo produced a fat, ready-rolled joint from his robes and took a step towards Stewart, whose eyes flashed ever more intensely. Taking a step back, Mo fished his lighter from a pocket, lit the joint — careful to not moisten the end — and passed it to Stewart, who continued to glower at him.

The friends waited as Stewart took a monumentally long drag on the reefer, hoping against the evidence of previous experience that the marijuana would calm Him, at least a little. Closing his eyes, Stewart exhaled for what seemed like five full minutes, filling the corner office with blue smoke.

Turning to face His son, Stewart opened His still-blazing eyes, fixing them on Jay's face. He made a gesture indicating that Mo should stand beside Jay, whilst He took another long toke on the joint. Angry as ever, He blew a vicious twin jet of smoke through His nostrils.

"They're done," Stewart said, spitting the words through the haze of smoke between Him and the friends.

Jay's heart sank. He knew who and what his father referred to and intended, but had to ask anyway. Swallowing hard, he spoke.

"Who? What's happened, Dad?"

Stewart's face twisted as He regarded His son.

"Those cunts." Stewart gestured at the wall, causing a large image of Earth from space to appear. "They've fuckin' had their chance," He spat. "Get that cunt Azrael in here. Now."

Mo disappeared through the doorway, to return a few seconds later.

"She's on her way, sir," he said to Stewart, who didn't acknowledge him.

Concern and dread etched on his face, Jay took a step towards his father. Standing at an identical six-four and with the same blue eyes, Jay was a mirror image of his father, aside from his own dark hair where Stewart had blond, but the two couldn't have been more different in temperament or personality.

Where Stewart was active, forceful, arrogant, Jay was passive, a calming breeze, humble. Where Stewart spat and swore and railed, Jay negotiated and pacified. Stewart expected and saw the worst in all His creations, constantly demanding that they improve... evolve. Jay was truly humble, in awe of his father's creations and in love with the living universe.

"Dad. Tell me what's happened."

Stewart's face darkened. His voice a growling whisper, He spoke.

"The same thing that's always happened and always will. Those fuckin' animals down there."

Stewart flicked his hand and the wall-screen began scrolling through images of war, children living in sewer pipes, mass graves, a Jihadist exploding in crowded streets, Christians *curing* gays with torture.

"That shite: war, famine, corporate greed, political corruption, religious persecution, basturdin' greed and vanity. *Why doesn't God help the poor?* While ten percent of them sit in luxury and the rest starve. *How can God let cancer exist? God's punishment on the gays?* They'll take no responsibility for themselves and attack each other using me as their totem.

"The whole while, yer good pal Nick keeps educating them in his Hell, sending the cunts up here for an eternity in my light, as though their entire fuckin' species isn't the most base of all creatures shat into the universe."

Stewart glared at His son, daring him to defend the humans.

"And you, fanny-baws. You and yer useless fuckin' pal there." He nodded at Mo. "Ye both had yer chance to straighten those cunts down there out. You, hipster-cunt."

Mo stepped forward, answering immediately to His new name for him. Not daring to look into Stewart's eyes, he bowed his head and stared at the carpet.

"You promised to lead your people to the Holy Land I provided. To teach them my ways, and to make those Hebrew bastards of yours worthy of being called my people."

Mo trembled.

"My lord..."

"Shut the fuck up," Stewart bellowed. Stepping forward a pace, He dipped his head to look at Mo's face which was still pointed at the carpet. Turning His attention to Jay, Stewart nodded sharply to Mo.

"Is he fuckin' greetin'?"

Jay nodded once.

"Well, fuck me. This cheeky prick had the audacity to go to his people with Ten Commandments carved into stone that he made up for himself after deciding that my single commandment wasn't fuckin' good enough for him and his people, and he's got the fuckin' impudence to kneel here crying now?" Stewart pulled at Mo's hair by the top-knot. "You weren't half so upset when you fucked me over on that occasion, were you, smart-arse?"

Mo shook his head. Tears burned tracks along his cheeks.

"What did I tell you? What was it you were supposed to share?"

Mo stuttered and wept for a few seconds trying desperately to swallow his fear and reply to Him.

"DON'T BE A fuckin' CUNT!" Stewart roared into Mo's ear, flecking it with spit. "That's it. Four words. Don't. Be. A fuckin'. Cunt! But no, spoiled basturd Moses lived in a bastardin' palace, thinks he knows better than I. Down he came with his ten.

"Don't covet yer fuckin' neighbour's sister's fuckin' goat and all that shite."

Mo was on his knees at Stewart's feet, a puddle of salty tears forming.

Jay fought the urge to point out his dad had just used five words.

"Why?" Stewart said, lowering his voice menacingly. "Cos you fuckin' shat yerself that my word wasn't impressive enough for a bunch of sandal-and-robe-wearing sheep-shaggers starving in the desert?" Stewart glowered down at the back of Mo's head, daring him to raise his head or argue.

Turning His attention back to Jay, Stewart returned to shouting.

"And you. You had the same message to spread, the same four simple basturdin' words. You had my living essence, my power flowing through you, Son of fuckin' God. You still fucked it." Stewart flicked

His cigarette butt at Jay, hitting him above the right eye. Ignoring the burning sting, Jay stared straight ahead at his father, giving Him his full attention.

"Aye, you did a better job of it than this wanker," Stewart continued, "but you let those fucking Roman inbreds down there string you up. You let them make you the dying god on the wood that they'd made up back when they were still fuckin' apes to justify their own flaws and deeds. You let every fuckin' pseudo-Holy-Cunt since then point at your sacrifice to excuse and absolve themselves of horrendous deeds.

"You were supposed to lead those cunts, hammer the bastards hard, show them my fuckin' word; not die for them. Did you really believe that your *sacrifice,*" Stewart made wee finger quotes in the air, "would convince them to believe in your message, to live a better life?"

Jay lowered his eyes, not due to fear of Him but to choke back on the growing need to argue, to justify.

"There's barely a war been waged since where that fuckin' cross of yours hasn't been flashed around to justify it first." Stewart punctuated his words with a jab of his index finger either at the screen or into Jay's chest.

Feeling uncharacteristic anger cresting in him, Jay asked, "What about Hammy? His lot have been just as bad. When's he getting hauled in here?"

The moment the question escaped his lips, Jay regretted it.

"Fuckin' leave Hammy out of it," Stewart spat. "Fuckin Islam has its issues, nae doubt, but Hammy's a good lad, and this shite started with you two cunts jumpin' on Nick's cause: *the humans have souls, they can attain heaven*. Arseholes, the pair of ye." Stewart threw a PlayStation controller at Jay, striking him on the left temple. Jay absorbed the blow, didn't react. Stewart jabbed him in the chest once more.

"Islam is a fuckin' stool-pigeon down there for all the rich white cunts that want to blame brown and black cunts for whatever the fuck suits their political agenda or to excuse their genocide. War against terror?" Stewart spat on the carpet. "Fuck sake!"

Despite the fear he felt and his father's rage, Jay stood straighter. "We did what we thought was right," he said calmly.

Stewart stuck a finger into his chest once more. "Well, ye were wrong, son."

He jabbed a thumb over His shoulder at the screen where an image of a sniper on a rooftop taking aim at a mother and child flickered.

"Fuck thum. Fuck the lot of thum. That's my New Testament, Jay."

Azrael appeared at the doorway. At over seven feet tall, she was one of the few Angels who stood taller than Jay and Stewart. Of course, as the Angel of Death, Azrael's intimidating appearance was inherent. In truth, Azrael's height was the only threatening characteristic the Angel bore. She moved like a dancer, looked like a Greek goddess and whispered like a lover. Everything about her emanated gentleness, peace. Peace was, after all, her purpose, depending on one's point of view.

On the floor, Mo had begun to sing a soft lullaby, forgetting most of the words. Some Hebrew shite about lambs. The broken stop-start song from the broken man on the carpet made Azrael grin.

"How may I serve you, My Lord?" she asked.

Stewart nodded at the wall-screen.

"Get rid of them."

Azrael's smile faded and her eyes lit with hope. She hadn't been summoned for her primary reason for existence in millennia.

"How many?" she asked. "Which countries?"

"The fuckin' lot of them. Every last man, woman and child, Az."

Azrael, dressed in a black Brookes Brothers' suit with stark white shoulder-length hair, clapped Stewart on the back.

"Brilliant. Thank you, sir," the Angel of Death sing-songed. "Any particular method? Fire? Flood? Disease?" she asked.

Stewart lit a Regal King-Size before answering.

"Couldn't give a fuck, Az, whatever you like. Have fun."

Azrael practically skipped from the office. Shouldering Jay aside as she went, she laughed.

"Bad luck, Jay."

Despite the anger Jay took his father by the shoulders.

"Dad, please, let's think about this for a while. Don't make this decision while you're angry."

It was a ridiculous request: Stewart was always angry. He worked angrily, ate angrily, shat angry shits and thought angry thoughts; hell, he even fucked with a scowl on his face.

Stewart was immobile and immovable.

Tuning his ears back into Paolo's singing, Jay grasped at straws.

"What about Scotland?" he asked, knowing his father's love for his homeland.

"What about Scotland?" Stewart parroted sarcastically. "Az won't touch the place, she knows better."

Jay searched.

"Well, what about all those souls that'll make their way here upon the death of almost eight billion humans? I thought you didn't want them here?"

Stewart's left eyebrow rose, mocking his son.

"Be lucky if ten percent make it straight here, Jay. Between their own fuckin' inability to see the woods for the basturdin' trees and Azrael's methods, most of the souls will be obliterated."

Jay winced, recalling the devastating effect that Azrael's sword or her bullets had on a soul.

Complete obliteration.

Stewart continued. "The rest will go to Nick and either suffer or learn their place and be allowed to come here and magnify my Kingdom. Either way, their time is over. I'll start the experiment again elsewhere."

Stewart turned to the screen and began flicking through galaxies and solar systems looking for planets on which he might begin his *experiment of life* anew.

Jay kicked at Mo who was still singing broken songs to himself. Looking at Stewart's face always made him this way. Mo looked up through tears to see his best friend's agonised face plead with him for help. With no little effort, he dragged himself off the carpet, onto his feet and stood beside Jay.

Placing one hand on his father's shoulder, Jay spoke softly.

"Dad. Please, for me. Give us a chance to fix things. Let us try one more time."

Stewart turned to face them.

Jay allowed a minute spark of the Holy presence within him to show in his eyes. Stewart picked up on it instantly — this fragment of His own being, His own presence. His power embodied in His son who was so very like He Himself, but... reduced. Jay really was a shard of Himself. The lad didn't show it often, but he was. Looking at the hazy reflection of His own being, of His presence in another's form, His son, Stewart softened slightly. He placed His own hand on top of His son's.

"Son, there's nothing to be done. They'll never change. They had a role... a fate to fulfil. They simply cannot."

It was the calmest, most honest Jay's father had been with him in two thousand years.

Jay choked back rising emotion and looked deeply into the eyes of his father.

"I know that they can, I know it. Allow us time. Give us the freedom to re-enter the world and minister to them as we see fit. One chance to do it our way, Dad. If we fail, no arguments. One chance, Dad."

Stewart sighed deeply.

"Son... Jesus, you will fail."

"You'll let us try?" Jay asked.

Stewart nodded once.

Jay punched Mo in the arm.

"Go tell Az to go back to torturing kittens."

Relieved to have an excuse to leave Stewart's presence, Mo ran after Azrael, leaving Father and Son alone.

Jay beamed at his father, causing Stewart's face to harden once more.

"You've a week. Seven days. Not a minute more. Not a second," Stewart said.

There was no point in or room for arguing. Jay nodded his head gratefully.

Stewart continued. "None of that Holy spirit, immaculate conception shite this time. Both of you will be placed in the body of someone who already exists. You may use whatever methods... whichever powers you wish."

Jay interrupted before he could catch himself. "What about the souls of those whose bodies we'll inhabit?"

Stewart raised his eyebrows. "What the fuck do you care? Of course, you could save them by not going," He said.

Jay waved his hands submissively.

"Okay, fine. Adult bodies."

Mo returned, a fresh scar emblazoned across his forehead. Clearly Az hadn't taken the news well.

Stewart pointed a finger at Mo. "You, none of yer shite this time, keep it simple. Keep yer own agenda well fuckin' supressed and follow his lead." He pointed at Jay. "You've seven days starting from arrival, but I'll tell ye this," Stewart's face twisted into a snarl. He looked like someone had made him a shite sandwich. "Fuck Earth. If you two cunts fail there, I'm scrubbing the whole cunting universe. Back tae square one, lad. Every planet, every galaxy, every atom of matter. Everything."

Jay was stunned at his Father's venomous brutality. Speechless, he simply nodded his agreement.

"Good," Stewart spat. "Noo, get tae fuck, the pair of ye, and nae fuckin' crucifixions this time, Jay."

Pure, clean, glorious and violent, light swept into the office in a whirlwind of brilliance and finality, and then disappeared taking the friends along with it.

Stewart lit another cigarette and looked around Jay's office, examining the mess and grime.

Clatty wee bastards.

Leaving the room, Stewart barked across the corridor to Jay's assistant. "Haw, strawberry pubes. Get Azrael back here and up tae my office."

3

Nick and Beth

NICK LEANED ONTO THE BAR, mirroring Beth's pose.

"I'm an Angel," he said, deadpan.

Beth laughed, clearly delighted, clapping her hands in mock victory.

"Oh my goodness, lucky me," she smiled at him. "And here I am, a post-grad in theology."

Nick raised an eyebrow. Sensing honesty he smiled at the irony before continuing.

"Well, Beth. That makes both of us very lucky."

Taking a sip from her vodka, Beth looked over the top of her glass at him.

"I take it you mean this literally, Nick?"

"Yes," he said.

"More specifically, I'm a fallen Angel, *the* Fallen Angel, actually."

Beth refilled her glass, a double this time, as she nodded along. "The Accuser? Beelzebub? Memnoch? Satan?" she asked playfully.

Nick gave her a glimpse.

A glimpse was what Angels called the moment when they chose to reveal a fraction of what and who they were to a mortal. Almost all the souls of humans who had ascended to Heaven had described the glimpse they'd witnessed as having a veil dropped from the world and a being of pure energy, absolute goodness, revealed to them.

Nick didn't doubt these accounts: this was exactly what a mortal would be likely to see when faced with a glimpse of an Angel's true presence, which was, of course, a minute flicker of God's flame. In reality, in Heaven Angels were flawed, warped mirrors of their Creator. Some were purely good, others were total cunts. God had his ways.

In Nick's case, he wasn't permitted to show his Angelic presence whilst on Earth or in Hell. Stewart had made that plain. It would simply be too easy to show his Angelic countenance and obliterate the flaws in any human, replacing them with the penitence and forgiveness required for entry into Heaven.

Stewart had enchained Nick, effectively hobbled him, decreeing that he could only appear with black, sooty wings and goat hooves. *Give the cunts what they expect from my Accuser. My Adversary.*

Nick didn't care. He worked. He converted. He saved those souls he could, regardless of the limitations and restrictions placed upon him by his Creator.

Beth gasped and looked around the room to seek confirmation that the bar's only other inhabitant had witnessed what she had.

"He's fucked," Nick said softly. "Besides, he's in a state of... somewhere else. So are we. We're in between the cracks. Think of it as a bubble."

Open-mouthed, Beth sweated and drank deeply on her vodka, mechanically refilling the glass.

Nick placed a hand over hers, which trembled.

"Yes, I'm real. Would you like to hear my story, Beth? I don't tell it often."

Beth blinked a few times as Nick smiled warmly, kindly at her. He gave her hand a squeeze. "Beth, I can leave now and you will not remember any of this, but I could really use a friendly ear right now."

Beth stared blankly at him. Sweat rolled along her brow and down her nose, landing with a plop in her vodka.

Nick smiled. "I could use a friend. Something's going to happen, something big, and I need some context. I need to remember why I do what I do."

Beth blinked hard, slow, several times. "Okay," she said dully. Shaking the fog, the fear and the adrenaline from her, she affected her previous confidence. It did not reach her terrified eyes.

"Go ahead, Nick."

Nick reached for her sweat-polluted glass, slipped it away and pushed a clean glass to her. He filled it three-quarters full with Grey Goose and smiled warmly at the frightened girl.

"Okay, kiddo. Let's proceed."

Nick took a deep breath and unburdened his conscience.

"And then there was light. That's what they say, isn't it? It's one of the very few things they got right. In the beginning there existed God... Stewart is His name. Stewart was, by His account, alone. Completely alone, the only entity in a universe of nothingness. No matter, no light, no sound, air or will except for His own. Can you imagine the stark isolation? The complete loneliness?"

Beth's eyes misted.

"He created another being like Himself, a being composed of light, of will and of passion, love, fury, anger, compassion and desire. A being who would reflect and share His own existence and whom He could study, examine. But one who would share none of His true power, only His light. A being I believe He brought into existence purely to determine how He Himself had come to be."

Nick looked into his glass, absent-mindedly tapping his fingernail against the side. Beth took his tic as a cue to top up his whiskey.

"Why the Irish whiskey?" she asked. "That's unusual for an Englishman."

As she said it, Beth laughed at her assumption that this being had a nationality based on his accent. Nick laughed also, out of politeness.

"Mostly to piss Him off," Nick answered, then gave a dismissive wave of his hand. "Anyway, that being was I. I gave Him companionship, camaraderie and brotherhood, within my imposed limitations, but I held no answers for Him on the question of His origins. He created more of Him... of us. Angels. Beings who reflected His magnificence. We have faces, form and structure, but we're composed of light, not matter. We see and sense our own and each other's limits and boundaries, despite the ethereal composition of our parts. The best I can describe us is as translucent. We look like larger, winged humans composed of light, because humans look like us and we look like Him. Such was the origin of the fracture in our relationship. Mine and Stewart's. Such is the reason I became his Accuser. But that came many billions of years later. In the beginning, there existed only us: God and His Angels and His Kingdom. We existed to love Him and serve Him. We did this willingly and gratefully. You cannot imagine what a pure and joyous gift it is just to stand in His presence. Even now, for me."

Nick noted a rise of Beth's eyebrows.

"What?" he asked.

"You describe the relationship like someone suffering from Stockholm syndrome."

Nick laughed. "I suppose that it must seem that way. It is, in fact, a very insightful observation. For a human. But we are not humans and our love for one another is not defined or limited like human love is. I assure you, I do not have to love Him. He's big on free will, y'know. I choose to love Him. We all do, His Angels."

Beth nodded, as though she understood. She couldn't but it didn't matter.

Nick continued.

"He basked in this love, this adoration from His creations. He fed on it and absorbed its power and grew ever magnified, above everything. He created legions, hosts of Angels, each reflecting a miniscule portion of His own perfection, each with no defined purpose other than the sharing of His light. Finally, despite our devotion, our worship and our love, we were not enough for Him."

Nick stared past Beth, as though observing the past amongst the bottles of spirits lined along the bar. Shaking himself from his momentary reverie, Nick took a mouthful of his whiskey, enjoying the warmth as he brought himself back into the moment.

"He created matter. Solid, liquid and gas — you've done science at school."

Beth smiled.

"Well, Beth, these states of matter are an everyday presence, boring in their ubiquity, their predictability for most sentients on Earth. You accept the presence of matter as eternally mundane. We, His Angels, were fascinated by matter. We were present at its creation. For beings composed of ethereal light, matter was and is a miracle; its different states are as artwork.

"At God's side we watched catastrophically gargantuan explosions send ripples through existence, birthing matter, gas, rock and liquid. Monumentally huge collections of gas collected and ignited, burning as uncounted trillions of stars throughout the new-born universe." Nick looked to Beth. "Imagine what burning stars, immense balls of fire, of light, meant to beings composed of light but still limited in size."

Beth looked as wonderstruck as Nick himself seemed at retelling his origins and those of the universe.

"Many of us thought these stars to be new Heavens, filled with creatures like ourselves. Perhaps beings like Him. Upon discovering the simple science of the burning of gas, our jubilation only increased for this was new, wondrous. The miracles of Heaven we had seen many times, so a new form of being similar to ourselves would have been exciting. But matter — burning matter emitting light — was simply wondrous beyond description. We were jubilant, humbled and completely in awe of what God had created.

"I recall commenting to God. 'What a wondrous new thing you have created, my Lord.' He simply smiled, kindly I suppose — He was kind then, in the beginnings of the universe. He smiled and said simply, 'This is only the beginning, my Angel.'"

Nick shook his head, dispelling some fog of memory that threatened to swallow him. Beth sipped her vodka, allowing him the moments he needed to rediscover the will to talk.

"It was of course merely the beginning... Genesis, I suppose." A sardonic grin flashed on Nick's face momentarily. "After the stars came solid matter. Elements, iron, carbon... all the rest, fused together. Molten cores formed and cooled. Sliding lava flowed and slowed, becoming tectonic plates. Gravity formed a shield around the floating chunks of cooling rock. Elements collided and combined at random. Liquids formed. Atmospheres emerged."

Beth's eyes widened. "You witnessed planets forming?" she asked.

Nick simply nodded.

"Whole galaxies," he replied. "This occurred in countless solar systems and galaxies. The process more often than not went nowhere. Perhaps halted by an explosion that sent thousands of tonnes of rock hurtling through space. Perhaps resulting in a giant floating shard of rock, orbiting a distant star. Occasionally — and I use the word in the context of huge, unfathomable numbers — occasionally, water formed on the surface of worlds. And where water came, life came soon thereafter."

Sunday

4

Jay and Mo

BLINKING HARD, JAY TRIED for the third time to focus his eyes, finding once again that the murky fluid of the world wouldn't shift. He closed his eyes tightly and rubbed at the lids with the middle knuckle of his index fingers, kneading the soreness behind them. Hair tickled his eyelids, the first sign that he had displaced another soul and taken its body. Jay sighed heavily. Part of him had hoped that his Father may have reconsidered the method by which he and Mo would re-enter the human world. Jay didn't like to cuss — Dad did plenty of that for the whole of Heaven — but several expletives escaped regardless in sympathy for the poor soul he'd disembodied upon arrival in the material universe. Earth, to be more specific.

Cricking his neck to the left and right, Jay prepared himself mentally for the imminent discovery of who and where and what he now was. A week, seven days, was not a great deal of time on Earth to bring about a change cataclysmic enough to delay God's decision to obliterate the universe and begin his grand experiment anew. It was all he had, though. Needs must.

Jay opened his eyes and observed the ceiling of the room he lay in. *Think, observe, examine,* he told himself as the ceiling came into view. The murkiness struck him once again, but part of his subconscious whispered that this was the haze through which human eyes perceived the world. His new body's eyes were working fine. This was all they saw.

Closing his eyes once more, Jay decided to let his other senses feed him the information he needed for a moment. He remembered from his time in Palestine, two thousand years previously, how very important smells and sounds were. Jay regretted the decision immediately as the unmistakable aromas of cold Chinese takeaway, stale farts and crusted spunk, far too nearby, filled his senses.

Choking back on the suddenly all-too-familiar sensation of a gag reflex, Jay focused on the sounds of the room. Traffic passing, nobody else at home and the gorgeous melodies of The Police wafting through the apartment? House?

Thank Dad he has some good music in the house, whoever he is.

Rising from the comfortable bed, Jay found a full-length mirror propped against the magnolia wall. He closed his eyes for a moment, bracing himself for the disappointment he half expected and then took in his new face and body.

He was a tall lad in his thirties, much taller than Jay had been in his 'God Incarnate' body in Nazareth. His new face was... okay. Just okay. Nothing remarkable, a bit dull looking if anything, but he had all his hair and teeth which Jay supposed was something at least.

A powerful cramp suddenly surged through his intestines, doubling him over. On porcelain in seconds, grimacing and sweating as his bowels emptied in a torrent, Jay eyed the stack of takeaway containers littering the floor in the next room.

What the hell's this guy been eating?

Jay's new body finished purging itself. Standing in front of the bathroom mirror, Jay took off the T-shirt the guy had been sleeping in. His slightly flabby body was covered in thick, wiry hair and hadn't seen much sunlight judging from the pastiness of his skin, but really it wasn't in bad condition at all.

Suddenly aware of the smells of someone else, Jay decided that a long, hot shower was due. The feel of hot water against his skin was pure bliss. Nothing as pleasurable as a simple shower existed on his last visit to Earth. His short life in the Middle-East had been one of heat and hunger and sand. One never felt truly clean in those days. In Heaven, of course, no matter existed, so showers were not required.

Stepping reluctantly from the steam-filled bathroom, Jay dressed himself in a Pink Floyd T-shirt and denims, which were the cleanest-smelling clothes from the pile lying in the bedroom.

The guy's house is a pig-sty, but at least he has taste, Jay thought, absent-mindedly shuffling through some letters on the dresser. Noting the name on a Scottish Gas bill, he made a *not too bad* face. *Garry Crawford, that'll do. Plain, ordinary, nowt flashy. Yeah. It fits the unremarkable face and flabby body nicely.*

Scanning down the little window of the envelope Jay's heart sank as he read Garry's address.

Motherwell... Bloody Lanarkshire. Dad, you are entirely sadistic at times.

Jay sighed and tried out his voice.

"Awright? Big Gaz here, how ye daen, mucker?" Jay closed his eyes and took a moment to compose himself before trying again.

"Hiya. Ahm Gaz. Good tae meet ye."

Better. Obviously Dad has stuck me with the accent, but at least I can smarten the dialogue up a bit.

Jay noticed a bass guitar resting on a black stands and rolled his eyes. *Couldn't even get a real guitarist,* he groaned. Returning his eyes to the mirror he spent the next few minutes staring into his new face, wondering how to paint an expression on it that would make millions, no, billions of people trust him, despite the Lanarkshire accent. Arranging his new features into a state somewhere between kindness and constipation, Jay shrugged.

Best it's going to get. Time to find Mo.

As he began searching for a phone, another cramp racked through his guts, sending him racing back to the little bathroom.

Got to get this guy on the salads.

∞∞∞

A spasm of pleasure ran along his groin, almost doubling him over. Leaning forward slightly, Mo rested his hand onto the lower back of a woman he'd just orgasmed with. She slid back along the length of his cock, tilting her hips a little to tease some life back into it. She needn't have worried; it had lost perhaps five percent, changing from rock hard to merely stiff and rubbery.

It'd still do the job.

Mo closed his eyes again, enjoying the sensation of bareback shagging. It'd been so long since he'd been on Earth, he'd forgotten the simple ecstasy of flesh and fluids connected and mingled. Turning his partner over — he wanted to look into her eyes — Mo fought back the distraction of her unfamiliar body. She was much thinner than the women of his era. She would almost seem fragile if she wasn't at that moment forcing him onto his back and positioning herself to ride him. Supposing her appearance was simply fashionable now, Mo shifted his awareness back to where they were connected and to her face, which was simply beautiful and oddly familiar.

Once again, the rush of orgasm came.

"Fackin' hell, Chris. You gone and spunked again?" She didn't sound angry, just surprised. "That ain't like you, love," she said, reaching up to his face to stroke his beard.

"Yeah," Mo replied, noting his cockney accent. "Sorry about that, darlin'."

She smiled, illuminating the room.

"Not to worry, got to get a move on now anyway, Chrissy," she said.

Rising from his weakening cock she placed a gentle kiss on his forehead before slipping off the bed and into the en-suite. The noise of a shower followed soon after.

Mo stretched back onto the bed, reaching his hands behind his head. Enjoying a long, feline-like stretch he smiled to himself. Rising from the mattress, Mo found a mirror and approached. His first look at his new body and face brought a wide smile to his face as it dawned on him why the face of the woman, his wife, was so familiar. Scanning along the tanned, slim and toned torso of his new body, Mo moved his eyes up to the bearded face and top-knot-crowned hair.

In his mid-twenties and handsome, his generation's most gifted footballer and spoken of as being in the same vein as Maradonna, Ronaldinho and Messi, the broad, bankable smile of Man United's goal-scoring machine, Chris Pillans, smiled back at Mo.

Mo stood grinning at himself in the mirror for a full minute. The moment was broken by the chorus of 'Uptown Funk' issued from an iPhone on the bedside table.

Retrieving the phone, Mo glanced at the screen.

FaceTime incoming.

Clicking connect, Mo rubbed at his beard as the call connected. The blue screen was replaced by the unfamiliar face of an angry-looking man in his forties with dark hair and very familiar blue eyes; his best friend's eyes. They took in Mo's new face, recognising it immediately. His brow creased.

"You fuckin' jammy bastard," Jay said with a thick Lanarkshire accent.

Mo managed to keep a straight face, for a moment. "You sound just like your daddy," he said.

Obscured by the sound of Mo's laughter, Jay barked, "Just gies yer address, bawbag."

Interlude

Saluzar and Miriam

MIRIAM PUSHED THE HEAVY MAHOGANY door open enough to peek through the gap into the office of the CEO. He spotted the movement immediately and made a subtle gesture that it was a good time to enter.

Padding barefoot across the highly polished marble floor, Miriam moved around the man in the leather armchair, seated with his back to her, facing Mr Saluzar. Nodding politely at Saluzar, she placed the tray she carried gently onto the oak desk between them.

"Thank you, Miriam," Saluzar said, softly. He didn't smile, he never smiled, but she could read the kindness, warmth in his eyes.

"You're welcome, sir," she replied. Turning, she nodded courteously at the man in the leather chair, who did offer her a broad smile, one that was well-practiced and as familiar to her as her own. A smile that never reached his eyes. Miriam returned the smile and moved past the man, making for the exit.

"Actually, Miriam," Saluzar said, "would you mind joining us for a moment?" Mr Saluzar indicated the vacant chair to Cameron's right. "The Prime Minister and I are having a minor disagreement. Your input would be appreciated, my dear."

Miriam nodded, fighting her natural urge to cringe when addressed by anything other than her given name. After ten years in Mr Saluzar's company, she knew for certain that such terms of endearment were merely a little tic of his personality and not meant to demean or belittle. He was a kind, good man who'd supported her professionally and personally so many times and had earned the right to show his affection whenever he chose.

"Of course, sir," she said, sitting lightly on the edge of the seat, legs crossed, leaning in.

Mr Cameron clapped his hands together, making her start.

"Excellent," he boomed, "thank you, Miriam, I'll let Mr Saluzar explain." The smile beamed again.

Face stoic as always, Saluzar tapped on the oak desk with his middle finger as he spoke, punctuating each word.

"This concerns the Mediterranean crisis, Miriam. The Prime Minister here believes that the current levels of financial aid made available are adequate."

"'Generous' was the word I used, Mr Saluzar," Cameron interrupted.

Saluzar regarded Mr Cameron for a moment, long enough for Miriam to wonder if her boss was angry enough to show it to the British premier.

Saluzar, around the same age as Cameron, was infinitely wiser in appearance than the man seated across from him. His dark skin, eyes and hair — lightly peppered with silver — and the warmth of those eyes set him apart from the perennially smug-looking Brit.

Saluzar closed his eyes in a long blink. "Yes... As you say, generous."

Cameron relaxed back into his armchair. Saluzar's demeanour unacknowledged, he smiled his smile.

"Generous it may be, Mr Cameron, but my company would like to push for greater input from your government." Saluzar looked at Miriam. "Mr Cameron does not accept that more assistance is needed. He has contributed almost three hundred million British pounds to the relief effort, which of course is... generous." Saluzar spat the word.

Cameron smiled warmly at him across the desk, offering a little nod of confirmation.

"What I would like to see is a commitment from the UK government that a percentage of the refugees in the Med are rehomed in the UK. Money to pay for boats and personnel to fish starving men, women and children from the sea is one thing." Saluzar glared across the desk at Mr Cameron, before blinking slowly once again and returning his eyes to Miriam. "The chance to establish their families in a safe, welcoming environment is quite another."

Miriam nodded along. "What's your position, Mr Cameron?"

"It's very simple, Miriam. The United Kingdom is not a haven for the waifs and strays of Europe, Africa, or any other continent. We have our own poor to... contend with."

Miriam's eyes narrowed. She knew how this man ran his country. There was no sense in arguing morality or compassion with him. He was one of those politicians, those men, who could justify any decision, convince themselves that their chosen course of action was for the greater good... *God, she hated that phrase.*

Both men sat quietly as she considered her response. Miriam could feel Saluzar willing her on. That's what he did for his employees.

Miriam had lost both parents in a flood during infancy. Another orphan roaming Delhi's streets and tunnels; another slumdog. Chance had brought her as a four year old to an orphanage owned by The Saluzar Foundation, one of his *Hope Orphanages*.

Where other orphans begged and robbed in rags on the streets, she was schooled, taught to read and write. Where thousands died from disease and starvation, she was kept clean, fed and loved.

Upon leaving the orphanage, Miriam had been selected to receive a scholarship to a United States college. She graduated with two degrees: one in economics, the other in business. Mr Saluzar attended her graduation. He did this with every single graduate who'd received the scholarship in his name.

Saluzar had introduced himself to her that day, explaining that he was the Head of the Foundation, having inherited the responsibility from his father. The company was widely regarded as an ethical supporter of developing nations and reputed to have invested billions in aiding small businesses, farms and entrepreneurs, as well as its continued provision of the orphanages and the education that Miriam had been fortunate enough to benefit from.

On the day Miriam had met Saluzar, she'd cried tears of real, true joy. She'd told him how grateful she was for the difference he had made to her life.

In his thirties at the time, dark-skinned, stern-faced, quiet and calm, truly calm, Mr Saluzar had taken one of her hands into both of his and said simply, "You, my dear, are most welcome."

She'd worked with and for him for almost twenty years since and still fought the urge to thank him every day. As his right hand, she was privileged to watch the man work, lifting people the world over from poverty.

Miriam ignored her dislike of the man to her left and smiled calmly at Mr Cameron.

"Mr Saluzar would be happy to finance the transport and rehoming of an agreed number of refugees. For a period of five years, he will provide employment for all who are able to work and an allowance for those unable, under condition that they enter full-time education. We have many businesses which employ a huge number of your citizens and pay a lot of taxes, Mr Cameron. We'd like to add to that."

"How many?" Cameron asked, talking to Saluzar.

Miriam bristled. Her smile vanished.

"As many as we tell you to, Mr Cameron," she said.

Cameron's smile disappeared for the first time. A flash of contempt showed for a second before he hid it. Looking back to Saluzar, he found an expression and gesture that said, *I'd listen to her if I were you,* before turning his attention back to Miriam who still smiled serenely at him.

"Within reason, of course, Mr Prime Minister." She made 'Mr Prime Minister' sound like *wanker.* "For each of the refugees we employ, we'll create a job for a British citizen. This will enable you to look compassionate, grow your economy and reduce unemployment, with no financial input from your government whatsoever."

The smile returned. "Deal," he said.

Rising from his seat, he shook Saluzar's hand and left briskly, ignoring Miriam.

Turing to Mr Saluzar, she raised her eyebrows.

"You didn't need me for that, sir."

The corner of Saluzar's mouth tugged a little. Ten years ago, Miriam would've hoped for a smile from him. After two decades in Saluzar's company, she knew better. The most generous, compassionate businessman in the world and he never smiled.

"No. I didn't need you," Saluzar admitted, "but he's such an insufferable prick. I wanted you to enjoy the moment."

Miriam stood. "Always a pleasure, sir," she smiled at her boss. "Will that be all, sir?"

Saluzar nodded. "Yes… no actually, Miriam. When was the last time we had lunch together?" he asked.

Miriam shrugged. "Yesterday."

"Really?" he asked, mock confusion in his tone. "It's been far too long then, my dear. Let's go."

Saluzar held the door for her, before following her out into the lobby of their office.

Feeling a shudder, he ignored the exit, walking instead to the north-facing floor–to-ceiling window.

Miriam reached the elevator before noticing the absence of her mentor and strode back into the lobby. Saluzar stood looking out at the city of London beneath, lost in his thoughts.

She gave him a full minute before placing a hand on his shoulder.

"Sir? Are you okay?"

Saluzar turned to face her, blinking dumbly, like he'd woken from a long sleep. "Yes, fine, Miriam, just had a weird feeling."

"Someone walk on your grave?" she asked, turning back towards the exit.

Saluzar followed along behind her. "Exactly that," he whispered under his breath to no-one.

5

Nick and Beth

BETH REACHED OVER THE BAR, placing a hand on top of Nick's. "Is it painful? Telling me your history?" she asked.

Nick narrowed his eyes, thinking about the question. Finally he said, "No. It's not, but it's hardly the first time I've vented to a stranger."

"Why me?" asked Beth.

Nick shrugged. "Mostly timing and circumstance. Right place, right time," he said.

"Mostly?" she echoed.

"We'll get to that later, Bethany," Nick said softly. "I have a story to tell first."

Beth's eyes flashed fear, but she hid it quickly behind a sip of her vodka and a smile.

"Where was I?" Nick asked.

Beth drained her drink before answering. She felt like she'd been drinking for days. Exhaustion crept over her.

"Water," she said. "Water and life."

Nick nodded once in thanks.

"Yes. Water and life. The moment when everything in Heaven and in the material universe was irretrievably altered."

Nick smiled warmly at her before continuing.

"Water, lightning and some chemicals, that's all it took."

"It was random?" Beth asked.

"Yes and no," Nick replied. "The lightning, the spark was intentional. He meant to begin the process. What came after, He left to chance... no, not chance — nature." A shadow of sadness passed over Nick's face as he spoke. "God made the atoms and molecules form into nucleic acid, DNA. Proteins formed, membranes, organelles. Cells combined, proliferated. Others went extinct. This simple snuffing of a cell shocked we Angels whose lives were unlimited by time or health or predatory chance. That a spark of life, even one so small, could be extinguished was abhorrent to us in our eternal lifespans. God reassured us that it was all *in nature. Part of life.*

"Billions upon billions of identical cells emerged from one common ancestor. Some adapted, some disappeared from the gene pool forever. Groups of cells formed bonds or fused together, forming tissues or other structures. The single-celled inhabitants of a pool of water adapted into a myriad of multicellular creatures. Simple organisms. Some photosynthesised food. Some didn't. Some hunted. Most perished.

"All that survived adapted in some way. Muscle, teeth, fins, gills. Some became simple worm-like creatures, or fish-like organisms. Others adapted to become plants. Hundreds of millions of years passed. Billions of organisms, whole species lived short lives and died.

"Angels wept for their brief existence.

"Adaptations, evolution continued. Rudimentary life found a way to survive, to adapt, to become complex life. Animals with eyes and mouths... faces emerged. Simple things that fed and bred and not much else, but they had faces."

Nick looked deep into Beth's eyes, causing her to shrink back a little.

"You cannot fathom the clamour that this simple development — a creature with a face — sparked in Heaven. Angels flocked to God. *'What does it mean? They have faces? Is it blasphemy? Does the existence of creatures with faces mock you, my Lord?'*

"It seems an absurd reaction I'm sure, Beth, but consider this. We were God's only creations, made in His own likeness by His own hand. We looked like Him. We had faces.

"That nature, evolution, had created organisms with a structure so closely resembling one of our own, by random chance, seemed a heresy."

Beth grinned.

"Yes," Nick said. "Seems ridiculous to you, I agree, but you were born into a world where a face is the first thing you see. In all of Heaven and God's good universe until that moment only God's creations, His Angels, had faces. That these random mutations of nature had produced a creature with such a structure was truly terrifying to us."

"Yeah, I suppose I can get that. Faces… terrifying," Beth said, sarcasm lacing her tone.

Nick rolled his eyes.

"God, calm as he'd been since our creation, spoke to us, His Angels, gently, reassuring us that all was as He intended, part of nature. '*Observe, my Angels. See what nature does next. Trust in me.*' Of course, we did trust in God and followed His advice. We witnessed the development of brains, simple but entirely functional. Ears, limbs, skeletons, nervous systems. Kidneys, hearts, livers pulsed and beat their way into existence. The rate of development was astonishing to us. You must understand, Beth, time is… different in Heaven. We existed for many millions, perhaps billions of years before God created the universe. Time passed for us, but didn't. Things changed, adapted I suppose, but nothing was diminished, only magnified by its passing.

"Change occurred in Heaven but only as we willed it, not at the mercy of nature and not on the scale that life was adapting in the universe. It seemed to us that time passing in the material universe simply meant death. Once an unnoticed companion to us in Heaven, time now seemed to stalk the material world. To us, the evolution present in the universe and the death that drove it was truly shocking.

"I've been talking about the evolution of creatures on Earth, but this was happening on countless planets, throughout the universe." Nick spread his arms in a broad gesture. "The unrelenting speed, the efficiency of nature in stimulating these frighteningly effective adaptations in animals and plants shook us. We returned to God once more, in greater numbers than before. '*Lord. Look what matter, what nature has done. Fish have grown legs and lungs and crawled onto the earth. Faces look to the skies. When will it stop?*'

"God's patience with us in our ignorance seemed eternal at that time. He merely smiled kindly and allayed our fears.

"As His first Creation, his closest companion, I was hurt in another manner by what unfolded in nature, so I asked God, '*There is a spark of life in them, a light, not unlike our own ethereal light. When they die, does it come home to you, my Lord?*'

"I had witnessed God create matter and I had witnessed it change and evolve from basic chemicals to the first cells and into a myriad of living animals and plants. The light inside each of the billions of cells was so familiar to me that it may as well have been part of my own self. I was in conflict. Where did this light go upon their deaths? Did their consciousness reside in the spiritual part of themselves, and, if so, how can God suffer them to die and this light to just dissipate? If that's what truly happened.

"I didn't really believe that He would allow these organisms to suffer such brief lives and their light to dissipate. That would be cruel. God was not cruel, He was the source of all love and warmth in Heaven and the universe. He was the Creator. But the questions remained as thorns in my subconscious.

"In creating this abundance of life, did God share his own light amongst them? He hadn't seemed diminished in any way by the act of Creation. If anything, he'd seemed magnified. Was he receiving the light of these creatures back into Himself upon their death? I knew for a fact that He wasn't because we would have witnessed the entry of such light in Heaven. Despite this knowledge, I was also certain that He must have a plan, a destiny for this light of life, otherwise the result of the whole experiment of the universe — life — was the cruellest punishment imaginable.

"Consider a brief life in the material universe followed by... nothing? I couldn't abide the thought. In hindsight, that moment was when I began to lose my trust in God and became His Accuser.

"I recall Him looking into my eyes. 'You must trust in me, my Angel. There is a plan.' I nodded and prayed and made all the right noises, Beth, but something crucial and irreparable had broken inside me. Despite this, it would take many years, uncountable trillions of deaths of living things and the evolution of humankind, to set me firmly on my course.

"God, of course, reassured us time and again that all was in nature. All was intended. Many Angels made a choice to trust God and merely observe. Other turned away from watching nature's progress altogether, returning to those concerns in Heaven that had busied them before God had created the universe. I resolved to be and remain The Watcher."

6

Jay and Mo

"C'mon shite-heap," Jay complained at the little Aygo for perhaps the thirtieth time in two hours.

Dropping a gear, switching off the AC and shoving his right foot, and the gas pedal, into the carpet, Jay eked every watt of power out of the little one-litre engine. Whining in reply the Aygo coughed out a few plumes of exhaust smoke and dragged itself a little more quickly along the M6.

Jay was aware that he was swearing out loud and in his head, frequently. Under normal circumstances he rarely swore and was putting it down to the Scottish traits left behind in Garry Crawford's body. He was having real trouble discovering his normally serene state of mind. It wasn't the Aygo — although Dad knows, that didn't help —it wasn't even that Mo had so characteristically landed on his feet with his new body. No, something else tugged at Jay's mind.

Barely an hour had passed since his Father had stormed into his and Mo's office and they'd convinced Him to allow them a brief opportunity to prove that the humans weren't irredeemable. Sure, by Heaven's standards an hour was a huge amount of time, but here on Earth it was fuck all. Urgency prodded at Jay. Sweat broke from his brow and pain lanced his heart.

Perhaps ninety minutes from Mo's Manchester apartment, Jay distracted himself by going over his plan once more. Seven days, that was it, but if things fell into place then it might... *might* be enough. Ignoring the ridiculously insincere face he'd been lumbered with — Jay could force enough of the Holy presence into his eyes and aura to compensate — he had to engage the humans on a scale he simply couldn't have comprehended in his Nazareth days.

People had so very much information at their fingertips now: data, news, gossip. The infinite stream of news was exactly what he needed to utilise, but Jay somehow had to find a way to shout loudly enough above the din to gain everyone's attention and then take it to another level, one that cut through their bullshitometers. That was the problem with twenty-first-century Westerners.

No superstition. Everything was explainable. Scientific rationale would determine the cause, and if it couldn't... then just file whatever it was away in a box labelled *weirdo*.

Jay had something *big*, something that couldn't be ignored in mind, but so many pieces needed to fall into place...

Mo.

He needed his friend's help. Son of God he may be, but Jay had never suffered from delusions of grandeur. Accessing perhaps one percent of the Holy power did that to a being; kept him honest. He needed his friends, always had. Ninety minutes and Jay would feel much better just being in Mo's company, despite the inevitable smugness from the former Pharaoh's son at his good fortune.

∞∞∞

"Do your part and introduce us."

Lorraine raised her eyebrows, reacting to the arrogance of the men in front of her. She'd interviewed some prima donnas in her time, but these two were something else. Fixing a genuine-looking smile, she moved her eyes along them as they bickered.

Dressed in white linen, Chris Pillans was actually more genial than he'd been the last time he had appeared on her morning show. On that occasion, he'd spent most of the pre-interview time Tweeting comments about her to his millions of followers, #MumsyAndShaggable, before turning on the charm when the red light above the camera blinked on. Seeing him with the big guy from Motherwell, well, he was a different man. They argued constantly, the language was terrible, but they were clearly good friends. Their effing and ceeing back and forth was beginning to grate, though. Lorraine decided to allow the Dundee lass in her out for a moment.

"You two sit down and shut the fuck up," she roared. "Yer doin' ma fuckin' heid in."

Chris Pillans and his Scottish friend's eyes opened wide, shocked into silence.

"Better," Lorraine smiled. "Count them in please, Amie," she said kindly to a producer off-camera.

Lorraine smiled into the camera, a faint sparkle of fuck *you* shining behind her eyes.

"Good morning, and welcome to 'Lorraine'. This morning we are joined by Manchester United forward, Chris Pillans, and his… friend, Garry Crawford, from Motherwell, Scotland."

Lorraine, completely in the dark as to why the Premiership footballer and magazine favourite Pillans had asked for the airtime, turned to the two friends.

"Chris, perhaps you'd like to tell the viewers why you're here this morning?"

Several very long moments passed. Chris Pillans looked to the big Scot with the gormless face to his right, who merely shrugged and turned to fix his too-close eyes on the camera lens.

Watching him look deep into the lens, Lorraine noted that his eyes held something… an undefinable sliver of honesty and simplicity that stripped away the roughness of his mildly dim-looking face. He stared into the camera, into the eyes of each and every one of Lorraine's four million viewers, and poured pure, simple peace across the airwaves and data lines.

With a gesture of his hand, Garry Crawford connected each and every news network, radio station, YouTube channel, vlog-feed, smartphone and tablet. Every single device connected to the net or by landline, 4G or Wi-Fi synched to the 'Lorraine' show. Twitter feeds and Facebook newsfeeds were awash with his face and words. In an instant, Lorraine's figures jumped from four million to in excess of four billion.

Garry Crawford's face and voice filled their screens and speakers. Sleeping devices pinged into life and began transmitting this face and voice to everyone who had access to the internet, radio or television globally. Every channel, every stream of data hijacked. Millions, billions of eyes looked upon him as he spoke. His words somehow translated to the local language wherever the transmission was viewed or listened to.

Garry Crawford, bassist, takeaway-eating borderline-alcoholic and apparent friend of the Premiership's most valuable player, deepened his expression and spoke.

"To everyone who can hear me, whether Christian, Muslim, Hindu, Buddhist, or any of the thousands of sub-divisions or branches of whatever religion you practice. I come to you with a simple message. I come to you for the second time and ask of you that you forgive your God for his callous abandonment of you."

Lorraine felt her heart tugged towards this simple man sitting across from her speaking so earnestly into the camera from the red sofa. In her decades hosting the morning show, Lorraine had met many big names: movie stars, football players, presidents, princes, queens and simple normal folk.

Many times she'd felt humbled. Many times she'd been angered or overcome with emotion, or caught the giggles. Lorraine had always, without fail, kept a genial, composed demeanour, guiding her guests smoothly through the interview and entertained her viewers. Genuine warmth, humour and professionalism were her trademarks and the reason for her longevity in an industry where her age and gender were a handicap.

A producer coughed, and the sound transmitted to the earpiece in her left ear. She didn't respond to the signal, so he spoke softly. *Wrap it up, Loraine. Get this nutter to fuck off-air.*

Lorraine wasn't listening; she was too busy looking into the eyes of the man on her red sofa. Too busy feeling his voice caress her soul. All professional composure gone, she was unaware of anything except this man and sat gaping at him, the cameras, her producers and her viewers a distant whisper.

It didn't matter. More than four billion people worldwide were caught in the same spell.

Garry Crawford closed his eyes, composing himself, clearly fighting emotion.

"God is finished with you. I cannot put it any more plainly. You have seven days to change your ways."

Garry swallowed hard.

"After seven days, God will obliterate you and the billions of other planets on which life proliferates. Such is your affront to Him, He is willing to annihilate life on countless worlds in order to see an end to your species. To begin afresh."

Garry filled his eyes with compassion, love, pleading. Leaning forward, he rested his elbows on his knees, made steeples of his hands, touching his fingers to his lips for a brief kiss. Looking upwards into the camera, the intense empathy in his eyes burned. He looked like a saint.

"My name is Jesus," he said. The hands lowered and turned into a palms-up gesture. "My friends," he nodded at Mo, "call me Jay."

Jay smiled warmly into the camera, allowing each of the people in the studio to *really* see him. *Feel* him. The people watching and listening to him across the continents, in the air or on the seas or oceans, wouldn't get the same glimpse — that would require too deep a pull on the Holy presence — but they would see that he was telling the truth. They would *know.*

Lorraine's eyes wandered around the studio. Each of the producers had grown quiet, caught in his eyes, held by his voice. Lorraine believed ever single word that Garry... Jay said. Every word. Lorraine *knew* that this man was who he said he was. She *felt* it. His presence filled the studio and every cell of each person present, bringing pure peace and love and acceptance. For a split second, each of them knew a fragment of Heaven.

When it was over, Lorraine became aware that he was quietly smiling into the cameras and had been doing so for a few silent seconds, bathing all in his presence, giving a glimpse of himself.

He was glorious.

Forcing as much compassion into Garry's face as he could muster, Jay spoke softly one last time.

"We have seven days. On the seventh day, this Friday, God will obliterate every..." Jay's eyes filled with hot tears which broke from the lids and streaked two silvery slashes along his cheeks. "On the seventh day, God will end everything. Every cell of life, every spark of energy, every atom of matter in the universe, unless you can show Him that you are worthy of His Heaven."

Jay bowed, closing his eyes to cool the burn of the tears. The people in the studio were crying along with him. Composing himself, Jay, face stoic, continued speaking.

"God hates you. All of you. Regardless of religion, race, sex, sexuality, nationality, or any of the other dozens of characteristics that you use to elevate or separate yourselves above or from each other. He hates you because you have souls. He doesn't want you in Heaven, but you do *have* souls and you *are* worthy... or at least you can be if you learn how."

Jay took a moment, as though deciding on his next words.

"Loving God is not enough for you to enter Heaven. Being sorry for crimes or transgressions or cruelty is not enough. He wants you to be honest and good and kind, yes, but doing those things will not elevate your soul after death. God simply does not want you in Heaven. Ever!"

Jay's cheeks were trembling, his eyes haemorrhaging intensity.

"But there are those who give their existence to gain entry for you. Who spend eternity dedicating themselves to seeing your species elevated. That is why we've come here."

Jay placed a hand on Mo's shoulder.

"To teach you how to forgive God for hating you, for underestimating your capacity for Heaven and for abandoning you."

Jay stood, ignoring the returning cramp in his guts. The cameraman snapped out of his daze and adjusted the lens to capture Jay.

"Mo and I will be conducting Mass. In stadiums and parks, we invite you to gather. Through cameras and smartphones, computers, radio, internet, we will try to teach you. I cannot know if we will succeed, but we will try."

Jay made a gesture and the global connection was lost. The studio fell silent, aside from the weeping. Mo stood alongside Jay and slapped one of Chris's heavy hands across the back of his neck.

"Fuck off," Jay yelped. "What was that for?" he asked.

"There's no way we can see enough people, never mind convince them in seven days."

Jay gestured at Lorraine Kelly, who sat staring at him in utter belief.

Mo fished in his pocket for a tin. "Yeah," he jabbed a thumb at the studio staff, "easy enough in person, but there's almost seven billion of the fuckers. You can't meet all of them. The fuck were you thinking, Jay? Just show them something... something big."

Rubbing at the back of his neck, Jay creased his face into a lop-sided grin.

"Trust me, Mo," he said.

Mo lit a joint, inhaled deeply and blew a long blast of smoke from the corner of his mouth, using the time to cast a cynical look in Jay's direction.

"They'll never listen, Jay. That's the truth."

Interlude

Saluzar and Miriam

THEY'D BEEN LISTENING TO THE MAN, to Jay's voice, since their tablets, smartphones and TV screens flickered into life filled with his face and their conference call with the Paris office began transmitting his voice. The boardroom had never been so quiet, silent in fact, aside from the voice coming from a myriad of tiny speakers around the room.

Spellbound, that was the only word for the state of those present. Simply rapt, completely spellbound, drawn by Jay's presence, his words. Those eyes, that voice.

Miriam watched and was lost in him and his words, like all the rest.

That is one hell of a charismatic performer, her inner-voice said.

Despite the effect Jay was having, those gathered were breaking from the spell as his speech ended, throwing each other conspiratorial grins. The uneasy laughter began, flippant remarks chuckled out, to shake the uneasy feeling that what they had witnessed was somehow real.

Hacker.

Tech illusionist.

Con man.

Prank.

Miriam grinned half-heartedly with the rest of them, but couldn't shake the feeling of warmth, of love, that Jay had projected. A crash broke her from the moment.

"Sir," Miriam screeched, running towards her mentor.

Saluzar, clutching at his chest, had fallen across the massive boardroom table. One hand shot out to catch himself, inches before his face struck. Miriam slung an arm under each of his armpits, helping him take the steps back into his chair. Once he'd been lowered, she spun around, finding the eight board members sitting, mouths gaping, in shock.

"Phone an ambulance," she yelled at no-one and everyone.

"No!" Mr Saluzar banged the desk with his left hand, his right still braced to his chest. He was sweating, shaking, his lips were blue and his face had paled. He was trying to stand despite the pain he was in. Trying and failing. Miriam ignored the voice screaming in her head and helped him up.

Standing at the head of the table, sweat forming the beginnings of a puddle on the expensive carpet at his feet, Mr Saluzar glared at those assembled. "No ambulance. Everyone out, now," he growled.

Finally those assembled shook from their state of shock and filed from the room. Each searched Miriam's face. *Should we call someone?* She shook her head each time.

When they were gone, Saluzar pressed a command on his tablet locking the boardroom door and frosting the privacy glass. Only then did he allow himself to collapse.

Miriam rushed to him. Kneeling by his side she supported the back of his head. "Mr Saluzar, tell me what to do," she said, panic rising.

Saluzar prodded another button on his remote and a hidden panel on the south wall slid open. He swallowed hard on what seemed like gravel. Raising his hand he pointed into the recess behind the panel.

"In there, Miriam. You'll find an oxygen tent with a bed inside. Get me in there and seal it."

Miriam's hands shook. She began to cry as she realised that Saluzar was dying. She'd seen heart attacks before.

"Sir, please... let me get help."

Saluzar closed his hand on hers, and suddenly she was very aware of how weak he seemed. The lack of grip in his hand convinced her to call for help. Saluzar spotted the change in her eyes.

"Please, my dear, I promise you that I will be fine." Saluzar's eyes pleaded with her. "Put me in there, close the door and come back in four days. I'll be fine by then."

Miriam searched his face. What he was asking was insane. He was dying: he needed a doctor and a damn good one. But this was Mr Saluzar. He was always prepared, his foresight was immense. He *always* knew what was coming and how to confront, avoid or survive, even thrive, beyond it.

She loved this man more deeply than any woman could love a partner, a brother or a husband. She loved him as a daughter loved a father. She trusted this good, decent man.

He saw her decide and croaked a thank you. "Four days, my dear. No less."

Saluzar flicked at the screen of his tablet once more.

"I've emailed you at the secure account. Open it immediately upon leaving here. Password: Second Coming," he said.

She nodded that she understood and willed love through tear-filled eyes.

Ten minutes later, she sealed the oxygen tent around the prone form of her mentor, who appeared to be taking his last laboured breaths in this world.

Miriam closed the panel, crawled under the table and cried until her tears dried.

Two hours after the forced exit of the board, Miriam, neatly rearranged and make-up reapplied, emerged to find a small gathering of board members.

Yes, Mr Saluzar is fine. No he doesn't want to see anyone. He left by his private exit. Gone away for a few days. Yes, I'll assume his duties in the interim. Just some heartburn. Working so hard.

7

Nick and Beth

SMILING ACROSS THE BAR AT HIM, BETH whispered, her tone conspiratorial. "You're supposed to be evil, y'know. The Beast."

Nick laughed loudly. "To some, I am, Bethany. Especially those souls in what you call Hell." Nick's voice was dark, but sad also.

Beth leaned back a little, subconsciously putting a space between them. "Hell's real then?" she asked.

"Yes, it is," Nick said solemnly, "and growing ever fuller by the second."

Beth's eyes misted with tears and memories of sins she'd been a party to. Nick had seen the reaction many times. That moment when humans really accepted who and what he was; when they realised that they really would go somewhere else after death and be held accountable for the decisions they'd made and the deeds they'd done in life.

This wouldn't do. Not at all.

Nick reached across to take Beth's handbag from behind the bar, retrieving a pack of cigarettes and lighter from it whilst she stood, shaking.

He lit two cigarettes and passed one to her, which she reached for numbly. Nick inhaled deeply on his own, savouring the burn and the head spin. He hadn't smoked a cigarette in twenty... no, thirty years. It felt good.

Reclining back onto his stool, Nick arranged his face, allowing genuine kindness to show and spoke softly to Beth.

"What is it that you imagine Hell to be, Beth?" he asked.

Nick had asked the question many times of many people across thousands of years. They all said the same thing Beth said.

"A place of torture, of fire and violence and punishment and death and resurrection. Lather, rinse, repeat. For eternity."

Beth noticed the cigarette in her hand and sucked hard on it, like an infant at its mother's breast. The toxins seemed to calm her.

Nick flicked his own cigarette to the floor, having tired of it. Crushing it beneath his shoe he smiled at Beth once more, accepting the inevitability of her answer, but as crushed as the cigarette he'd discarded. *When would someone understand?*

As he moved to speak, Beth interrupted.

"At least that's what the *books* say." She made little quote marks in the air with her fingers. "Having met you in person," she continued, "I can't see how a being such as you would preside over souls suffering those violations for eternity."

Nick's eyes danced with excitement. "Go on."

Beth shrugged. "I really don't know, that's the point. I can't imagine a place of torture with you, fork in hand, reigning over it. Not now." Beth smiled at the notion. "But having said that, you are Satan, the Accuser, the Adversary. You're unlikely to show me your true nature."

Nick nodded. "Quite right, Beth, but I already told you, I'm not permitted to show my true self on Earth."

Beth gave a curt nod.

"Yes. So that leaves me with an obviously good being in front of me who also runs Hell." Beth stubbed her cigarette out in the manner Nick had. No ashtrays in British bars these days. "So just tell me, Nick."

Pouring himself another whiskey, Nick shook his head. "Later," he said, "I'll even take you there if you wish, Bethany."

Fear emerged in her eyes once again.

"Relax. I have plenty more to tell you first," Nick said quietly. "Pour yourself another."

"Plants and animals and insects and microbes came and went. Life continued to adapt to the challenge of simply existing. Angels continued to weep at the mass extinction and extinguishing of the flame of life in each and every insignificant existence lived.

"God continued to placate. 'Trust in me. It's all part of nature. You will understand. Be the Watchers.'

"Reptiles, great beasts of the ocean, ancient plants and trees, plagues, miracles of nature came and went. Finally mammals emerged. Small, insignificant, weak and scared, they scurried in the cracks and gaps, filling a single niche that the much more widespread and gargantuan lizards had left vacant. Tiny shrew-like creatures hugging each other and their young in burrows while monstrous reptiles shook the earth above. They seemed doomed, ill-equipped for survival in this wild, oversized landscape.

"They hid and bred and adapted. They remained underground as the meteor cracked the planet, sending a decade-long cloud of dust and death into the atmosphere. As the giants roaming the planet fell — such huge beasts with such big appetites and so little food — the mammals made gluttons of themselves on insects who had themselves feasted on the carrion of the dying giants.

"The mammals survived, underground and over-fed, the greatest cataclysm to strike Earth since Creation itself."

Nick paused for a moment, realising Beth was still quaking in fear.

"Bethany, I will not hurt you today. I am not evil and I never lie. You will see and hear many things during our conversation, but I'm not here to trick or harm you." Nick's face relaxed as he realised the truth of his need to vent to this woman. "Something big is coming. I don't know if I have the strength for it, or even care enough to witness or fight when it comes. I just need to rediscover why I do what I do. I just need a friend right now."

Beth steeled herself and nodded that he should continue. "Mammals," she said. Her voice was strained.

"Mammals," Nick repeated. "They survived the extinction of so many organisms so much more complex and numerous than themselves. They emerged into a barren world of ashes and grasped the opportunity *nature* had given them." Nick smiled bitterly at the word. "The mammals filled niches previously unavailable to them, now vacant because the dinosaurs were dust. They did what all life does and adapted to the challenges and opportunities they found themselves pressured by and offered. They grew, they shrank, and they took to the seas, to the land, to the air and to the trees. They became the undisputed rulers of the planet.

"Over many millions of years the mammals spread and adapted to every niche on the planet. Jungle cats, rodents, sea mammals, even polar mammals. They also claimed the trees as monkeys and then... as apes."

8

Jay and Mo

"Lorraine… Lorraine!" Amie shook the host gently by the arm.

Blinking heavily, Lorraine cleared her thoughts. Her eyes moved from Jay's face for the first time since he'd begun his monologue. Dreamily, she turned them to Amie.

The young producer was speaking, but Lorraine couldn't comprehend her words which seemed abstract, diluted from the real word somehow. The stage door crashed open, shoved hard by Mike the director who rushed into the studio.

"Lorraine!" he roared at her. Lorraine snapped from the spell, startled by the shouting of a normally gentle man.

"Yes," she said, "yes." Another long blink after which her eyes fixed more certainly onto Mike's face. "I hear you, Mike," she said.

"Get those two down into the press conference room, right fucking now, Kelly," Mike screeched.

Instincts honed by Lorraine's long years in media took over. "Who's here?" she asked.

"Better to ask who isn't," Mike said excitedly. "CNN, Sky, Reuters, fuckin' New York fuckin' Times, Al Jazeera... Basically every news agency you've heard of, and dozens you haven't, have sent a reporter.

Despite her confusion, Lorraine nodded, acknowledging the situation, the opportunity. "How did they see the transmission so quickly?" she asked.

Mike's face beamed. "The interview, his monologue, was transmitted through phones, PCs, tablets, TVs, radios... virtually every electronic device on the planet." Mike's eyes were halogen lamps.

"Billions, Lorraine. Billions of people," Mike added before spinning around.

Lorraine watched as Mike approached Jay and Mo who were smoking and arguing. Placing an arm around Mo, Mike attempted to usher them towards the conference room.

Mo shrugged Mike's arm off. "Fuck off and give us a minute here, mate," he said.

Mike trudged back over to the presenter.

"They need a minute," he said, blushing.

Lorraine simply nodded. She was thinking clearly again at last, but still couldn't tear her eyes from Jay's. He noticed her and smiled warmly. Holding his hand up, he mouthed *give us five minutes* to her whilst Mo continued to barrage him with potential obstacles.

Lorraine sighed.

"Look, I hear you, Mo, but it is what it is," Jay said bluntly. "We're here now, and we're doing things my way, okay?"

Mo's right eyelid twitched in annoyance, but he'd been friends with Jay long enough to know when he'd made his mind up.

"Yeah, okay," he said grudgingly. "But if you think I'm gonna let these cunts put you on a cross a second time, you're off your fuckin' head, mate."

Jay smiled broadly at him. Grabbing at his beer gut with one hand and a medium-sized man-boob with the other, Jay laughed. "No way am I up for being paraded through the streets with this guy's body. What a brassneck," Jay said.

Mo smiled but didn't laugh. "I mean it, Jay. We do our best, give everything we have, but I won't watch you tortured again. Not in person and not from Heaven." Mo looked around the studio. "Not for them."

"I'll try, Mo, okay?"

Before Mo could offer any further warnings or admonishments, Jay turned from him, retrieving a vibrating phone from his trouser pocket. Flipping the screen he looked back up at Mo. "Fucking thing has been going non-stop since we transmitted."

"Yeah, mine too. Got a call, actually."

"Right," Jay said. "Let's take a minute to see what the reaction is then go meet the press."

As Mo connected his call, Jay scrolled the screen of Garry Crawford's smartphone. A little icon showed one hundred missed calls. The phone was vibrating almost continuously. It was impossible to distinguish between calls, texts, Facebook and Twitter notifications. Jay slid the *airplane mode* icon across and breathed out with relief as the phone finally went silent.

Figuring that he should begin with Garry's relatives, who must be wondering how and why one of theirs was all over every media outlet on the planet, Garry selected the text icon and began scrolling through messages.

Woody: Whit the fuck are you up tae noo, ya mad cunt?

Marc: You look a right fat bastard on telly, mate.

Del: Get thae tits sorted 'Jesus'.

New Century Bar: Round here and get thay Jesus hands working on my water, fuckface...

Jay shook his head, closed the messages and selected Garry's Twitter feed, by far the busiest with notifications.

@GarryCrawford6

Motherwell lad, Musician.....#the45

Jay groaned at the Motherwell FC profile picture.

Noting the number of Garry's followers was slightly over four million, Jay flipped aeroplane mode off and counted to three, with Mississippis. The device began vibrating madly again until Jay flicked it back into aeroplane mode.

Garry's Twitter profile now had in excess of two hundred million followers and several hundred thousand tweets addressed to him.

Jay steeled himself and began scrolling through the Tweets Garry's account had received in the four minutes or so since he had transmitted his message:

@glampire

@GarryCrawford6 Peace and love, my Lord. #TrueBeliever

@aidanthorn

@GarryCrawford6 You can buy my shorts here: http//www…

@Krusty

@GarryCrawford6 I've always wanted to fuck the son of God. DM me.

@AngieWalker999

@GarryCrawford6 Get tae fuck, son. #FullAyShite

@Robcow63:

@GarryCrawford6 Welcome to earth, man.

@justinbieber

Let's make the world a better place, brother. #WhatDoYouMeanOutNow #Belieber

@knntom

@GarryCrawford6 If you're really the son of God, what's the best ale on earth? Oh, and do gingers have souls?

@MissyTee

@GarryCrawford6 Yaldi! Knew you were real. Fancy a toke?

@pike_star

@GarryCrawford6 How do I defeat the Riddler boss-level in Arkham City on most difficult level?

@silibil

@GarryCrawford6 Every cunt knows I'm bigger than Jesus GTF. #LetsDoLunch #ApologiesFromThe Jews

@GarethSpark1

@GarryCrawford6 You will suffer torment in hell for eternity, blasphemer.

@TheEndFanzine

@GarryCrawford6 We'd love to interview you, mate. You in Manchester soon?

@charliestOnes

@GarryCrawford6 Been having identity issues of late and hoping you can offer some insights. #TheSwitched

@IrvineWelsh

@GarryCrawford6 Keepin' it real. #LeithMassive RT?

Groovydaz39

@GarryCrawford6 How the fuck can you allow the Tories to exist? #EndAusterity

@tasha71

@GarryCrawford6 Looking for tickets to SXSW this year?

@Scatterofashes

@GarryCrawford6 We have naked pictures of you. See who sent them. Follow this link...

@MichaelLogan

@GarryCrawford6 Murmur is pleased to see you on earth, my Lord. Coffee? #Wannabes #CaffeineDrip

@GayleR28

@GarryCrawford6   Fuck   off!   Jesus   ma   erse. #CuntyBaws

@Squigmeister

@GarryCrawford6 Give that Chris Pillans boy a slap. Burst ma coupon last Saturday.

@WBCSaysRepent

@GarryCrawford6 You will suffer for eternity. Obey His Holy word. Are you a sodomite?

@BabsWilkie

@GarryCrawford6 Is this a reality show?

@STVEdinburgh

@GarryCrawford6 Would love to catch your show at the Festival. DM details?

@Dynamomagician

@GarryCrawford6 Great work, Bro. Let's do lunch. #HowTheFuck?

Jay closed the app and opened Garry's Facebook feed, but only for long enough to confirm it contained similar comments. A long sigh escaped his lips.

Jay approached Mo who was red-faced, yelling into his phone.

"Look, just do your fucking job, mate," he screamed before jabbing disconnect.

"How do you turn this off, Jay?" he asked, handing him the smartphone.

Jay flipped the phone onto plane mode and jutted his chin questioningly at Mo.

"Pillans' agent," Mo growled. "Total wank. Set him straight, he's gonna get onto the club and get us a crowd and cameras at Old Trafford for 7:30. That cool?"

Jay nodded. "Aye. Thanks, Mo." He nodded across at Mike, still blushing, shuffling his feet nervously.

"Shall we?" Jay asked.

The friends spent the rest of the day fielding questions from the world's media in a sweaty conference room in Manchester. By early evening, the frenzy had grown. Each news channel, talk show, topical daytime magazine show, online news outlet, vlogger and blogger in the digital world was running the story, a live feed to the conference or offering expert comment and analysis. They picked apart every word Jay had spoken on Lorraine's show, debating, ridiculing and dismissing them and Jay himself.

Local news stations and online media were ripping apart every aspect, each minute detail of Garry Crawford's life. Chris Pillans was being treated with a little more respect, mostly because the media suspected that the Lorraine interview was a publicity stunt designed to elevate Pillans' already-huge profile and brand.

Jay and Mo sat in the player lounge at Old Trafford scanning snippets of reports and headlines from a range of online news, blogs and media outlets.

New York Times:

Tech genius hijacks world media.

Guardian:

Second Coming of Jesus: Artist/Magician stuns the world.

The Times:

Satirist baffles tech experts.

Daily Mail:

'Jesus' conman linked to ISIS.

Telegraph:

A new Jesus; only the Scots!

Daily Mash:

Of course the son of God is Scottish.

Saints and Sinners Blog:

He is arrived.

Heat Online:

Has Jesus let himself go?

Westboro Baptist Church Bulletin:

Moses, Nazi Jew on Earth in collusion with the Anti-Christ.

Mo's face was tracked with tears. He'd been laughing so hard for so long he was holding his sides in genuine pain.

Jay scowled at him. "Give it a rest, Mo."

Mo cackled and snorted like a teenager in a lingerie store for a few more seconds before finally composing himself.

"I told you, Jay. They won't listen."

Jay's face showed not a trace of humour. "You know the consequences if that is true," Jay said.

Mo flushed with embarrassment. "Yeah… sorry, mate."

Jay rose from his seated position. Resting his hands on the window ledge he looked out across the stadium, taking in the electronic advertisement on the stand opposite. Playing on a loop on the electronic board was a highlight reel of Chris Pillans' goals for Manchester United against Liverpool from the previous four seasons, captioned with *Parting the Red Sea*. The speakers blared 'God Gave Rock n Roll to You' by Kiss.

Mo joined his friend. Looking out over the grass below, he placed a hand on Jay's shoulder.

"I hope you've something special in mind for tonight, Jay. These cynical bastards might be beyond saving."

Jay smiled sadly. "You know that I'll never accept that."

Interlude

Saluzar and Miriam

ONE AT A TIME, MIRIAM MUKHERJEE closed each of the live windows she'd been scanning. Her eyes had grown dry and irritated reading reports of the Scotsman who called himself Jay. Miriam fetched a small black case from her desk drawer and made a pinching motion at her closed eyelids, loosening the contact lenses beneath. Each lens took a few dry nipping grabs to remove. She squirted a little soothing solution into each weary orb, sighing in relief as she slipped her glasses on. After a long day reading and researching, the comfort of her spectacles was akin to slipping one's shoes off and stretching cramped toes.

Her head reeled with the information and disclosures she'd been forced to absorb since sealing Mr Saluzar in his oxygen tent earlier that day. The seemingly imminent death of her mentor, her father figure, had focused her beyond even her normally intense commitment to work. Upon leaving Mr Saluzar, Miriam had followed his instructions precisely by taking care of the day's business before accessing the secure mail server as he'd instructed.

Despite being privy to what she'd believed were all of her mentor's business dealings and personal secrets, Miriam still felt a dizzying mixture of stunned and numb at the contents of Saluzar's email. She brought the email up and reread it for the fifth time.

My dearest Miriam,

I'm so very sorry that I've placed you in the position of asking you to open this email. Please trust me when I say that were there any other option, I would choose it. I never wanted this for you. Unfortunately, it seems it is out of my hands.

What follows is the truth. Please believe. It will be difficult, but trust in our history. Know that I have never lied to you and have only tried to do good in this world. You may think me mad, but I swear to you that everything I write here is true.

The man who is all over the news (I'm presuming here that this is how he will choose to announce himself in this modern world) is exactly who he claims to be. Jesus Christ. Jesus of Nazareth. The Son of God Incarnate.

If I were to disclose to you in writing how I know this to be true, you would believe for certain that I'm insane. I am not. I knew… I know this man. He is the sole reason I exist and my motivation for aiding the poor and destitute.

If you can, Miriam, I ask that you put aside your disbelief of my own assertion, and his, that he is Jesus risen once again. I do not need you to trust in him or believe in him. As well as we know each other, I know that this is an impossibility for you. What I ask is that you trust in me, your friend, your surrogate father, and do as I request.

I do not know why Jesus has returned. Two thousand years ago, he came to save us. That much the New Testament was correct in, and whatever his current mission it will be for our benefit. I do not know how Jesus will choose to engage the world, but however he proceeds you must put the entirety of our resources at his disposal.

I will be back with you in four days, as I doubtless promised you. Do this: trust in me, in our history.

Your Friend

Saluzar

Miriam sighed wearily. Pushing her chair away from the desk, she allowed the wheels to skitter the chair back a few feet before standing. Looking out across the city below, Miriam cast her thoughts back to her childhood. Fast-forwarding through her teens, early twenties and up to the present day, Miriam found her life's achievements, joys and triumphs all connected in some way to Mr Saluzar.

Ever-present in spirit, if not in body, Saluzar had brought strength and hope and genuine happiness to her world. He'd enabled a street orphan to utilise her vast intellect and iron will. Without Saluzar she'd have died before her thirtieth birthday, perhaps unmourned except by a pimp or a john. Trusting Saluzar came easily to her, but he had taught her also to look at every aspect, to question, analyse and evaluate, coldly.

Everything was telling her that Mr Saluzar couldn't be right. That he must be mad. She did not believe in Jesus or God or any other prophet or deity. An agnostic since childhood, she could never accept what her mentor claimed the charismatic, alluring man on TV was: the Son of a God she didn't believe in.

Miriam shoved a thumb and forefinger up under her glasses and massaged her eyes once more. She was torn between her own instincts, the skills her mentor had assisted in developing and her loyalty to the man who defined her world.

Miriam summoned an image of herself and Mr Saluzar before her mind's eye. It was a recreation of an old photo, housed in a glass frame on a wall in her apartment. Mr Saluzar's and Miriam's smiles beamed in the photo. Miriam wore her graduation robes and Saluzar wore joy like a second skin.

She flicked mentally through other images of them; in offices, celebrating deals together, hard times, good times and everything in between. Miriam examined the lessons of her life, not from the perspective of a daughter, an orphan or an employee, but with the cold analytic eyes of the businesswoman she was. She knew beyond all doubt what she had to do.

9

Nick and Beth

"Monkeys and apes, evolution right enough rather than creationism? That's what we're talking about, right?" Beth asked.

Nick shrugged. "Evolution sparked by Creation, Bethany. God set the spark, as I said, but He allowed nature to unfold and adapt as pressures forced or allowed. In fact, his insistence upon allowing nature to proceed, how that process resulted in humans and His assertion that humans remain part of nature are how I came to be His Accuser." Nick swirled his whiskey glass again, lost in his own thoughts.

After a short pause, he continued.

"We weren't just Creator and Creation, master and servant, He and I. We were, and still are," Nick smiled sadly, "at least outside office hours, best friends."

Beth simply nodded along, not wishing to interrupt the flow of his monologue. She was beginning to feel fatigued, despite the situation and the revelations she was hearing. Despite the presence of a being like Nick. She had no clue how long they'd been in the *bubble* he'd created for them. Drinking, talking. As soon as she acknowledged the exhaustion, something crackled in the air and it vanished. Her muscles, mind, spirits were all refreshed with a surge of adrenaline.

Nick's doing?

She didn't bother to ask; instead, filling her glass, she felt too sober all of a sudden. Beth nodded for Nick to continue.

"The mammals branched out, *divergent evolution* your scientists call it." Nick grinned, something tickling him which he chose not to share. "They adapted to fill thousands of vacant niches. Land, sea and air, as I said, they also became adapted for life in trees. Hands for gripping, teeth of varying size and shape for a myriad of functions. Groups formed, adaptation proceeded. Monkeys began to evolve further. Apes of various size, demeanour and type emerged. Tails shortened and disappeared. Hands lost muscle and gained dexterity. Brains increased in size. Tools were invented, new food sources exploited. Brains grew in size exponentially, but only in one particular branch of the great apes."

Nick tapped his knuckles on the bar in a manner that mimicked an ape.

"Animals," he said, "still animals, then three things changed that sent a wail of outcry through Heaven unlike any before." Nick raised his eyebrows, looking at Beth in a questioning way.

Beth smiled.

"Faces?" she guessed.

"Yes," Nick said, sadly. "Faces was the first."

Nick took a drink from his glass, enjoying the burn for a moment before proceeding.

"Hairy ape faces — sloped, prominent brows, wide nose and large jaw — adapted to accommodate the growing brain, for sure, but the hair, that was what sent the Angels running to God once more.

"Hair receded from faces, exposing them like never before. Ape facial characteristics also receded, succeeded by a more feminine-looking, much less ape-like visage. The females lost all hair from their faces and most of their bodies. Their curves flowed, replacing the harder functional muscle of their ancestors. Their eyes widened, their gaits changed, their stature adapted and they stood. But it was the faces once more, especially the females' faces that sent the Angels to His feet.

"Lord, they cried, *look what the apes have become. Their faces are hairless and gentle. The females, Lord, the females are beautiful and kind. They look like us, more than ever.* Can you guess what God told them, Bethany?"

"Observe. Part of nature. Trust in me," Beth replied.

"Exactly so," Nick said. "And they did. They watched, His Angels, as several species of human developed, competed and thinned out to fuse genes and characteristics, forming one dominant species of human from all who had existed. Homo sapiens."

Nick smiled warmly at Beth.

"Were they stood in front of you now, the first Homo sapiens would appear ancient to you in their similarity to the apes they descended from. To us, their appearance was astonishing, a wonder beyond anything our imaginations or intellects could have predicted. I, of course, approached... accused God also. I, of course, resumed my watching, and began to wonder as to God's true motives. This was a new state of mind for me — questioning his motives, his intentions — and I did not like the loss of certainty that I'd previously possessed. I'd lost the capacity to accept whatever He said, without question. A cavity the size of the universe had opened up in me at the loss of that trust.

"Billions of years of doing... what I do haven't replaced an atom of that loss."

The air crackled once more, and Beth could feel the loss, the bereavement, emanating from Nick as he spoke of God. She broke the moment, guiding him back to his monologue.

"What were the other two events that changed your relationship with God?" Beth asked.

"Ah, those," Nick's voice dripped bitterness. "I'd turned my face for a time from the events taking place on Earth and chosen to observe other worlds: worlds less developed. Further back on the evolutionary process, if you like. Unexpectedly, I found a comfort in looking back at the beginnings of evolution unfolding at a different pace, or following different paths, on other worlds. The randomness of nature still startled me, but the predictability of life's capacity to adapt and to survive eased my mind and made me believe once more that God's insistence that nature would find a way, that life would adapt, was correct. The evidence of God's viewpoint could be observed throughout the universe, on countless worlds. Unicellular, multicellular, reptiles, mammalian equivalents — they were all there, pushed along, forced by nature to adapt to survive. Many species only existed on certain worlds. Others were common on millions of planets.

"Only Earth held humans. Inevitably, I returned to check on their progress."

Nick jutted his chin at a vase on the end of the bar, which held some sad-looking wilted flowers.

"Those were fresh this morning," Beth whined, puzzled.

"Time's a little different in here," Nick said. "Anyway, flowers. That was the second event."

Beth blinked a long deliberate blink, attempting to clear her puzzlement.

"Right," he said, "flowers. I returned to watching Earth, finding the number of Angels who now shared that particular pastime to have increased to unprecedented levels. I recall asking Michael what the sudden interest in Earth was. He looked at me sadly.

"Better that you return to your other pursuits, he told me. I wish that I had listened. That was the day I lost my Angelic form. The day that I was named *Accuser*. The day that I was banished from Heaven."

10

Jay and Mo

THE CENTRE-CIRCLE FELT FAR TOO CLOSE to the rows of seats reaching up into the stands around Jay. Despite the apparent vastness of Old Trafford, now, tonight, the football shrine felt oppressive in its confined quarters, such was the number of people gathered. The stands were filled, but the organisers had also arranged rows of seats, ten deep, on all sides of the pitch between the advertisement boards and part of the playing surface. Perhaps close to eighty thousand people were inside the stadium. Billions more would soon be watching through one of the many lenses pointed at Jay.

 As he scanned the faces assembled, confirming his fears for the event, Jay's heart sank. One word could summarise the type of person present... rich.

Jay had expected this to be the case, but disappointment stung him anyway. The audience, which had gathered mostly out of curiosity, indignation and excitement at being present for the next big thing, consisted mainly of the very wealthy, very famous or political leaders from a variety of countries. Chris Pillans' agent had boasted to Jay moments before he'd stepped onto the pitch that those in attendance had paid extravagant sums of money to witness his *show*.

Outside the stadium a sea of people congregated. Parted by a valley of Greater Manchester's finest, two factions waved boards and banners at each other, either condemning Jay and Mo or praising them. Many had come just for the spectacle: *what would he do next?* Many came asking him to save them.

Taking in the faces of footballers, Russian businessmen, media moguls, bankers, prime ministers, presidents and European royalty, Jay felt a chill vibrate up his spine.

Mo walked through the tunnel behind Jay and placed an arm around his shoulders. Joint dangling from his lips, Mo sneered, "Hope you've got some pretty words, matey. This lot are predators."

Jay nodded once, but did not speak. He gestured with his hand, a movement insignificant to anyone who caught it, but one which connected the cameras and internet feeds once again.

He closed his eyes.

Breathing deeply, Jay accessed the reservoir of power available to him. Not deeply enough to merge his consciousness with that of his Father — doing so was never advisable — but instead Jay allowed a long, gentle trickle of God's power to flow into him. Sensing the change in his friend, Mo stepped away.

Immersing himself in the light, Jay raised his arms slightly at his sides, basking in it. He permitted an infinitesimal portion of the Light of Heaven to show in his face.

Gradually those assembled in the stadium grew aware of the change in his appearance. People prodded and shooshed each other, pointing at Jay's face as he stood there in the centre of the pitch. It had taken on an ethereal quality, not a glow exactly, more a radiance that shone so clearly it hushed the crowd. Nothing... no-one moved. The entire stadium of people held their collective breath. The air itself seemed to vanish. The gentlest whisper escaped Jay's lips that no-one in the stadium heard, but each felt.

"Understand."

The fabric of the world flickered, like a glitch in the universe that suddenly corrected itself. Almost as though the whole of humanity had blinked at the same moment and opened their eyes to the very same reality as before, but one in which something unprecedented had shifted.

Everybody felt it. Every person in the stadium. Every human who had access to a digital feed. No-one could define it.

Jay had not known what would happen until he decided upon it. Thought and deed were one in Heaven and the fraction of Heaven's power that he had access to had moved to make his wish a reality. Jay smiled gently and opened his eyes as the cries began.

A stadium, filled moments ago with the rich and the famous, the morally corrupt, the lucky, the ignorant and the scheming, now held tens of thousands of children whose voices filled the air with joyful panic.

In the director's box Mexican children from Hidalgo County, United States, whose parents had been exploited for decades and who lived in abject poverty, raided the tables, heavy with rich foods, and banged the windows, whooping in delight.

In Hidalgo, businessmen in suits found themselves playing in the dirt.

In Khayelitsha, South Africa, pampered celebrities found themselves in the heart of the slums, a hangover from apartheid, surrounded by disease and three-foot rats who hunted babies in their cribs. The actors wept whilst the children of Khayelitsha ate their food and danced in the aisles of the Sir Alex Ferguson Stand.

In the Upper East Stand a young boy bit hungrily into a pie. He alone from his shanty, La Saline in Cite Soleil, Port-au-Prince, Haiti, had been brought to Old Trafford. He cried in shame as he ravenously devoured the mutton pastry, devastated that he was eating whilst his family was starving at home.

In Haiti one hundred Premiership footballers experienced the violence the boy had endured for all of his ten years in the shanty.

Bankers and lawyers who'd paid thousands of pounds to attend Jay's gathering cowered in the pipes of Dharavi, Mumbai, India. Many vomited in reaction to the smells and sights around them. Rapists stalked them.

In Manchester the Chawls and pavement-dwellers, most under ten years old, also cowered under the seats of most of the West Stand. Ten thousand children, freed from the sewer, too frightened by the daytime they found themselves in to emerge.

The stadium emptied and filled in the blink of an eye, at the whim of the Son of God.

Orphaned, abused, abandoned, destitute, unwanted and unnoticed children from Kibera, Neza-Chalco-Itza, Maharashtra and many other slums of the world changed places with the most blessed of the Western world.

Jay looked over each of their frightened, joyful and bewildered faces and collapsed to his knees in the centre of the playing field.

Mo rushed to his side. "Fuck. What have you done?"

Jay was exhausted. He always was when he accessed Heaven in this manner, but the greater strain came from the pain he felt from the children filling the stadium.

"Given them a glimpse of each other," he said softly. "With any luck, made them realise who we are and what they've done."

Jay fell face-first to the grass while the world realised what had taken place and lost its collective shit.

Monday

Interlude

Saluzar and Miriam

MIRIAM GLANCED OUT AT THE BRIDGES spanning the Firth of Forth beneath the Gulfstream IV and smiled, satisfied that she'd made the correct choice. The rising sun hanging behind the bridges amplified the sense of new beginnings she'd been feeling.

 The media's reporting of the Old Trafford Event had been predictably dismissive, sensational and scathing, all at once. Saluzar's connection in the Greater Manchester Police had reported Jay's whereabouts to her that morning.

 Whatever unfolded in the next few hours, however she approached Jay, she could be confident that choosing to ignore her misgivings and to trust the man who'd raised her had been the right thing to do, regardless of what may come.

Three more days. Please keep your word, Mr Saluzar.

11

Nick and Beth

"Flowers, for fuck sake, Beth. How many relationships or friendships have ended over flowers?" Nick was grinning, forcing humour into his face, but his voice was strained, the hurt evident. "Michael could see that I had no intention of returning to my other pursuits without checking in with events on Earth. He placed a hand on my right cheek and told me simply, *I'll come stand by you.*

"I made my way to the tear in the fabric of Heaven through which we observe Earth. I gasped. Sounds dramatic, especially for beings with no need for air, but it's the only way I can describe my reaction. I gasped, my whole ethereal being flickered. I thought that I would cease to exist. Afterwards it seemed that I actually had, momentarily, and had reformed as something — someone else. Someone angry and embittered. Someone who felt betrayed by his Creator.

"I observed the ancestor of Homo sapiens. They looked much like they had some hundred thousand or so Earth-years previously, the last time I'd observed them. Their faces were smoother, even the males', radiant. Their whole demeanour had softened: they possessed something previously unseen in nature on any world I'd observed. A self-awareness. The next event I saw made clear to me what changes had taken place to bring about this awareness.

"Flowers.

"They gathered around one of their dead. A male. He looked elderly. He looked like he'd had a hard life. His hands were rough and calloused, his face weathered, his body carried many scars.

"These creatures were the very first of your ancestors, Bethany. Millennia before agriculture developed, before animals were kept as livestock, seeds sown or lands claimed. They were nomadic hunter-gatherers. It was a hard life and they died young. That this man had lived forty-plus years was exceptional at that time.

"He lay there, dead, gone from the world, but a gathering was around him. His people stood in a circle around his body. Some looked solemn, some laughed and celebrated his life, some cried. His body was laid on an altar. It was covered in flowers… flowers, Bethany. These people, these animals, as God insisted they were… they mourned their dead."

Beth remained silent, but her face wore a *so what* expression.

Nick's patience was limitless.

"Flowers, to mark the passing of a loved one. Grief, sadness at the loss of that individual. These were new. These were not things demonstrated by any other creature on the Earth. Not in the whole, entire universe, Bethany. Countless billions of forms of life, and here on this insignificant rock in an unremarkably minor solar system around a young star, a life-form recognised loss and mourned it.

"I fled, straight to God and demanded of Him, 'You see what the humans have done, my Lord? They mourn, they grieve the loss of their own, they consecrate with flowers.'

"He smiled patiently at me, as always. 'Do you imagine that I do not know this, my Angel? Do you think that this is not intended?' he asked me. 'All is as nature allows. All is as I wish.'

"I was stunned at his dismissal of this monumental development of the human state of existence, but I could not find the words with which to reply. Looking back, I think that I knew at that moment. I think I knew that He was simply wrong. I knew it but I buried it into my deepest subconscious. This was a blasphemy — God couldn't be wrong. These creatures, all things in the universe, only existed because He wished them to. Who was I to argue with the Creator of everything?

"'Return to watching, My Angel,' he told me.

"I did. God forgive me, but I did.

"Many years passed on Earth. I witnessed humans continue to mourn their dead, to place markings and flowers and items from the person's life beside their loved-ones' bodies. They began to bury and cremate the dead. Some consumed the flesh of their dead, the brain or the heart. But however those left behind chose to mourn, grieve or honour their dead, something had changed. Something irrevocable.

"From their actions it was clear that humans now believed that their dead became something else, or went elsewhere after death. The concept of an afterlife had formed. The remarkable thing was that they were absolutely correct."

Nick raised his eyebrows at Beth, a question implicate.

"Ghosts?" she asked.

"Spirits," Nick replied. "Souls."

Beth subconsciously covered the lower half of her face with her hands. Her eyes, wide and sad, peeked over her fingertips. A tear hung on her lower eyelid and then broke, running along her fingers.

"He meant for that?"

Nick shrugged. "Part of nature," he replied. "I watched a group of them, humans, mourning their dead. They sang, they celebrated and they prayed. They prayed, Bethany. Not to a God or a deity, but to their ancestors. The belief that their dead somehow lingered in the atmosphere beyond the death of their body had taken hold. They did not need, want or believe in a God. Not yet. Instead they accepted death and the afterlife and held fast to the belief that those who had gone before protected them, watched over them."

Beth interrupted. "Did they?" she asked.

Nick considered his words. "Yes and no," he replied. "I watched a single soul rise from the form of a man at the moment of his death. The outline of his physical self, it seemed. Transparent, fabricated of something other than matter. Not an Angel, no. Too small, not radiant enough for that, and it did not ascend to Heaven as an Angel might, this soul, but most definitely it was Angel-like.

"More so than ever before, the humans had adapted, evolved, to become more nearly Angels, alike as to God Himself. Even in the state of horror I was in, I restrained myself from running once more to God and making demands of Him. I resolved to observe as I had promised Him I would.

"The soul of the dead man rose, not quickly but slowly, as though confused or perhaps saddened by the new form it had taken. A swirling thing, becoming less distinct as each moment passed, the soul still clearly held the intelligence of the man it had resided within. The eyes of the soul told me this. They were fixed on the dead man's grieving relatives. No tears fell, but all the hurt in the world was concentrated there to see.

"Humans cannot perceive us. God and His Angels are elsewhere, hidden from human perceptions. Giving them a glimpse of Heaven in showing them our faces or allowing them to hear our voices was not possible. The Light of Heaven was too powerful for them.

"I'd whispered in human ears on many occasions, but simply to appease myself. They simply could not see or hear me. If I allowed them too, it would destroy them. Despite this, I wished to comfort the soul. I spoke the words. 'They will be fine, my friend.'

"The soul's entire form contracted into the tight outline of a human once more. It looked around, clearly searching for the source of the voice it had heard. I shrank my presence, not hiding exactly, but protecting it from my glory.

"The soul took a moment and then ascended. Not into Heaven, but to a murky place where other souls had gathered over the centuries in the upper atmosphere. I followed, dread in my heart but a seed of hope also."

Beth's eyes were wide once again. "You wanted to guide them to Heaven?"

Nick shook his head. "No. Not at that moment. I simply wanted to observe, as I had been commanded. I imagined in my observations that I might find the kernel of evidence I needed to convince God that humans had evolved beyond nature, so I watched and listened and I wept for them."

Nick once again lit a cigarette for himself and for Bethany. They smoked together in silence. Nick smiled a little, sadly, pondering how the simple act of smoking with someone rather than on one's own created a bond, a warmth, between people.

Blowing the last of the smoke through his nose in a weary gust, Nick continued.

"I went there, amongst them, beyond and beside them. Souls from centuries before, souls from that very morning. The souls of the young, old and new-born lingered. Male and female souls, though they were only barely distinguishable in their spirit form. As in matter, in spirit the females were more nearly Angelic than the males. Some souls retained their very human dimensions, their physical characteristics from life, represented in immaterial form. Most had dissipated, becoming loose swirls of entities that covered large parts of the sky.

"Immaterial, invisible and largely discorporate, the souls of humans lingered in a murky soup. Purposeless and abandoned, they seemed unaware of each other, completely without identity. Except for a very small number who gathered in the upper levels.

"They called themselves The Enlightened."

12

Jay and Mo

"Jay?" Mo said softly.

He placed a hand on his friend's right cheek, the contact causing him to stir at last.

Jay had slept until noon after collapsing onto the Old Trafford turf the previous evening. Mo had lifted his best friend up onto and across his shoulders as the stadium erupted around them. Stewards and police had no chance of preventing the flood of children surging towards Jay from the stands. Mo, assisted by Pillans' agent and some club physios, had barely made it to a waiting car. Once clear of the crowds outside the stadium, Mo lit a cigarette and relaxed a little.

Accompanied by three plain-clothed police officers, two men and a woman who had been assigned as protection detail, Mo and an unconscious Jay had sped from Manchester north to Scotland. Jay had barely stirred throughout the trip or during his subsequent transfer from the car into the little cottage in South Queensferry.

"C'mon, pal. It's time to shift yourself," Mo said, a little more gruffly.

Jay rubbed at his closed eyes with the heels of his hands and groaned.

"How long?"

"'Bout seventeen hours, Jay."

"Shit," Jay said. Raising his head from the pillow, Jay found himself in a rather old-fashioned room. Low, wooden-beamed ceilings and white walls surrounded him. The bedroom held dozens of little glass ornaments, arranged carefully along shelves and on a dresser. The bed was an old metal frame with a crochet blanket over. It looked like an old lady's cottage.

"Where?" Jay croaked.

"South Queensferry," Mo said. "One of the coppers... Dougie, it's his granny's place. Left it to Dougie in her will. Nobody knows we're here."

Jay sat up. "I take it that's a good thing, Mo?"

Mo cocked an eyebrow.

"Eh, yeah," he said. "It went fuckin' mental after you conked out, mate. We barely got you out of the stadium."

"The kids okay?" Jay asked.

Mo grinned and nodded. "Yeah. Most have been housed in royal residences."

"Fuck off," Jay said.

"No, really. The Queen stepped up, really came through. Currently Buckingham, Kensington and St James's Palaces and Windsor Castle have hundreds of refugee kids roaming the corridors, having the time of their lives."

Jay's eyebrows lifted. "Fuck me. A result of one of her own being sent to Haiti, you reckon?"

"Na," Mo replied. "I think she was genuinely moved by what happened. Lots of people were, you'll see. Besides, it was only that prick Andrew."

Jay laughed.

"Can't all be good news, Mo."

"No, it's not," Mo admitted. He jutted his chin at the door to the living room. "C'mon," he said.

Led by Mo, and wrapped in the heavy crochet blanket, Jay padded his way on bare feet through to a comfortable living room dominated by a fifty-inch TV. Dougie was flicking through news channels.

Hearing the men enter, Dougie jumped to his feet and performed an awkward gesture. Half bow, half curtsey, Dougie's face burned red as he stammered, "All yours, My Lord."

Mo's face creased with laughter. "What the fuck was that supposed to be, Dougie?"

The big copper's eyes were wide and didn't leave Jay's face.

Jay gave him a reassuring smile. "S'cool, big man," he said. "I'll take the other chair."

Dougie flicked his eyes at Mo for reassurance.

"Sit down, you massive soft shite," he said, joining Jay on the sofa. "Owt changed, mate?" he asked Dougie.

Dougie snapped himself out of his funk.

"No. Same stories on repeat... Oh, there's been another mass suicide in Alabama."

"Fuck them," Jay muttered. "Extremist pricks."

Dougie's eyebrows shot up at hearing the Messiah curse.

"Eh, yeah... Fuck 'em," he agreed uncertainly.

Mo patted him on the back.

"That's the spirit, Dougie."

Jay shooshed them and made a gesture to Dougie that he should pass the remote for the TV. Spending the next forty minutes flicking through news channels and swiping through articles on Dougie's tablet, Jay absorbed the world's reaction to the previous night's event at Old Trafford.

A mass hysteria had taken hold in all the cities and countries he had expected to react most strongly to his arrival.

In America Rednecks, Bible-thumpers and survivalists in Tennessee, Florida, Texas, Kentucky and Louisiana had begun heavily arming and organising themselves. A strong *Kill dis summbitch* rhetoric prevailed. Jay's assertion that God was the bastard of all bastards had not gone over well with them.

A similar reaction from Isis, the Taliban and Al Qaeda was evident. Effigies of Jay and Mo burned. Threats were issued.

In Vatican City the Pope had condemned Jay's use of Christ for entertainment purposes, but had urged restraint.

Likewise, Jews the world over were outraged at a premiership footballer claiming to be their deliverer, Moses. Benjamin Netanyahu had issued a decree that both Jay and Mo were never to be permitted to enter Israel and made a request that the United States restrict them also.

A handful of churches and cults, cities and towns in the States and across Africa, India, Brazil and Spain had declared Jay the true Messiah and prayed round the clock for the mercy of Heaven in the coming days.

Some had formed and perpetrated suicide pacts, the coming apocalypse at the forefront of their minds.

Calais and the Channel Tunnel had been overrun, the barriers and fences trampled by thousands of refugees who'd been camped nearby for months. Starved of hope as much as nutrition, the men, women and children had watched The Event — as it was being referred to — in Manchester on large screens in the docks and recognised Jay for precisely who and what he was, and what he represented to all of humanity: hope.

A legion of the poorest, most desperately abandoned walked the length of the tunnel, a purpose at last... perhaps somewhere to belong.

The news channels — BBC, CNN, Fox, Al Jazeera... dozens more — interviewed their experts on religion, forensics, illusions, psychology, confidence tricks and scams, and also police and government ministers.

Heresy.

Preying on vulnerable, scared people.

Insanity and narcissistic tendencies.

Mass, shared delusions.

Drugs in the stadium. Possible chemical agents used.

Terrorist.

Greatest illusion in the history of humankind.

Forensically, these people appear to have genuinely been switched. Traces of mud from India on the children. Minerals only found in those regions. The GPS on many of the switched persons' smartphones corroborate them moving instantly between countries and continents.

We cannot explain it.

Jay gave his attention to a man talking on BBC who called him and Mo *the most well-prepared, convincing and talented con-men in history.*

The mainstream media and news outlets gave airtime to only those incidents and people who would dismiss or debunk the event in some way. The internet told a different story.

Across social media platforms, people were beginning to consider whether Jay and Mo really were who they claimed to be. Across Europe and North America users were questioning the official story, sharing accounts, videos and pictures of The Event posted by people who were there. Lady Gaga, who had been switched with a Peruvian orphan, had been sharing images of her experience on Twitter which had been retweeted by millions. #SaintGaga was trending globally.

That idea, the acceptance that the stadium event had been real, not a trick, was slowly taking hold in the virtual world, but like political analyses, or human rights activism, the real, material world seemed happy to dismiss the event as a spectacular illusion or stunt, perhaps pre-arranged for years.

People appeared to be waiting for the *big reveal,* or for Jay and Mo to be exposed.

Too few were actually worrying about God's promise of an end to humanity.

Mo handed Jay a mug of coffee.

"Hate to say it, Jay, but your dad was right. These fuckers don't deserve Heaven. They care more about a scratch on their new sneakers or fuckin' Beyonce's bunion than they do about each other or about Heaven, Hell or God."

Mo eyed Jay, who stayed silent.

"They're fucked, mate."

Jay sipped at his coffee for a few moments, eyes unfocused, deep in thought.

"South Queensferry, you said?"

"Yeah," Mo replied, "Just at the foot of the bridges over the Firth of Forth."

A lopsided grin began to form on Jay's lips.

"That a fact?" he said.

Jay took his coffee outside with him. Still wrapped in the blanket, he pulled it closer to him and gazed up at the rail and road bridges spanning the Forth. His eyes followed the line of the road bridge north to where it plonked down into Fife.

Sensing that Mo stood nearby, Jay spoke without looking away from the bridge.

"I assume that the press want to speak to me?" he asked.

Mo eyed the back of his head suspiciously.

"Look, Jay. It doesn't matter what you say to them. It won't matter if you convince every single human on this planet that you are Jesus, Son of God, and that His wrath is coming. They're too fucking stupid to care."

Finally Jay did turn to his friend. His eyebrows were knitted into a frown.

"You sound just like Him."

Mo scratched at his beard. "Yeah, well… It's true, Jay. We're wasting our time here."

Jay was angry — as angry as he got at any rate. He fought back a vicious comment and spoke softly to his friend.

"Do you trust me?"

"You know I do, Jay." Mo jabbed a thumb over his shoulder at Edinburgh behind. "It's those cunts I don't trust."

Jay nodded. "Doesn't matter… I believe in them. You don't have to."

Mo's mind flashed back almost two thousand years ago as he'd watched from Heaven as the humans tore the flesh from his best friend's torso with a whip. He'd screamed as they brutalised Jay, as they nailed him to a cross to suffocate and suffer… as his muscles and tendons and ligaments were pulled and ripped past their natural limits. He'd watched until he couldn't bear it a moment longer and begged God to intervene as Jay was sacrificed to human superstition.

He could not, did not have the resilience to allow it to happen again.

As though reading Mo's mind, Jay placed a hand on his friend's shoulder.

"It's not like last time, pal. This time I have a friend."

Salt-sting made Mo rub at his eyes with a knuckle as he looked out over the Forth and chewed his lower lip.

"What do you want to do?" he asked with a sigh.

Jay squeezed his shoulder… a thank you.

"Ask that agent of Pillans' to get the press to the Esplanade at Edinburgh Castle. One hour."

Jay strode purposefully back into the little cottage. Watching him go, Mo said a silent prayer to a God he knew didn't care to prevent his best friend from being hurt.

13

Nick and Beth

"I watched them, these distinct, purposeful souls. Watched and marvelled. They gathered in a group of perhaps fifty. Each of them serene… calm. None of the turbulence, or even the torment around them seemed to register in their manner. They embraced each other, they danced playfully, fully in control of their spirit forms and clearly revelling in them, the flesh of their previous lives unmissed.

"Most incredibly, some of them visited their descendants. Some even attempted to answer their prayers."

"They thought that they were gods?" Beth asked.

"The people on Earth or The Enlightened themselves?" Nick replied.

"The spirits," Beth said.

"No. They did not," Nick answered. "They merely answered the cries and the celebrations of their kin."

"They communicated with humans?"

"Yes," Nick grinned. "In a small, but impactful manner, that is exactly what they did, Bethany. The Enlightened had learned to affect matter from the immaterial plane they inhabited. Small things like making fires flare up, little movements of cups, that sort of thing. They did not do these things to frighten, or to garner worship; they did so to reassure their kin that some part of them did survive beyond the death of their bodies."

Beth covered her mouth again, her eyes widened in horror.

"The people, they thought that the spirits were gods answering their prayers," she said flatly.

"They did," Nick confirmed, "but The Enlightened wanted no worship, as I've said. They withdrew completely from their communications with humans and never returned. Other souls, less *Enlightened*, had no such moral restraint.

"Spirits, sometimes in great number, sometimes benignly, sometimes with great malevolence, made it their eternal mission to communicate with, torment, even influence the humans. This occurs even now, in your time, Bethany.

"Many of those spirits saw it as their ultimate destiny, a reason for the afterlife they found themselves in. A purpose. Some declared themselves gods, or portioned a territory on Earth within which other spirits were not permitted. The humans were to worship only one god in those zones.

"These would-be god-souls gave their names, whispered them to their followers. Conflicting rules, rituals, dogmas and demands for sacrifices emerged in the various valleys and mountains now resided over silently by men who communed with their gods."

"The birth of religion," Beth gasped.

"Precisely. Men knew that something survived beyond death, they knew it. They spoke to entities claiming to be Divine. Sometimes these entities possessed their bodies, spoke with their voices. The world and humans were changed forever. Immoral men took advantage of the power religion brought. Honest men fought wars over differences in beliefs.

"The evolution of a soul and the evolution of that soul in the afterlife, its adapting to re-enter the material world in some way — these things took humankind out of nature, made humans believe in, aspire to, something more than a limited earthbound life. They developed the capacity for and yearned for Heaven.

"That was the beginning of the death of my blind worship for my Creator: the evolution of the human soul.

"If I could change that moment, the choice I made to return to watching earthly matters, I would. That single decision saved more souls than even I can count, but separated me forever from the Source. From God."

Beth reached for him to place a hand on his, hesitated, then steeled herself and placed a soft, warm hand onto the back of his.

"I'm sorry, Nick."

He willed the tears to dry from his eyes and nodded his thanks.

"But," Beth continued, "I don't think that's true at all. I don't think that you would change that decision, lose all those souls you saved. Not for anything, not even for His love."

Nick acknowledged her remark with a smile, but did not reply. After a moment, he said, "Regardless, everything changed. God Himself changed… because of what I did."

Nick's eyes suddenly looked very human, every part of the hurt he felt was being expressed. He hated at that moment that she'd seen it.

Nick looked into Bethany's eyes.

"These are not huge revelations to you, Bethany. You're a clever girl, you've pondered the beginnings more than once. Especially after your uncle."

Beth's face became stone.

Nick simply shrugged. "Did you think that I could be *who* I am… *what* I am, and not know everything about you, Bethany?" Nick let the question hang between them, sending a plume of cigarette smoke up to join it after a few long, painful minutes.

Black-mascara tears slashed down Bethany's cheeks. She did not make a sound in her weeping. When she could trust her voice, that the fear hadn't obliterated it, she whispered, "What do you want with me?"

Terror made her knuckles white around her empty glass.

Nick slowly, deliberately, filled her glass to the top.

"I told you, we'll get to that later." He nodded at her glass which looked as though it might crack under her grip any moment. "Have a drink," he said. "I have more to tell you."

Bethany drained the glass, feeling her head spin almost immediately.

Nick made a gesture and she sobered, but only enough to allow the sickness to pass. He left her inebriated enough to dull the urge to tear her skin from her face with her fingernails.

Sadness passed over his face. Sadness and regret.

He reached for her hand, wincing as she flinched. Taking it softly, he squeezed her hand in reassurance.

"I'm sorry, Beth. I'm feeling particularly bitter at present. I did not intend to frighten you."

Beth managed a single, curt nod of her head.

Nick leaned in. "I promise you that I will not hurt you in any way, Bethany. You're in no danger from me. Okay?"

Again the nod, but her eyes lost their panicked edginess. Nick reclined back.

"I went back into the swirl of souls. They called it Sheol. I returned and searched its entirety for more souls like The Enlightened but I found none. I wanted to speak to them, I needed to. I wanted to know what they desired, what they believed their purpose was. I wanted to understand them — how they could be so passively serene in the turmoil of Sheol. I did not have the courage."

Nick stared off into the distance for a few moments.

"Perhaps it's more correct to say that I did not have the means. It was not within my power to reveal myself in all my Heavenly glory to these *earthbo*und souls. In hindsight, that was correct. Had I been able, I would have and that would have meant disaster for them because I held no real answers for them, simply because I could not give them access to that for which they were so ably adapted. I could not admit them into Heaven.

"In any case, I did not reveal myself to these souls. I knew in my heart that God, who loved His Angels so, somehow could not be completely aware of the new stage of evolution that the humans had attained. Had He known, He would have certainly welcomed those enlightened souls, so very like His Angels, into Heaven with warmth in His heart and open arms. I was completely certain of this. I made for Heaven with this certainty. That once He knew what I had witnessed, He would see, and He would accept those glorious souls and all who came after.

"I flew. Away from Sheol, escaping the material realm, I slipped into our existence and welcomed the return of my true form, which I'd missed during my time on Earth.

"Angels clamoured to me. 'What has happened? You are glowing with a new light,' they said to me. I could not perceive what they referred to and assumed that I simply looked invigorated by my discovery of the human soul.

"'Come. I will tell God, and in my telling, you will hear also,'" I told them.

"God embraced me. His being merged with mine, His glory entered me, became me, surrounded me. Pure love flooded all present. Every need fulfilled, every desire sated. This is what it means to be in God's presence, Bethany.

"Still, I felt the stab of need. Not my own, but that of humanity. I recall thinking, *why do I have to care? Let me be happy to worship Him once again.* Of course, I wasn't that being any longer.

"I broke off, causing a flicker of His presence.

"Anger.

"This was the first occasion that God had felt, or at least shown, anger, and I was the cause of it. In His unmistakable voice, with that accent, but much harsher than previously, He asked me, 'Why do you pull away from me, Nicholas?'

"I remember brushing His question aside, which only increased His anger. I began talking, too fast, too impassioned and too demanding. That's what it was, but it was all I had to offer on their behalf. I told him. 'My Lord, the humans have souls. They have perceived these souls from Earth and pray to them as we pray to you. They are immaterial, like us, but earthbound.'"

Beth had become lost in the story, and had forgotten her fear. "He already knew," she stated.

"Yes," Nick replied. "Of course He did. He attempted the same patience, the same love He always offered, *trust me, watch what nature does,* all the old platitudes. This time a tinge of anger tainted the words. He was restraining Himself, forcing calm when anger was all. My being was repulsed at the change I'd brought in Him with my endless questioning of His will. His universe. I did not stop, though. Humans meant that much to me, and they still do.

"'They are of nature, Nicholas,' He told me again. 'Their souls are not our forms. They never will be. They are as the skin a snake sheds and leaves in the sand.'

"I was horrified. 'But they long for ascension, My Lord. They need it. Why create this evolution of an immaterial soul for them if they are not to join us here in worship of God?'

"'That is not for a fucking Angel to know,' His voice blasted from Him. 'These are my fucking Creations, as are you,' he pressed a finger into my body, bruising the immaterial form. Heaven literally shook at his anger. Angels fell, their faces to the floor, their voices raised to placate.

"Forgive him, My Lord, Nicholas loves you. Forgive, mercy.

"'You, of all my Creations, you — my first and best and truest — you question me?'

"His voice, His anger, threatened to rip my being apart. I wanted to stop existing. I wanted to become one with Him once more and forget everything about humans and His entire material universe. I wanted to turn away and be the happy Watcher once more. I could not.

"I fought the fear and the threat to my sanity... my very existence. I glared back at Him as He glared at me. I was created to be His image. His image I was.

"Both of us the absolute antithesis of our true selves as we stared each other down. I was horrified that My Lord's face could take such form. Anger, malice, absolute malevolence where once only love and acceptance and eternal patience had been.

"I should have dropped to His feet and begged forgiveness. Instead I showed Him that reflection of Himself."

14

Jay and Mo

"Thanks for everything, Dougie," Mo said, slapping the big copper on the shoulder. "You did some job getting this organised in an hour."

Dougie's eyes scanned the throng of journalists, demonstrators, worshipers and police officers held behind some very fragile-looking metal barriers. The Esplanade was filled, overfilled really, across its breadth and the crowd led back out onto The Royal

Mile. Every minute that passed brought more people funnelling into the cobbled area leading up to Edinburgh Castle.

Dougie spoke quietly from the corner of his mouth, his eyes still busily assessing the mood and movement of those gathered. "More than just me involved with something this size," he said.

"Yeah, but I know how hard you've worked to co-ordinate all these people." Mo nodded over at Jay who sat on a short wall near the Castle entrance. "And keep the good Lord over there safe."

Dougie's eyes darted nervously at Jay for a second, as though he'd be struck down for nodding absent-mindedly at Mo's comment.

Mo punched him on the upper arm.

"He can't hear us. You're some man, Dougie."

Dougie returned to surveying the throng of people across and along the Esplanade.

"Respect, mate, innit," he said, trace of a smile.

Mo grinned broadly. "Well, thanks anyway, Dougie, see you afterwards, 'kay?"

Mo broke off and made his way across the front of the crowd. Hands reached over the barriers to touch him. Mo smiled warmly at each of the people, regardless of whether they carried signs that damned himself and Jay or begged them to save them.

Shaking hands as he moved along — Helen, a colleague of Dougie's, following in his wake and shoving away hands that grasped rather than welcomed — Mo marvelled at the power of social media. Fifty-seven minutes had passed since he'd stood with Jay at the foot of the Forth Rail Bridge. Less than an hour later and every major news organisation in the world had a representative present. A hundred thousand people were crushing along the Esplanade and the cobbled streets beyond, hoping to hear Jay speak, perhaps witness another miraculous illusion.

Mo thanked a man who had shaken his hand and wished him the best before stepping back from the barriers. Along with Helen, he made his way towards Jay, currently resting an arse cheek and a foot against ancient stones outside the Castle.

As ever when he was nearby these sort of structures, Mo felt a mixture of wonder at the inventiveness of man and despair at the lengths they'd gone to, at how sophisticated their war-making had become since his life in Egypt so many thousands of years before.

Jay sat against the stonework, face turned to the sun, soaking up its warmth. A momentary flashback of standing in a Nazarene street, kids playing around him, came painfully to mind. He'd been seven years old that day, a part of the chaos and innocent fun around him. They ran and tussled and learned. It was a perfect moment on what seemed a perfect day. The day he, a child, had gained full awareness of who he was, and what he had to face in the years that followed.

Jay recalled his seven-year-old self, trying to convince himself that the newly surfaced knowledge and powers were merely a child's fantasy; to convince himself that they were nothing more than the product of a happy boy's overactive imagination. Jay had allowed his young face to soak up the sun's goodness for a few short seconds. When he'd opened his eyes again, he was no longer one of them. He'd accepted what he was and that the child he'd been moments before would never exist again.

"You look a right gormless prick, Jay," Mo said as he sat himself next to his friend. "Honestly, mate. That face... your dad must be pissing himself laughing at the body he lumbered you with."

Jay broke his moment of reverie and smiled at Mo and Helen. "Disnae matter..." Mo's eyebrows shot up in amusement at the accent, so similar to God's. Jay coughed. "Doesn't matter," he enunciated, sounding all Hugh Grant.

Mo laughed loudly.

Jay turned from him, smiling wryly.

"Doesn't matter," he repeated, "actually, it's sort of fitting."

Mo nodded. "Yeah, I suppose so." Nodding downhill to the restless crowd, Mo asked, "Ready, matey?"

Jay didn't answer, but rose to his feet. Mo could felt the air shift as Jay accessed Heaven, allowing its presence within him to show once more. Helen gasped, but Mo didn't hear it, hidden as it was by the collective gasp of a hundred thousand people who'd felt the change also.

Jay closed his eyes. Scanning the depths of history at his disposal, the feelings of everyone present and many more across several continents, Jay assessed the mood, the soul of as many as he could comfortably examine.

Some felt aggressive, others passive. Some were openly hostile, either towards him or each other for their opposing views. Many souls were tainted by fear. Fear that he was a blasphemer and that they were somehow complicit for beginning to believe his words. Fear that he was correct, that God hated them. Fear that there would be no ascension to Heaven for any of them. Fear tainted with excitement at the prospect of being a participant in a switch similar to the Old Trafford Event.

Some, comfortable in lifelong atheism, were afraid that Heaven and Hell existed after all. Others cringed at the choices they'd made in life. Many, far too many, showed only excited amusement in anticipation of what the *famous illusionist* may do next.

Jay opened his eyes and walked with calm, deliberate steps up the stairs of the hastily-constructed little stage to take his place at the microphone. More than four billion people hissed at each other to shut up as Jay's image appeared on their devices.

The crowd writhed silently.

Jay gave them *that smile.* The one Mo recognised as a less snide but as wholly immersive version of God's own.

"Thank you for coming here today, brothers and sisters," Jay said. "We have little time to prepare your souls." Jay looked deep into the camera lenses, allowing the wonder of Heaven to show in his eyes for the people watching. Those present in the Esplanade narrowed their eyes as though staring at the sun.

All doubt was gone from the minds of each present. No-one close enough to hear or see him doubted at that moment that he was the Son of God. All fear, anger and excitement had vanished from the crowd, replaced by an eerie, calm acceptance. A fulfilment. Their souls saw the glory of Heaven inside the tall, simple-looking man speaking to them and responded with longing.

Jay continued, "But prepare them we must."

Jay's eyes moved over the faces of reporters, activists, the poor, the wealthy, the destitute, religious zealots, atheists and agnostics. He *saw* each of them as they really were — their trappings meant nothing to Jay and melted away under his gaze.

Jay looked into their souls and saw the kindness, humanity, cruelty, greed, generosity, evil or goodness that constituted the discorporate part of themselves and bathed each of them in a portion of Heaven's magnificence. People swooned or gasped. They cried tears from the depths of their hearts and surged forward, bending the steel of the barriers. They *felt* him as he searched their souls and knew for certain that Heaven was real. They knew also that they might never feel this complete fulfilment ever again.

The sounds of joy, weeping, wailing, begging began to grow and echo along the cobbled streets.

"God does not want you in His Kingdom. He does not want your eternal souls to experience Heaven, which I assure you is infinitely greater than the infinitesimal glimpse I've given those present today. God believes that you are not worthy, that you are mere beasts of nature who will pollute His realm."

Jay's eyes blazed as he did nothing to disguise his anger at his Holy Father.

"My friend Mo and I *know* that you *can be* worthy of Heaven." Mo came to Jay's side. Standing, hands clasped behind his back, he arranged his facial expression to show calm, agreement.

"We wish to show you how," Jay said, eyes still blazing. "God has promised to utterly obliterate the entire universe. Everything, every atom and cell, every electron and strand of DNA. Billions of worlds... trillions, and an almost infinite number of lifeforms will cease to exist."

Jay lowered his chin, but did not break eye contact with the silent people assembled.

"All depends on you humans, here on Earth, gaining the insight, the peace and the capacity to ascend to Heaven upon your deaths.

"Every. Single. One. Of. You."

Jay went silent, allowing his words to echo along the wide Esplanade and out onto The Royal Mile.

Millions listening across the continents fell to their knees.

Teach us, Lord... Save us.

Many more shot rifles, raised swords, punched at walls or at family or animals.

Lies. Heresy. Infidel.

The vast majority of those watching shook off the diluted glimpse of the Divine they'd witnesses an instant after Jay dimmed his Heavenly presence. Laughing nervously, they looked around at each other, convincing themselves and those around in a second that Jay, his words, were all part of an audacious illusion or prank.

Isn't the technology thing amazing? How does he do it? What a man. Greatest illusionist ever.

They scenarios being played out across the world were represented by those assembled in Edinburgh also. It took the crowd a few moments longer. Long, silent, strained seconds where those assembled either accepted his words or became incensed by them.

Men and women moved through the Edinburgh crowd, whispering admonishments in the correct ears, inciting hatred, inflaming all the basest of fears.

"Blasphemer!" a voice rang out from somewhere in the throng.

"God is good... let Him decide." Another voice.

"Allahu akbar."

"Y'hei sh'mei raba m'varakh l'alam ul'al'mei al'maya."

The air was suddenly charged with a very different and much darker energy as the crowd's mood turned. Soon, violence erupted. The barriers, and the stewards stationed at them, suddenly gave way and were trampled. Men and women fell to join them and were crushed by the surge of angry protestors and by the worshippers who attempted to halt the aggressors' progress. Blood began to flow in rivulets along and between the cobbles.

Jay and Mo ran back towards the Castle entrance, barely ten paces ahead of the front wave of attackers. Jay heard a woman scream. Whipping around he watched her skull crack open under the weight of a man's boots. Her eye plopped onto the cobbled Esplanade. Jay started towards her, but was pulled back by Mo who had both his arms hooked through Jay's own, dragging him back towards the Castle on his heels.

A woman lunged from the crowd. Slashing at Jay, she opened an eight-inch gash along his chest. Jay, unable to bring his arms round to block the attack, screamed in agony as the blade carved across and through his pectoral muscles, scratching against the bony breastplate and ribs beneath.

Mo pulled him, from behind, to the ground. Stepping over Jay, Mo threw a hard punch into the woman's face. She had been at the end of her slashing movement and took the blow full force to her cheek. She recovered her footing.

The woman snarled at Mo, changed the grip on the bloodied kitchen knife and lunged at his chest in a stabbing motion. Mo threw up his hand to protect himself. The knife slipped through meat, popping out through the palm of his hand.

From behind, Dougie grabbed her head with two large hands and shook it before smashing it onto the cobbles. He delivered a brutal kick to her for good measure, before stepping over her prone form and dragging Mo to his feet. Dougie shouldered past a small group of people who'd reached them, pulling Mo Jay back up onto his feet.

A swarm of officers had begun to position themselves between the Castle entrance and the front line of assailants. Riot shield raised, they pushed back against the crowd, buying Dougie the seconds he needed to get Mo and Jay through the gates and into the relative safety of the Castle courtyard.

The officers in riot gear had succeeded in slowing the attack, but sooner or later they would be pushed back into the courtyard. They simply did not have the numbers to cope with this many angry people in such a funnelled space.

Dougie assessed their options and Jay's physical state quickly. With strong, sure hands, he dressed both Mo's and Jay's wounds with a swift confidence. He led both men, Jay one arm hooked round Dougie's neck, up the Lang Stairs.

Reaching an open space in the Upper Courtyard, Mo searched the area frantically with his eyes.

"What now, Dougie?" he screamed.

Searching the cop's face, Mo realised that Dougie had been on autopilot, dealing with the wounds and the immediate threat. Now that they had a moment to reassess, it was obvious to all three of them that the crowd would overwhelm the officers below and would catch up to them in minutes.

"Good time for one of those miracles, Jay," Dougie smiled apologetically.

Jay, despite the wound, was calm as ever. He held Dougie's hands between his own and gave the big cop a reassuringly serene look.

"Dougie, "he said," ye'll be fine, son." Jay nodded over Dougie's shoulder just as the cop became aware of a familiar-sounding chopping noise.

Mo laughed loudly as the three men, joined now by Helen, turned to see a small helicopter hovering down into the courtyard.

"No sooner said than done, Dougie, m'boy," Mo said slapping Jay on the shoulder.

Jay grimaced at the pain, but managed a smile.

"Not my doing," he said.

As the helicopter touched down, a door slid open and a stoic-looking woman, hair tied tightly in a bun at the top of her head and immaculately dressed in a royal blue skirt suit with expensive-looking black shoes, stepped confidently from the aircraft. She stooped slightly until clearing the blades, making her way quickly to the group.

Striding over, she shouted above the engine noise, "Come with me if you want to live."

Mo, Dougie, Helen and Jay stood blank-faced, her joke clearly lost on them.

The woman's stern disposition vanished as she laughed nervously.

"Sorry, always wanted to say that line." Shoving a hand out in front of her, she said, "I'm Miriam Mukherjee. I've been sent by my employer, a Mr Saluzar, to offer you transport and logistical support for the duration of your mission."

Dougie stepped forward but felt Jay's hand tugging at his elbow.

"It's okay, Doug," he said, looking deep into Miriam's eyes. "We can trust her. She works for an old friend."

Miriam cocked her head to the left quizzically, but decided that now wasn't the time to ask questions.

"Right, well, c'mon then," she said, turning to make her way across the grass towards the helicopter.

Jay and Mo boarded the chopper, collapsing into the large seat facing the pilot. Miriam stepped lightly into the cabin behind them.

Jay leaned his head through the open door.

"Dougie," he yelled, waving his hand in a *get in here* gesture. A tearing pain made him wince.

Dougie came in through the open door. Crouching on the metal floor he looked to Jay questioningly.

"Going nowhere without you, Doug," Jay said through gritted teeth.

Dougie grinned. Mouthing *thank you*, he pulled at the door, sliding it into place. Turning he jabbed a thumbs-up at the pilot and clipped his harness over his shoulders.

Jay pointed behind him and tapped the earpiece of his own headphones.

Retrieving a pair, Dougie jutted his chin up.

What's up?

Jay pulled his mic into place as the chopper banked up and over the courtyard below.

"Will they be all right down there?" he asked.

Dougie scanned the courtyard and Esplanade before answering.

"Yeah," he said. "Look, word's obviously spreading that you're gone." Dougie pointed at thinning sections of the crowd. "There'll be a few scraps between factions, but it'll fizzle out quickly now that the focus of their obsession is gone."

Jay nodded his thanks.

"Where are we going, Miriam?" he asked.

Miriam gestured to the port window.

"Edinburgh Airport. We have a private jet which I've been instructed to place at your disposal. We have contacts, agents, politicians... anything really, in all the major cities of the world. I'd like to utilise them, get you in front of as many people as we possibly can."

Jay smiled warmly.

"Thank you, Miriam."

Miriam gave him a polite nod.

The remainder of the descent into the airport, as well as the transfer to the waiting jet, was done in silence.

Once aboard the luxury jet, Miriam asked, "So, where first?"

Jay answered instantly.

"Vatican City."

Tuesday

Interlude

Saluzar

The monitor blipped, reminding Mr Saluzar that he was still in the room... at least some of the time. Focusing on the Darth Vader-sounding respirator, he listened as it pushed air into his lungs. He'd only allowed his consciousness to return for a few moments, but was already tiring of the monotony of the machines that kept his body from decomposing. Saluzar tried moving his eyelids. Unable to manage even a slight flutter, he decided that, like all the other times, there would be no early reprieve for him.

Two more days.

Mr Saluzar said a silent prayer for his Miriam then allowed his consciousness to leave the room once again... Back to Sheol.

Two more days.

15

Nick and Beth

"Standing in His presence, I should have been enveloped in Heavenly adoration and love. In His complete and unending love. Instead I glared into His face, my own fury rising to almost match His.

"'You would stop existing for these fucking animals?' he roared at me.

"I steeled myself and raised every ounce of courage He'd given me upon my Creation and forged in the suffering of human souls in Sheol.

"'Give me one chance to show you that these souls can enter Heaven, that they can magnify your glory in doing so.'

"God seemed to shrink in that moment. It wasn't just that His anger ebbed, although it did, it was also His true self emerging once more, peace and love flowing from His being once again. More had changed: He had been lowered, reduced somehow in my eyes. He was not the perfect being we had thought Him to be. This was plain to me and it lessened Him in my eyes.

"He was wrong. That was the crux. In regard to human souls, He was just plain wrong. He didn't understand the depths of His own Creations. This changed everything. I pressed Him further. 'My Lord, I discovered a group of souls, only fifty, who are so wondrously at peace, serene in their state of eternal nothingness, that they are a reflection of ourselves.'

"His eyes narrowed and filled with malice. 'Do this thing.' He hissed the words at me. 'Do this, if you must, Nicholas, but there will be repercussions for your actions.'

"I stood once more, rising to meet His eye-line, 'Thank you, my Lord. I will bring these souls to magnify your glorious Kingdom.'

"His eyes widened and looked upon me with compassionate sadness, but only for a moment. They narrowed again so quickly, I wondered if I'd imagined the moment.

"He turned from me. 'Three,' He said, 'bring only three of these souls you are willing to risk so much for. No more. If you cannot find one who is worthy from their number, you will join them in Sheol, stripped of your Angelic power and awareness for eternity.'

"I was stunned. I wanted to fall at His knees and beg forgiveness for a nature He'd given me which compelled my compassion and empathy for the humans. I wanted so very much to forswear those souls in Sheol and simply absorb my essence back into the glory of Heaven. Instead, I left His Kingdom for the last time as a true Angel."

Nick stood from his stool, stretching his legs as he lit another cigarette. Beth gave him the time he needed to steel himself to continue. Partly because she was frightened of interrupting his thoughts, but mostly because she needed a break from his revelations. Time to process.

Instead of returning to his stool, Nick walked to the nearest table and rested his backside on it, folding his arms across his chest, moving his right hand back and forth as he smoked.

Beth walked around from behind the bar, joining him in the main lounge. She pulled a chair from behind her with a hooked foot and relaxed into it, her back thanking her for a surface to lean on after so long propped rigid on a stool.

When Nick had finished his cigarette, he dropped it to the floor, extinguishing it with a press of the sole of a shoe. He spat onto the smouldering butt of the cigarette for good measure.

"I felt heroic on my departure. No other word can describe my mood. I, of all His Angels, had been given perhaps the single most important task in the long history of His Kingdom. I knew this, even if other Angels did not, even if He Himself did not." Nick looked at Beth whose face wore a cynical expression. "Yeah, I know," Nick said, nodding, "for an ancient being, witness to all of Creation and history that followed, I was pretty fucking naïve."

Beth laughed, for the first time since he'd deliberately frightened her. "I told you, abusive relationship," she said, only half joking.

"Yes, well, off I went, trumpets blasting, chest puffed out, flags waving, arsehole puckered." Nick mocked himself and felt good in doing so. His spirits lifted again. He liked this kid. He liked her a lot actually.

Shaking the thought, Nick resumed.

"I was thoughtless in my urgency to prove to Him that I could bring to Him worthy souls, though at that moment I had no idea as to what criteria they would be judged upon. I simply relied upon my knowledge of what was good and pure and that which magnified the Heavenly structures I'd been surrounded by for my entire existence. Again, in my naïvety, I assumed that the human souls would be judged by eyes filled with the compassion, love and inclusiveness that God's had always been. I had not reckoned on the new visage which the Lord had shown me that very day in Heaven. His wrath."

Nick raised his eyebrows.

"That's the word that humans use, isn't it? Wrath?" he asked.

Beth shrugged. "I suppose," she said. "Seems a big enough word for Him, doesn't it?"

"No," Nick said flatly. "It does His anger... His vile malice no justice."

Nick seemed to shrink momentarily, like he expected to be struck for his words, before recovering again so quickly that Beth questioned her perceptions.

"I shot from Heaven, straight into Sheol in all my glorious, Heavenly form. The murky souls at the edges and even at the middle of the swirling mass of spirits ran from me. Burned, they seemed, by the sight of me. They did not return. Those ancient souls, who thought themselves deities, attempted to attack my Angelic form. I did not move against them. They crashed against me and were repelled, diverted, obliterated as waves upon a rock. My Heavenly Light burned through legions of furious souls who did not want a being such as I in their midst.

"When it was done, only a few malevolent souls remained. These entities fled, leaving only a comparative handful. The Enlightened."

Nick smiled warmly at Beth.

"These souls were not frightened, threatened or in awe of me, they were simply accepting. They looked at my form and were curious, but that was all.

"As they gathered close to me, I spread my form to its full glory, enveloping them in Heavenly radiance. 'I am Nicholas, First Angel of God. I have been sent by the Creator of all things to determine which of you is worthy of entry into His Kingdom.'

"Several of the souls flashed with anger. I had not expected this. 'There is a God, an Almighty? This being has suffered us to live and die, to roam eternally the skies as fragments of our former selves?'

"The once-serene souls, now stripped of their assurances and self-constructed fantasies of the purpose of their existence, became enraged. I had not foreseen any of this: it had not occurred to me, the insult I represented. The arrogance, the callousness my mere existence and previous absence represented to these abandoned souls.

"The sentiment spread quickly amongst the group. The change in their state was terrifying. Some were consumed by anger and vanished into the ether of Sheol. Some tried to strike me as their kin had moments before and were obliterated by my Heavenly Light. Shame coursed through me. All who remained fled — their peace, their contentment shattered forever.

"All but six.

"Six souls, still shining and whole in form, still radiating the same peace and serenity, moved closer to me. They bathed in my Holy light and were magnified by it. In turn the essence of Heaven, the infinitesimal fragment of God that composed my own form, grew in response to their light. These were worthy, each and every one of them. That they could bathe in Heaven's power in my presence, that they could add and magnify it in me, meant only that they had the capacity to do so in Heaven.

"For God.

"I swept them up in my Heavenly Light, tore the fabric of their reality and transported them in a fragment of an instant directly to Heaven. Directly to His presence."

16

Jay and Mo

Mo woke groggily. Reaching up to rub the crust from his eyes, a throb of pain lanced through his hand and brought him fully awake. Mo concentrated on the pain, making it melt away, and cursed Jay for not healing his wound.

They have to see we are committed.

Bollocks, thought Mo. *Suffer all you like, mate, but why do I have to join you?*

Mo made his way into the lounge of their suite in the Hotel Alimandi Vaticano. Dougie was snoring on the couch, Miriam was talking at speed into an iPhone, and Jay stood at the large windows, hands resting on the sill, looking out onto the street below.

Mo checked the clock on the mantel — *eleven am* — then joined him, resting his backside on the sill, his back to the window.

"Fuckin' hand's throbbing."

Jay turned to face him.

"Sorry, Mo."

"Not sorry enough," Mo said, jabbing the middle finger of his injured hand at Jay.

Jay smiled. "It's important, mate."

"Yeah, it always is," Mo replied. Changing the subject he nodded over at Miriam.

"What's the story, there?" he asked

Jay sat on the wide sill beside his friend.

"She's arranging a meeting with Pope Francis," Jay said.

Mo's eyebrows lifted. "She's that connected?" he asked.

Jay shrugged. "Is that so surprising, considering who she works for?"

Mo shrugged in response. "I suppose not. When's it happening?"

Jay checked his phone, "Forty-five minutes. She's arranging discreet transport."

"Tell me you ain't meeting in the Sistine Chapel. Fuckin' depressing place, that is."

"Naw," Jay said. "In his chambers, I believe."

Mo nodded. "You trust her? That she is who she claims to be? That she works for Mr L?"

"Aye. Knew it as soon as I clocked her," Jay replied.

Mo nodded. "Right well, better get a shave if I'm meeting the Head of the Catholic Church."

∞∞∞

Jay entered the Pope's chambers, followed by Mo and Miriam. Dougie wished to stay outside the rooms, and was chatting with a Swiss Guard. Pope Francis smiled very warmly as he rose to his feet to offer a welcoming handshake. He spoke in Spanish.

"Bienvenida, mis amigos."

Clutching Jay's right hand in both of his own, Francis looked deep into Jay's eyes, assessing him. Jay accepted the examination without guile.

This was a good man, a humble pope. Something the Church had badly needed for decades, perhaps for centuries. This was a pope who knew that religious inclinations were but a single route to being a good person. A pope who was accepting of people from all backgrounds and lifestyles. In short, he was a lot like Saint Peter, whose church he represented.

Jay smiled as Francis' eyes widened — a sliver of recognition? Still clutching Jay's hands gently, but firmly; still looking into his eyes and clearly examining Jay's reaction and comprehension of language, Francis spoke in English this time.

"After Miriam made her calls to arrange our meeting, I was warned by my Cardinals, my advisors, that you are, at best, nothing more than an extremely talented entertainer and, at worst, a despicable con-man who preys on people's fears. I can see that the latter is not true. You are clearly a very good man. But the Messiah returned?"

Francis shook his head. Switching to Italian, he replied, "Non la penso così."

Releasing his hold on Jay's hands, Francis still wore a smile of acceptance, but had clearly satisfied his curiosity.

"Why don't you tell me what it is you want from me, my son," Francis said in English again as he returned to his armchair.

Jay was growing bored with Francis testing him. He took a few steps towards Francis' chair, then took a cross-legged Buddha position on the carpet at Francis' feet.

"I want you to announce a Mass. In one hour, right here in Vatican City. From your balcony I want to talk to as many people as we can gather in St Peter's Square below. I want to make them understand what they face and how their souls might survive what will come in a few days."

Jay placed his hands on Francis' knees.

"I want to prepare them for Heaven."

His eyes filled with compassion, Pope Francis smiled sadly down at Jay as one might a harmless idiot carrying the sandwich board with the legend, *The End is Nigh.*

"My son," Francis said gently, "I can see that you believe what you say and that you only wish to help people, but you are quite wrong and quite deluded."

Francis rose to his feet, smoothing his white robes along his legs. He offered Jay a hand and helped him up onto his feet with a strength that belied his appearance.

"I shall make sure that you get the help you need," Francis said, placing an arm around Jay's waist. Clearly the meeting was over.

Mo sissed through his teeth. "Told you," he said. "They're too fuckin' stupid. What did you expect from an institution with the history these paedos have?"

"That. Is. Enough!" Jay roared.

Mo's eyes widened, stunned at his friend's uncharacteristic anger.

Jay closed his eyes momentarily. Rediscovering his calm, Jay said softly, "I'd like a minute alone with Pope Francis."

Francis moved towards the door. Clearly not in the mood for any more talk from Jay, he intended to summon the Swiss Guard outside his chambers.

Jay stepped into his path. Placing a hand lightly on the older man's chest, he filled his eyes with deep earnestness. "Please, Francis. Allow me a minute more of your time to convince you of my words."

Deep sadness showed in the pontiff's expression. He radiated sympathy.

"All right, my son. One minute, but I insist on my guard being present... and your friends stay too."

Jay nodded his approval.

Mo opened the doors. "Dougie, bring your new pal in. The gaffer wants you both." Mo had recovered quickly from Jay's rebuke. Having been friends for millennia, they'd disagreed many times. Still, Jay's words had stung more than usual.

As the single Swiss Guard entered the room with Dougie close behind, the tall, heavily-built Special-Forces officer threw a questioning glance at the pope.

Jay watched an unspoken exchange take place.

All's fine for now, but stay close.

Jay closed his eyes, transferring that part of him that was a sliver of God to the immaterial plane where Heaven existed. Unlike the moments during the Old Trafford Event or at Edinburgh Castle, Jay did not allow the Light of Heaven to show in his physical being on Earth. Instead, he summoned a portion of his Father's power, searched the life of the man in front of him and made his decision. Finally Jay opened his eyes.

"Jorge, figlio di Mario José Bergoglio," he said in Italian, before switching to English once more. "I have two gifts for you."

Pope Francis' face flooded with cynicism. His father's name was pubic record. He was beginning to lose his patience.

Jay decided to push his buttons.

"È un regalo da tua madre," he said, placing a hand onto Francis' chest.

The Swiss Guard stepped forward, but Francis pushed a hand out.

"No, Alfonso. It is all right."

Francis closed his eyes, examining the sensation of warmth he felt coursing through his thorax. After too short a time, Jay removed his hand.

Speaking in Spanish, he said, "Respirar profundamente, mi hijo."

Francis filled his lungs with air, his entire lungs, and laughed in joy at the impossibility.

Looking concerned, Alfonso pleaded, "Holy Father, what is happening?"

Francis beamed at his guard. "My lungs, Alfonso. I am filling my lungs."

Alfonso squinted at the pontiff, uncomprehending, but Francis had already turned his attention back to Jay.

"Lungs I lost a portion of to pneumonia at twenty-one years of age."

Jay nodded calmly, confirming what Francis felt.

Francis spoke to everyone in the room. "My lungs are whole again... He... he made them grow back."

Mo grinned, as did Dougie. Alfonso stood stunned, watching the Holy Pope dance a victory jig. Finally Francis realised the full implication of what had occurred.

Reaching for Jay with both hands, Francis gripped the taller man by his elbows.

"I cannot... I..."

Jay smiled, accepting the processing Francis needed to go through. His entire faith had been validated and destroyed in the same instant. This good, decent man had believed in and committed his entire life to a Church that preached that Jesus was the Son of God and had sacrificed himself for humans.

True.

Francis' face fell as he realised that if he accepted that Jesus and his act of selflessness was fact, and that this man standing in his presence was truly Jesus returned, he also had to accept that the God he'd worshipped for decades was a sadistic, cruel being who cared nothing for his creations and that his life's work meant nothing to that entity.

As the series of revelations and realisations hit him, Francis fell to his knees in front of Jay. It was partly an act of subservience, or perhaps worship, but mainly he was just a man overwhelmed.

Jay reached down, cupping Francis' right cheek with his left hand. Lifting the pope's face, he came down on his haunches, bringing them eye to eye.

"The second gift is from your father, Mario," Jay said softly.

Jay took Francis' right hand and dropped an object into the waiting palm.

Francis stared at the impossible. The wedding ring his father had been cremated wearing some twenty years previously.

By four o'clock the entire party stood behind Pope Francis on the balcony, listening to him attest to Jay's authenticity and introduce him to the thousands packed into St Peter's Square below. Francis requested that all one point two billion Catholics scattered across a huge number of nations and several continents, accept Jay — as Francis himself had — as their returned Messiah.

Francis begged them to listen to Jay's Mass with an open heart and act on his instructions for entry into Heaven.

Jay spoke for a mere ten minutes. By the end of his speech, billions of people had felt his words tug at their souls and accepted him in their hearts as their savior returned to guide their souls.

17

Nick and Beth

"My return to Heaven was made with far less pomp and with infinitely more humility than my departure had been. I was badly bruised in spirit by the deaths of the souls in Sheol. I knew for certain that God knew of my calamitous entry into Sheol and my failure to foresee the affect my Heavenly presence would have. I should have made myself smaller, less glorious in presence. This action had not even occurred to me, so detached was I in my distance from earthly matters. I had thought myself their champion, when in fact I'd appeared a mere demon to them. The personification of the Creator's detachment from them. His disdain.

"The human souls gathered by me fell to their knees upon entering Heaven. Songs of pure joy came from them, drawing Angels from all parts of Heaven to us. Their joyful voices drifted through Heaven, affecting the substance of it. Their elevation magnified Heaven as I'd hoped it would. However, Heaven's light did not enter them. I turned to face God who had come to us.

"The Enlightened raised their voices once more in worship of the Creator. Each of them thanked Him for His mercy and for the lives they'd had on Earth.

"All loved Him.

"I stepped forward and raised my arms to indicate my little group of refugee souls. 'They are of Heaven, my Lord. Look how their souls are growing, look how your Kingdom welcomes them and is magnified by their love.'

"God gave a gentle nod.

"'Just so,' He said.

"He cast His eyes across their faces smiling warmly at them, searching them, but only for a moment.

"Fixing his eyes on one of them, a man in life, perhaps forty when he died, He asked of the soul, 'Tell me, human, what do you want from me? What do you want from Heaven?'

"My whole being shook with anger, just as it had when He and I had confronted one another earlier that day. *Why is he testing them?* I remained silent.

"The human soul did not hesitate to answer.

"'To worship you, Creator. To remain here and add to your glory.'

"The soul had spoken the truth. His compatriots nodded along, also.

"'We wish only to worship and to take our place here in Heaven, in your service,' the soul said.

"God smiled warmly once more. 'But you are human," He said gently. 'You have no place in Heaven.' The smile changed into the malicious grin He had used when addressing me earlier that day. He allowed His anger to show.

"'More than a billion humans have existed on Earth. Half of that number have passed into Sheol in spirit form. By my will, nature gifted you eternal life as a soul, anchored to your planet, able to watch over your ancestors. You are the only creatures in all of my universe to have evolved a soul, and you have the fucking arrogance to come here to my domain and tell me it isn't enough? Who the fuck are you that I should let you into my Kingdom?'

"God's voice was a hurricane that threatened to tear the fabric of their very forms apart. God's face had contorted to a bitter reflection of His normal self. Angels cowered, but worse, some nodded agreement with Him.

"The human souls were irreparably altered.

"Two of the six were destroyed, utterly eradicated, by the force of His fury, the storm His presence had become.

"Three others stepped towards Him, faces a mask of rage fuelled by millennia in Sheol and His casual casting aside of their suffering and their love.

"'How can such a God as you exist?" a male cried. His spirit form, his entire soul, was falling apart, but he found the courage to demand this of his Creator. The two others joined him, glaring at The Lord.

"'You are a callous deity.'

"I was frozen in fear. The courage of these simple human souls shamed me more than I could bear.

"God's face became hate itself. 'Get tae fuck!' He screamed into their faces. His voice, his vile anger, removed the souls from existence.

"He turned on me. His rage threatened to bring me to my knees. I forced myself to stay on my feet: to glare back at Him as I had in the recent past. I, an Angel, His first Angel, I had to match, to honour the courage the humans had displayed moments before.

"'You see?' He asked me. 'You see how limited they are? Their glory is not our glory. A simple question and their serenity is stripped away to reveal the hate underneath. They are animals, Nicholas. Of nature, nothing more. They are not worthy of Heaven.'

"My fear was changing into a rage that matched His. I fought to control it. I wanted to take this anger that had infected He and I both, and crush it. I wanted to be its master, to be better than Him.

"I recall the thought striking me hard: *it's not every day one finds that their Creator is flawed.*

"I swallowed a lump of hate along with a thousand curses and condemnations and softened my face.

"Pointing to my right I asked God, 'What of that one?"

"God glared down at the single remaining human soul in Heaven. A woman, mid-twenties in form, the single survivor of Sheol's Enlightened, she cowered, face pressed to the floor.

"God shrugged. 'Take her back.'

"'No,' I told Him, growing calmer still in the act.

"His anger flared once more.

"'Do what you're fuckin' telt,' He roared.

"I nodded respectfully at Him.

"'She has not grown angry, or afraid. She has not demanded anything of you. Neither to stay in Heaven nor return to Sheol. She wishes to worship, to remain in Heaven, yes, but she did not raise her voice in protest when you told them that humans had no place in Heaven.

"God's eyes narrowed. He addressed the female soul.

"'Right, hen. Get tae fuck back tae Earth. You're not wanted here.'

"The soul nodded slightly in deference.

"'Yes, my Creator. Thank you,' she replied.

"God's laughter boomed.

"'She's a coward. A fuckin' shitebag,' He said.

"'No she isn't,' I said respectfully.

The soul spoke again.

"'I'm not afraid, my Lord, I merely wish to honour you. I forgive you that you are pitiless to your creations.

"She vanished, not destroyed like the others, but absorbed into Heaven's structure, its fabric. She became a permanent, an eternal part of His light, against His will. Her soul added structures to Heaven of the like we had never seen.

"God roared in fury at the space she'd stood in.

"'Cuuuuunt!'

"I took no pleasure from her elevation nor His anger. I was heartbroken in truth, that He was so small, that He had adapted as surely as the humans had, changing His very essence into something arrogant instead of accepting, and furious instead of serenity itself. God's recent change in mood was as altered by recent events as Heaven was by a single human soul. He had been altered by the elevation of that soul. Heaven was Him and He was Heaven.

"He turned on me.

"'This is what you wanted, Nicholas. A human in Heaven.' He spread His arms wide indicating the changes the human soul had wrought. His eyes blazed at me, challenging me to defend what I'd done.

"'Yes, my Lord...'

"'No!' he shouted into my face. 'Do not address me as such: you have forsaken me. You have brought about a change in the very fabric of Heaven that was not to have been.'

"The human acts of courage as my inspiration, I steeled myself.

"'I'm glad of it," I said defiantly. 'The humans deserve this existence. You were wrong to deny it to them.'

"God's face grew angrier. The changes to His presence, His language, His demeanour, His very countenance, magnified in that moment and have not returned to those I'd known for so many countless eons before.

"His accent, always his, unchanged in billions of years — what you Humans call a Scottish brogue — became more coarse, horrible really, as did His language and temper. God had discovered His wrath. All benevolence towards life was gone in a micro-instant.

"'I'm fuckin' done with you. Nick.' He spat the words through gritted teeth. 'You've put your love for a herd of fucking animals before the love of your Creator. You point to the changes that your single human soul has made to my Kingdom... to me, and tell me it's a change for the better?'

"'Lord, I love...'

"'Shut the fuck up!' God's anger threatened to eradicate me. I shook in place but remained on my feet. Silently.

"When He regained control of His temper, He spoke.

"'You were my First Angel, Nick.' His face softened. 'My best and truest friend. Why?'

"It was one of those moments that would change everything. He knew it and I knew it. We stood there for several long seconds looking at each other, the shared history passing between us in a stream of images in our minds' eyes. We had been together for so long. I had been created to end His isolation. We had spent billions of years alone together before He added to the Angel's ranks. We were as one for an age.

"I did not know then if He had sent the images or I had, and I don't know now. Never bothered to ask Him in the millennia that have passed. It didn't matter. We were both hurting. Both of us wanted to be who we had been before human souls had evolved. Neither of us would or could change what we had become.

"I replied to Him as honestly and earnestly as I could.

"'They are not of nature, they are beyond it. I believe this with all of my being. I believe, simply, that you are wrong in denying them this elevation. I cannot exist knowing that their souls may never attain Heaven.'

"I watched God fight back the urge to give in to His anger once more. After a few seconds He spoke calmly to me.

"'Fine,' He said, voice barely audible. 'You have been my Accuser since the humans appeared. Be my Accuser. Tell them how terrible I am... tell them whatever you wish. Be their teacher, their guide and their torturer. Make them worthy of my Kingdom, as worthy as the single soul from one billion who has gained entry today.'

"Hurt emanated from Him as He spoke. Angels began to gather closer to hear the exchange.

"'You are no longer my First Angel, Nick. You aren't an Angel at all from this moment forward. You are denied a home here in Heaven. You will exist in Sheol with your students. You may leave Sheol only to visit Earth or Heaven.'

"I was stunned. Separation from Heaven was incomprehensible to me. Like Him, I was part of Heaven and it of me. What He had decided was worse than amputation. I reminded myself of the courage I'd seen from The Enlightened I'd brought to Heaven at the moment of their destruction and simply bowed my head in acceptance.

"'You are not permitted to show humans your Angelic form, not on Earth and not in Sheol, though I will allow you to be your true self when you come here to my Kingdom. That mercy I give you.'

"I wanted to scream. I wanted to rush to Him and beg forgiveness for my argumentative nature, beg to remain in His light.

"I did not.

"'Thank you, my Lord,' I said from habit.

"He grinned at me then, that horrid, detestable smile He had made His own.

"'Call me Stewart,' He told me. 'You will offer souls for assessment by me as and when you feel they have fulfilled the criteria required. Those you send to me who fail will be returned to you for re-education. I will not destroy them. You may try to elevate them as many times as you have the stomach for, Nick.'

"'I will send them to you by the millions,' I said.

"He laughed loudly. 'Good luck. But I don't think so, Nick. Your odds haven't been good up to now. One in a billion?'

"My resolve hardened. 'They have me to teach them now.'

"He nodded. 'That they do, lad. Teach them well, do whatever you must to get them to my criteria.'

"'What standard will they be judged by?' I asked.

"'Simple,' he replied. '*Don't be a cunt.*' He grinned at me, sending a wave of revulsion through me.

"'That's a bit broad,' I said.

"He shrugged.

"'It is what it is. You saw what was required of the soul already here in Heaven. There ye have it,' He said. 'Send me them in a trickle, send me them by the shitload, I don't give a fuck, Nick, but know this: you will not return here to Heaven in your true form, a permanent part of my Kingdom, a true Angel again, not until every soul that vacates its material body comes straight to Heaven and there is no longer a single soul in Sheol.'

"The cruelty of my best friend, my Creator, stunned me.

"'Now, Nick, get tae fuck. I'm sick of looking at you, sick of listening to you and want you gone.'

"I was broken down into the basest of the components that constituted my Angelic being and rebuilt on Earth, a fraction of my Angelic presence. My access to Heaven was limited. My broad sight of the whole universe gone entirely. I could see and sense souls, know their history and view the entire history of the Earth and its inhabitants. I was also privy to Heaven's history. That should have been a blessing but served only to sharpen the pain of separation from my home.

"My appearance was altered also. Black, sooty feathered wings and goat hooves. He gave me these as a nod to the images of devils humans had created to explain disease and misfortune on Earth. I held this form in Sheol. I still hold it, and proudly. I made it a symbol of hope for the souls in Sheol.

"On Earth I can pass as human. Another mercy." Nick's voice dripped with bitterness.

Beth looked horrified. "He sounds horrible."

Nick shrugged. "He is what He is, Beth."

"How long ago did this happen?" Beth asked.

Nick raised his eyebrows thoughtfully.

"Time has a fluid meaning for us, Bethany," Nick said. "Best guess, maybe five million years ago."

Beth placed a hand over his, which rested on the table between them.

"You've been in Hell... in Sheol all of that time, educating, saving souls? Completely separate from your home... from everything you ever loved?"

Nick shrugged. "Yes," he said simply.

A few moments passed in silence. "Is it a terrible place, Hell?" she asked.

Nick appraised her for a moment. "What do you imagine Hell to be? Now that we've spoken, that you know why it was brought into existence?"

Beth considered her response.

"A school for souls. That's what I imagine it as. A place for souls to learn to be better."

"Better?" Nick asked. "Better than what?"

Beth's face darkened. "Better than Him," she replied.

Nick laughed. "Well, Bethany, for sure there are sections of Hell that contain rooms filled with exactly that. People being tutored."

Nick's face took on a sadness, but an ugly one, tainted by millennia of doing what was necessary. "There are many more levels to hell, to Sheol, in which souls are in torment, lost, perhaps forever, in absolute agony, mental and physical pain, eternal. Your books got that part correct."

Beth's face became a mask of terror.

"What did you expect, Bethany? A place where I stand at the entrance telling each soul who enters, *Oh, God's a wanker, He doesn't care about you nor does He want you in His kingdom. Go find a way to forgive Him for fucking you over and I'll let you in the back door to Heaven*?"

Nick stood over a seated Beth. Moving around Beth, he placed his hands onto her shoulders sending a shiver through her.

"Hell is a truly horrific place, Bethany. It is a place of learning, of rehabilitation, but it is also a place of punishment."

Nick released his light grip. Coming to her level he knelt, facing her.

"Imagine the souls who come to me, to Sheol. The damage needing repaired; the work required to strip them of their arrogance, their disillusionments, the outrage and abandonment they feel.

"Men of war who were told that they fought on the battlefield for God only to find themselves in Hell, tortured by and for their stupidity in life.

"Holy men and saintly women, humble in life, given over completely to their religions, who are tortured on the lowest levels of Hell for thousands of years for their arrogance. Pious monks, virginal nuns, dedicated priests, all who've given entire lives to Him. Can you imagine the injustice they feel when they discover He does not care for their prayers; that He does not want them? They watch atheists ascend before they themselves do, these holy men and women, simply because the non-believers have less anger in them at His abandonment of humans.

"The murderers and rapists and paedophiles, some take millennia to elevate, most never leave Hell, but a few, who care nothing for Him and His Kingdom but who find a conscience upon seeing the horror of Hell, pass straight through His gates. Can you imagine the fury this betrayal ignites in those good souls who came to Sheol in worship of Him? Can you fathom the countless years I have to work just to get these souls to a point where I might begin the process of their elevation?"

Nick's eyes burned with pain and rage. Sweat beaded on Bethany's forehead and ran along her spine. Her eyes spilled molten lead tears. Unable to summon the words to speak she simply sat and shook, crying at Nick's words and pain.

Nick stood.

"Despite this, despite every obstacle He has placed in my way, each injustice He perpetuates and His callous criteria by which souls may enter Heaven, I am winning, Bethany. I'm sending souls to Him in a torrent where once a trickle and then a flow existed. Heaven is larger, grander, more glorious than ever because of the addition of these souls, and He Himself shines brighter than ever.

"That most humans are growing beyond the need to believe in a God, to worship Him, means that my methods in Hell work so much more effectively. Humankind is moving into an age of reason rather than superstition. I have so much less work, not having to undo the damage that religion does to souls. I *am* winning."

Nick smiled. It was not a victorious smile.

"His wrath grows ever more dire. He is magnified, no doubt, but He still resents the souls that come to Him and His patience is ebbing. Something is coming. Something... final."

A long silence followed during which Bethany attempted to process the disclosures Nick had given. It was all just too… big. After ten minutes of silence, something prodded her curiosity.

"Nick? If God truly attempts to keep humans from Heaven, aside from those He marks as *worthy,*" Beth made little finger quotes in the air, "why send Jesus or Moses or Mohammed to guide us? Or is that just human input?"

Nick smiled warmly at her.

"No, it isn't," he said. "Those men did exist and were sent by God. Those were good men who tried to elevate human souls. Men who believed in the worth of those souls. They still do."

Beth's eyes widened, the theology student in her delighted at the confirmation of the three prophets' existence.

"Why send them, then?" she asked. "Why send these men to aid humans in their understanding of Him, if not to assist the elevation of their souls to Heaven? Surely that must indicate that on some level God wants, or perhaps needs, human souls, regardless of what He says."

"It's a good question, Bethany. The simple answer is that He did not send them, not really. Two of them,

Moses and Mohammed, begged to be sent to Earth to assist *me*. Jesus... well, Jesus was different, Jesus *is* different. Unique in all the universe and in Heaven. He genuinely is the Son of God."

Beth's face broke out into a wide smile which Nick returned.

"Yeah, that's the usual reaction," he laughed. "Jesus is a fragment of God. He exists as a part of Him, but as a separate entity with free will and a portion of the Lord's power. Jesus can access a flicker of the Creator's light, powerful but minute in comparison to God's glory. Should Jesus try to access a larger portion of the power, merge his being with God's to a greater degree than they are already linked... well, it isn't really possible."

Bethany's eyes shone. "They share a consciousness?" she asked.

"Sort of," Nick replied, "but only on a very small level. Think of Jesus's access to God's knowledge and His power as a computer technician accessing one megabyte of a one Googolplex hard drive. He can comprehend the data in front of him, he can even comprehend the huge reserves at his disposal, but if he tried to utilise the data?"

Nick bowed his head.

"It would be the end of Jesus were he to attempt to access a deeper reserve of his father's power."

Beth sat open-mouthed, gaping.

"He's still got a fair portion, trust me," Nick smiled. "Not that you'd know it, the kid's as humble as they come. He's a pure soul. Never lies, only wants to love everyone."

Nick shook off a threatening reverie.

"Can you tell me how the three of them came to Earth? What they tried to accomplish, if they succeeded?" Beth asked.

Nick's eyes narrowed.

"Yes," he said, "but for now, I have something else in mind."

Beth's eyes narrowed also.

"We're going on a trip. I want you to understand everything. You're coming with me... to Sheol."

18

Jay and Mo

IN THE AFTERMATH OF THE MASS IN VATICAN CITY, the media erupted and stories filled all outlets.

In the hours following the Mass, long into the darkness of night, Pope Francis sat in his chambers, speaking earnestly about his encounter with Jay and Mo, and how his beliefs had been validated, but painfully altered. The pope was tireless, insisting that this was how he could best assist Jay in reaching more souls. In the Sistine Chapel, a score of Cardinals met, whispering plans to remove Francis.

The media frenzy made the surge of attention after Old Trafford seem like a minor trickle in comparison.

The tabloids raked over Garry Crawford's life, highlighting his irreverent Facebook group *Baws 2* as a racist, sexist den of bullying and sadistic sexual outlet.

Chris Pillans was also being metaphorically crucified by the tabloids. A stream of models had emerged selling stories of brutal and bewildering sexual liaisons.

The broadsheets, *The Guardian* and *The Independent* in particular, focused on the Vatican Mass. Questions were raised by the journalists investigating both this and The Event.

Had the pope gone mad?

How did these men fool Francis?

Cults forming?

Could Jay really be the Messiah?

Social media was awash with conspiracies, outraged Christians, Jews, Muslims, and Hindus. The list went on. Across millions of threads they commented, accused, threatened and argued. Keyboard crusaders had never had it so good.

A few groups sprung up that had attracted millions of followers within hours.

Christ, Man, was a group of stoners who were generally elated that Jay had confirmed during the Vatican Mass that their *peace, man... cool with everything and everyone* lifestyle seemed to guarantee them VIP entry into Heaven.

RSVP Heaven, with ten million members, had been founded to organise gatherings for those who needed support in following Jay's instructions. People of all nationalities and faiths formed its membership. A picture of Jay from Old Trafford, arms open and face filled with Heaven's Light, graced their banner.

Britain First had rebranded as *God First.* They filled their subscribers' newsfeeds with images of booted feet kicking puppies and hands around chickens' throats, throttling them, and broken crosses and windows outside churches.

Almost invariably, Jay's face was crudely Photoshopped into the corner of the images with captions like *God loves all creatures* and *Garry*

Crawford wants to destroy your faith splashed across them.

Theologists, sitting in large leather chairs, debated the impact of Jay's appearances and of The Event in Manchester. Most agreed that, at this point, it mattered little whether Jay was the greatest con-man in recorded history, or indeed the Messiah returned. The events he and Mo had put in motion, the questions, fears and guilt they'd provoked would have far-reaching, unprecedented consequences on society.

Physicists, scientists, geologists and engineers frantically examined The Event on documentary channels. Their commentary was as endless as the number of opinions and theories they offered to explain how The Event had occurred.

Theoretical teleportation.

Camera trickery.

Collusion with those present in the stadium.

It seemed that the scientists involved could find no end to the number of ways they could dismiss the evidence that The Event had really been as simple, as miraculous, as it had seemed.

∞∞∞

Jay closed the laptop, sighing at the stream of news he'd been scanning for most of the flight. Miriam looked up at him from the seat across the aisle in response to the sound.

"Everything okay?" she asked.

Jay smiled. "Aye, just a little disappointed," he said.

Miriam's eyebrows met in the middle and pushed down. "Seriously? You've accomplished so much — convinced billions in two days."

Jay rubbed at his temples with a thumb and forefinger. "Yes, but we have so little time and most of the planet's population think I'm a well-intentioned nutter. A talented one, for sure, but a nutter none the less."

Miriam didn't argue.

"Well, we have a Mass at Hyde Park, London, tomorrow morning, over to Paris for another at the Arc de Triomphe. Then onto Berlin in the evening. The day after that we have seven Masses across South America—"

"And the day after that," Jay interrupted, "we're fucked."

Miriam nodded. "Perhaps, but we will have Masses across the African continent and Canada to complete first. Get as many souls as we can, before… y'know."

Jay grimaced. "We just don't have the time. What about Asia, the Middle-East, Australia?"

Miriam's eyes misted. "This is all we can fit in, Jay. We have to hope that your message continues to spread and grow across social media, television and radio." Miriam rose. Reaching over, she lifted Jay's chin to bring his eyes up level with her own. "Have a little faith," she said, smiling.

Jay looked like he might cry.

"If I can't get all of them, every human on Earth, He *will* end everything, Miriam. Everything."

Miriam returned to her seat without further comment.

After a few painfully silent minutes, she asked, "Why go back to Scotland then? We could divert somewhere else, perhaps Madrid, or Barcelona. Be back in London for the morning."

Jay looked down at the Firth of Forth and the bridges spanning it. He nodded towards the structures.

"I have something in mind. Something their scientists won't be able to explain with physics or anything else." Despite the tension and creeping despair over the impossibility of their task, Jay grinned.

"Okaay," Miriam said, uncertainty in her tone. "Media?" she asked.

"Please," Jay replied. "One hour, at Dougie's granny's wee house at the foot of the Forth Rail Bridge."

19

Nick and Beth

BETH NEVER SAW HIM MOVE. He was on her in an instant, wrapping his arms around her. He changed again, this time into the tall being with the blackened wings he'd described. Beth screamed as she felt her body come apart. Just like that, every cell in her ceased to be matter and was converted to... something else.

Aware that she was someplace else, Beth stopped screaming. She felt her face, whatever that meant now, pressed against his chest. No heartbeat comforted her. No warmth emanated from him. From Nick.

He released her from his grip, holding her at arm's length to look into her face. She had expected to be panicked, shaking uncontrollably, all reason lost. None of these things happened. She did, in fact, feel a peacefulness she'd never known. All hunger was satisfied, every desire fulfilled. She just *was* and felt joy for the gift of its simplicity. She looked at Nick.

"Am I dead?"

He shook his head.

"No, your soul has been separated from the flesh of your body. It will be returned when we are done here... if that is what you wish."

Beth took a step away from him and moved her eyes over the place she found herself in. They stood in a very modern-looking office complex. Pods with neck-high separator panels stood all around, separated by wide corridors and open areas. In each of the large pods various people worked at computers and on telephones. Some played video games on a fifty-inch screen in the centre of the office which seemed to be a communal area. Others milled around the coffee lounge, chatting, laughing. The office had a lively feel, a productive vibe.

Music played in the background and the workers dressed casually. The office and its occupants looked like one might expect the people and complexes of Google or Facebook to. Meg scanned their faces, her eyes widening and the steel rod her spine had fused into relaxing a little.

Nick smiled at her, humour shining in his eyes.

"What did you expect, Bethany? The Big Fire?"

The words struck her.

The Big Fire. Uncle Harry.

He had called Hell exactly that. Told her she that would go there. Beth fought back a rising panic attack. Taking a deep breath she held it and the threat of unleashed emotion back, refusing it, and both Nick or Uncle Harry, that power over her. She felt Nick watching her, gauging her response. It made her angry and doused the fear under cold intent.

"You're a bastard, Nick," she said flatly.

Nick gave a single curt nod in the affirmative.

"Yes. But not enough of one to take you to the lower levels," he said.

His eyes darted away from her face to a person who was approaching from behind her. Beth turned to face the being. Dressing in denims, long-sleeve-T and with Cons on her feet, a blonde woman, very pretty but with concerned features, approached carrying an iPad.

She handed the device to Nick, who gave her a warm smile, completely at odds with his Hellish appearance. He greeted her.

"What do we have here, Meg?"

An apologetic look creased her face. "Bit of an anomaly, sir," she said. "To be honest, we're glad you're here — we were about to call you anyway."

Beth stood with her arms folded in a hug around her body wondering what constituted an anomaly serious enough in Hell that its ruler would need summoned. Nick's eyebrows knitted together as he scanned the information Meg had presented to him.

"They've been here since… when?" he asked.

"Four days now, sir," Meg replied, subconsciously worrying at a scar on her neck with the nail of her right index finger. Despite her obviously good relationship with Nick, she looked faintly terrified at his prospective reaction.

Beth could relate.

"And they've been in that same room since, together, no contact with any other souls?"

"That is correct, sir, although they did spend twenty-four hours in a re-education booth."

Nick raised his eyebrows.

"Ah well, that can't be helped now. Thanks for bringing this to me, Meg, you did the right thing in calling me."

Meg relaxed visibly. "Oh, and Mr L is here also, sir."

"When's he due to return to Earth?" Nick asked.

"The day after tomorrow... Earth time."

Nick nodded. "Ah well, in that case I won't have the opportunity to drop in. Give him my regards please, Meg."

Meg nodded and scurried off, disappearing into a throng of workers gathered in the coffee lounge.

Nick tucked the tablet under his arm and returned his attention to Beth.

"C'mon," he told her, flicking his head towards a door to their right, "I have a little problem to deal with before we can continue the tour."

∞∞∞∞

A few paces behind Nick, Beth moved her head from side to side, taking in as much of her surroundings as she could process whilst they walked towards the elevator. The clacking of keyboards, sounds of laughter, chatting and general productiveness comforted Beth, reassuring her that this was just another busy office.

Following Nick into the elevator, she flicked her eyes towards the control panel. According to the little electronic panel above the buttons, the elevator currently sat on Level Two. Scanning the buttons, of which there were easily two hundred, Beth skimmed though to Level Seventy-Five before Nick broke her concentration.

"Push Level Seven please, Bethany," he said.

Finger hovering over the panel, Beth's eyes flicked to the button designated Level One, which had a key slot.

"That what I think it is?" she asked Nick.

"Just push Seven," he said, without looking at her.

Beth poked at the button sending the lift the opposite way she'd expected. As the lift descended, Beth gave a sardonic laugh at having expected an elevator in Hell to do anything other than descend.

Nick stood impassive, watching the numbers rise, chewing at the inside of his lip.

After a few moments, the elevator binged, its doors sliding open to reveal a much grimmer-looking level than the one they'd left above. Following Nick out into the corridor, Beth noted the change in colour scheme, dimensions and general atmosphere. Stark white tiles covered the floors and walls. The area was lit by an off-ultra-violet coloured strip of light that lined the walls the length of the corridor. No music played, no workers busied themselves; no one was present at all.

As she followed Nick along the corridor, she could feel his mood darken as they passed a series of doors labelled with people's names and a year. The doors did not have handles. Nick came to a stop at a door labelled *Crawford and Pillans, July 2015.*

Reaching for a small panel, Nick paused. Retracting his hand, he turned to face Bethany.

"Beth," he said quietly, "please don't be afraid. I will not allow anything to harm you here in this place, but you may see things you do not... approve of."

Nick searched her eyes for a moment. Beth did not react.

"If you can, just trust me. Once I've dealt with this, we'll proceed with your tour."

Beth nodded her agreement.

Nick offered her a half-smile and pressed his hand to the door's panel. Instantly the door slid open and an angry Scotsman appeared at the threshold.

"Whit in the name ay fuck are you guys offering us now? A hydrochloric acid enema?"

The guy, dark hair, over six feet in height, clearly used to getting his way, attempted to push past Nick into the corridor. He may as well have been shoving against a marble statue. Fear filled his eyes momentarily, sending him backing up into the room to join another man inside.

The other guy wore his hair in a top-knot. He was tall also, with a beard; very handsome and extremely familiar-looking. Top-Knot placed a hand on the Scotsman's shoulder.

"Calm down, mate. This is the gaffer 'ere. It'll get sorted now." He spoke with a cockney accent.

The big Scotsman did not calm down.

"Sorted?" he demanded, eyes filled with disbelief and anger. "You think these cunts can make up for what's been done tae us here?"

He drilled his eyes into the cockney, daring him to argue.

Nick and Beth entered the room, Nick standing with his back and one foot up against the wall, clearly entertained by the Scotsman.

"Well, I'll fuckin' tell ye this, son," he continued talking to Top-Knot, but was pacing and scanning the room with angry eyes as he spoke. "Waking up in a shitehole, the likes ay which even a Lanarkshire-man wouldn't enter-fuckin-tain, tae be set about by two scabby-looking basturds in hooded robes, scalpels and dildos in hand might be your idea of satisfactory accommodation, Mr Premiership Wank-Face, but where ah come fae," he searched for the words to express his outrage, "well… it just isnae on. Ma hole's in basturdin' tatters here."

His eyes bulged and moved from Nick to Beth and back to the cockney, who stepped forward to placate him once again.

"Mate, you're right, I ain't arguing wiv ya, I'm just saying they admitted they made a mistake, innit? The guvnor's here now. Let's hear him out, Gaz."

Shoulders hunched, fists clenched, Gaz clearly wanted to hurt someone, but having already failed to budge Nick, he simply stood inert, snorting through his nose, trying to calm himself.

"Aye, right," he said, flicking his eyes back to Nick. "But if one mair ay your workers comes near ma erse again…"

Nick laughed loudly, making Beth jump.

He stalked over to Gaz and the cockney, towering above them.

"You're in my hands now," he said, his voice a sadistic lover's caress. "Let's get to the bottom of this," he turned to Gaz. "No pun intended, son."

Gaz shuffled uncomfortably alongside the cockney, still furious, but quiet for a change.

Nick made a gesture and a panel opened in the wall of the unfurnished room. A sofa slid through the open panel, banging into the back of the men's legs, causing them to fall softly onto the cushions. Both men grimaced a little but stayed silent, eyes on Nick who stood over them, arms crossed across his chest.

"So you two came here a few days ago, went straight to…" Nick fished the tablet from under his arm, "Level Twenty-Eight?" He made a whooshing sound through pursed lips. "You pair must've been right lively little bastards before you died to deserve Twenty-Eight."

Gaz's eyes lit up again. "Look, mate, I done a lot ay shite things in ma life, but fuck all tae deserve what's been done tae me here."

Nick pressed his face close to Gaz's.

"That is not for you to judge, Mr Crawford. We do not make mistakes with the placement of a soul. The treatments you've received in Hell since you arrived are exactly what is required upon your death if you are to be redeemed, and precisely what you have to look forward to upon your actual death." Nick growled the words.

His black wings ruffled behind him, sending a spasm of fear through the human inhabitants of the room.

"However," Nick said," it does seem as though neither of you gentlemen were scheduled to depart the material world just yet."

The cockney fought his fear to speak up. "You mean we ain't dead?" he asked.

"No, Mr Pillans, you are in fact not dead, but *are* the first two souls in history to have entered my domain without either dying first or at my invitation."

Beth shuffled her feet nervously.

"It seems that your souls were displaced to allow other entities to inhabit them," Nick said. "It has happened before, the disembodiment of souls, and normally by one of the many ancient, malevolent souls who want to return to the flesh. Humans call them demonic possessions."

Nick searched the faces of Gaz Crawford and Chris Pillans.

"The disembodied spirit, however, does not enter Hell, instead remaining earthbound until its body is vacated. In your case, entities powerful enough to eradicate your bond to the material universe have shunted you from your bod—"

Nick's eyes narrowed as something occurred to him. Sweeping around, he spoke with urgency.

"Beth, come with me, we're leaving."

Gaz was on his feet in a heartbeat.

"C'mon tae fuck, chief. Whit about us? Ye cannae just leave us here, we've done fuck all."

Nick's eyes glinted, reflecting the violet light of the corridor.

"I'm afraid you're here to stay, chaps."

The door slid closed, Gaz Crawford's voice roaring through.

"Ya fuckin' durty basturd!"

Nick sighed and reopened the door. Moving with the purpose of a living statue, he shoved Gaz back into the room, then pulled the big man into him bringing them nose to nose.

"You have entirely too much to say for yourself, Mr Crawford."

Caught in Nick's grip, physically and mentally, Gaz did his best to glare back defiantly. His eyes misted, but he spat out the words, "Get tae fuck."

Nick calmly pressed a single finger gently to Gaz's lips.

Beth felt something shift in the air as Nick touched the Scotsman. Nothing physical, but something...

Nick was now leaning back, surveying Gaz's face. Beth's eyes widened in shock, then narrowed in curiosity as she took in the change in the man.

Where his mouth had been, a wrinkled, badly torn anus now protruded. Several damaged haemorrhoids sat dangling onto his chin. Gaz's eyes darted from Nick to Beth. All arrogance had left them and been replaced by undiluted fear as his hands moved to where his mouth previously sat.

As his fingers confirmed what his mind already knew, they recoiled in revulsion from the orifice. A muffled voice came from Gaz's trousers.

"Whit... Whit the fuck, man?" Gaz's bluster was all but gone, his voice stifled as much by growing fear as by the fabric of his underwear and trousers.

Nick spoke into a cell phone. "Meg, my dear, could you send Mr Michael Clark-Duncan to pay a visit to Mr Crawford on Level Seven?"

Nick smiled warmly at Gaz whose eyes had begun to fill with tears. Holding a finger up in a *quiet for now* gesture, Nick responded to Meg, "Yes, that's correct, standard sexual torture for both Pillans and Crawford." Nick stole a glance at Gaz's mouth. A grin tugged at the corners of Nick's mouth. "Tell Mike to start with a blowjob from Crawford."

Nick disconnected his call. Taking Beth gently by the arm, he left the room, closing the door behind him. The beating of fists and a flatulent chorus came from its inhabitants, causing Beth to startle.

Nick did not look back.

Tugging at his arm, Bethany asked him, "Nick, you look worried, what is it?" Nick's face had lost all humour and was stoic.

"Remember I told you that something big was going to happen?" He nodded back at the door to Gaz and Chris's cell. "Those two clowns are the start of it. I needed to see them in person to be sure, but only God could've sent their souls straight to Sheol without death occurring."

"Why would he want to? Why them?" Beth asked.

"A better question is, who did he send to take their place?" Nick said.

Headed back to the elevator, Nick called over his shoulder, "Come along, Bethany. We've work to do."

Wednesday

20

Jay and Mo - South Queensferry -1:15 am

FOR ONCE, THE SKIES OVER THE FIRTH OF FORTH were clear of cloud, jet black and unpolluted by lights from below. Scattered across the picture-perfect sky, stars twinkled and shot. Below Jay and Mo once again stood in front of the cameras of the world's media.

Mo stood at the shore, where the pebbles merged with the cold, murky water, speaking into his phone, casting the odd glance at Jay and the myriad of reporters and police officers present; checking every face for signs of hate or fear or worship. Feet away from him, bobbing on the Firth, a Grey Zodiac sat tethered to a wooden mooring, ready for their departure either when Jay had finished whatever he had planned — or if things went to shit again like they had at Edinburgh Castle.

With Dougie by his side, Jay approached the bank of reporters who were being joined by a growing trickle of people who'd heard about his presence through social media. Catching movement from Mo, Jay glanced over to his friend who pointed up to the streets above and the road bridge overhead, clearly worrying about the number of people headed down to the little beach outside Dougie's granny's cottage. Mo tapped his watch, mouthing, *Whatever you're gonna do, make it quick.*

Jay nodded his understanding, and his thanks, before turning back to face the reporters.

With his feet near the lapping waves, his back to shore, Jay faced inland, taking in the faces of the gathered media. There was a cynicism, an almost predatory feel in the air. These men and women were utterly desperate to discover and reveal the truth behind the con-man in front of them. The eager desire to debunk him was almost as powerful as the excitement they felt at being among the chosen few present at the shore. To Jay, a man who had been in the presence of true evil many times, they stank of unsavoury intent. They were not bad people; they had just deserted their morals to *do their job*.

Jay blocked out the negative feelings emanating from them. Closing his eyes, he searched for the strength to accomplish his intent. The ethereal tether he maintained with Heaven, even with his Father, pulsed and surged with the strain, the unprecedented pull on Heaven's power he that he made.

Jay felt God at the periphery of his reservoir of Heaven's Light. Having never pulled so deeply on Heaven before, Jay had expected that he might encounter that part of Heaven, of his own self, that was also his Father.

Jay gasped as God's disapproval burned him furiously.

Despite His displeasure, God was true to His word and did not intervene. Jay sensed an almost sadistic curiosity emanating from his Father's presence.

Drawing on His power as strongly as he'd ever dared in his long existence, Jay felt the air change catastrophically around him.

The people present were instantly silenced, humbled by the feel of the air. On automatic pilot they focused cameras on Jay, held microphones out, adjusted lights, but never once did a sound disturb the little pocket of charged air.

To Mo, standing a few feet away, it felt as though Heaven itself had dropped an electron-sized piece of itself onto the stony little beach.

Jay opened his eyes. Turning his back to those gathered on the pebbles, he looked up at the road bridge.

In the centre, the exact centre, of the giant structure, a bank of very clean, white fog grew. The speed of its appearance and remarkably precise placement of the cloud of fog, which was a rough sphere perhaps two hundred feet in diameter, was startling in its unnatural arrival and growth.

Continuing to spread itself along the suspended carriageway north towards Fife, the fog cloud enveloped the bridge structure, clinging to the road, the underside and the towers, but never leaving to stretch out over land or onto the sea beneath.

By the time the fog settled, the bridge structure looked like a digital artist had very deliberately painted a clinging cloud to the structure.

Facing out across the Forth, Jay made a broad gesture with his arms that made the muscles in his new body's shoulders ache with a muscle-memory they shouldn't have. Being suspended on a wooden cross with nails through your wrists and feet put a tremendous pressure on a person's chest and arms: enough, it seemed, to be remembered across two thousand years and through the body of another man with a mere gesture.

Ignoring the pain in his outstretched arms, Jay focused the tremendous torrent of power he was funnelling.

A gasp rose from those assembled as the sun rose over the mid-point of the Forth Road Bridge. Not an illusion, actual daylight appeared in the exact centre of the road bridge spanning the Firth of Forth.

In the sky, a strip of blue shone with the early evening sun peeking at the edge. A scar of daytime, perhaps six hundred feet wide, slashed into the black night sky. A few fluffy white clouds drifted past, pushed on a light breeze, much gentler than the one rushing across the Forth.

A news helicopter jinked to the south as the strip of day appeared, violently trying to avoid it. The startled pilot found his courage and flew across the slice of day in the night sky. The cameraman and reporter in the cabin sent a live broadcast to STV as they flew through night to day to night in three seconds.

Jay lowered his arms and made a sweeping gesture with his right hand. To those standing behind him, it appeared that he'd physically drawn his hand along the length of the road bridge, sweeping the fog from where it had rested. As the clouds of mist disappeared, the people on the beach, along the bridge, across the shore in Dalgety Bay and in Inverkeithing, Rosyth and Dunfermline, began to realise that something had happened to the bridge underneath the length of day that disappeared off into each horizon — west out to Kincardine and east out to the sea.

The bridge itself had changed. Impossibly, although that word had new meaning this day, the colour and structure on the north side had changed from grey-silver to a deep red-orange. The road surface, towers, elevation — all altered.

Slowly their eyes drifted along the carriageway, onto the road as it met the shore, eventually fixing on the line of unfamiliar cars emerging onto the land in Fife.

∞∞∞

Paddy Sheehan

San Francisco

Golden Gate Bridge

Five pm

Rush Hour

Sitting in the back of a yellow cab, Paddy Sheehan grinned to himself. Despite the rush hour, the heat, the absolute shite the cab driver had been chatting for the length of the journey, Paddy was a happy man.

His first visit to San Francisco had been filled with plain, simple fun. At seventy-three years old, it was his second visit to America. Unlike the first, a holiday to Florida, this visit had been more than a simple break in the sunshine.

Brought up in Belfast in the fifties, Paddy had moved to Glasgow in the sixties along with his brothers and sisters, mother and father. Economic and political motives compelled the migration. Paddy's oul' da' had been heavily in debt and even more in the shit with his ties to the very active IRA.

Paddy had joined the British Army as a teen, served his time with gusto and educated himself in maths, English and whatever else proved useful. In contrast to his siblings, he hadn't been content to settle for the relatively easier life of mainland Britain and wanted to work hard to educate himself and the daughters he had in time. Education... that was the key. Paddy wanted an office job for his kids, none of the manual labour he'd had to toil through.

Pulling onto the Golden Gate Bridge, Paddy Sheehan grinned once more as he looked out over the bay. His youngest daughter lived in San Francisco. An accountant, she'd lived and worked all over Europe for years, and had eventually married and settled in the States, using it as a base to work across South America and Africa at times.

Paddy's eldest daughter was a solicitor and had given him and his wife two wonderful grandchildren whom they adored: Patrick, who always made Paddy grin, and Cara. Two kids who had all of the opportunities and choices in front of them that Paddy had dreamed of giving his own children.

He was a happy man.

Letting out a contented sigh, Paddy felt a little adrenaline rush as the cab bumped along to the midway point of the Golden Gate Bridge. Seventy-three years old and tunnels and bridges still made him excited.

Paddy lowered the window. Breathing in the warm air, he watched the sun glint off the water below and along the rooftops of cars in the unusually light rush hour traffic.

Another beautiful day to commit to memory and tell the grandkids about.

Brakes and tyres screeched all around as the cab lurched violently forward and the world stopped making sense. The air, suddenly cool, smelled differently — wetter and more... familiar than the Californian breeze he'd got used to these last few weeks.

Paddy shook off the confusion. At his age, he'd grown accustomed to his brain taking a few seconds to catch up to events. Paddy gave the glass screen separating him from the front of the cab a gentle rap with his knuckles.

"Ye all right in there, son?"

The cabbie was staring out at the sky and either hadn't heard or had chosen to not respond.

Paddy rubbed at his forehead, suddenly aware that a bruise was forming. Deciding that he must've walloped it in the violent stopping of the cab, he looked out the open window, finally aware of why the world felt so wrong.

The clear blue sky had been replaced with a night-time one, filled with twinkling stars. Scanning along the traffic, Paddy's eyes were drawn to the metal of the suspension bridge. Once orange but now grey, Paddy recognised the structure immediately. Out of habit, he turned right to take in the Forth Rail Bridge, lit up at night, shining red in the night sky.

Paddy shook his head, grinning at his own imagination, then knocked on the glass separator again.

"Son, I think this bang on my head's a wee bit worse than I thought."

∞∞∞

Tracy Stewart

Forth Road Bridge

Northbound

1:18 am

"Fuckin' stupid bastard." Tracy rolled her eyes at herself in the mirror for perhaps the fourth time.

She'd woken from a deep sleep, the thought that she hadn't locked the steel shutters at her little newsagent's entrance nagging her sleeping mind.

Unable to rewind her memories to confirm whether she had or had not locked the shop, and all too aware that it was Sunday the next day, meaning the shop would be closed with nobody returning to check the building until Monday morning, Tracy had dragged herself from a warm bed, pulled a nightgown over her pyjamas, and climbed into her little car. Cursing her own poor memory, she made the fifty-minute drive from Bellshill to Dunfermline to check on her shop.

Tracy caught herself in the mirror and threw a few more curses at her reflection as her little car began working its way up towards the halfway point of the bridge.

The bridge was very quiet, headed northbound. Only a handful of cars were joining her on the road over into Fife. Tracy's eyes widened as a long line of cars suddenly appeared on the southbound carriageway. Unfamiliar, each car was an American model, complete with driver on the opposite side of the car and American registration plates.

Tracy narrowed her eyes as the drivers began clicking on their lights.

Must be some sort of convention, she thought, reaching the highest point of the incline.

Light pierced Tracy's eyes as she crested the hill. Lifting her foot from the accelerator, Tracy pulled her visor down, cursing at the cars opposite to lower their full beams. As her eyes slowly adjusted Tracy stamped hard onto the pedal, bringing her car to a screeching halt.

She caught the cynicism in her own eyes smiling back at her in the mirror.

"You are fucked in the head," she told herself. Laughing, she stepped from her car out onto the carriageway of the Golden Gate Bridge.

Shielding her eyes from the sun, Tracy scanned a line of rush-hour traffic making its way off the bridge onto the unfamiliar shoreline. Three seconds after she'd decided that she was still in her own bed in Bellshill having a wild, cheese-induced dream, Tracy Stewart's face met the tarmac of the famous San Francisco structure.

Her last conscious thought was, *What about my shop?*

21

Nick and Beth

RETURNING TO LEVEL TWO VIA THE ELEVATOR, Beth followed Nick through the open-plan office she'd arrived in earlier. A few faces looked up from their screens, coffees or games to greet Nick as he passed. Nick acknowledged each of them without breaking stride.

Entering a corner office, Beth sat in a large, high-backed chair which Nick had nodded to. She watched as he took his own seat behind a mahogany desk carved with images of Angels. As Nick clicked away at his computer, Beth surveyed the room.

Plain in décor, the office was what some people would describe as *minimal*. White walls, grey carpet, chrome and mirror and glass. But for the images adorning two of the walls it could have been an office in any corporate tower.

Beth caught Nick's eyes. Nodding at the images she asked, "Mind if I wander over and have a look at those?"

Concentrating on his task, Nick flicked his eyes up to acknowledge her and nodded his agreement before returning to tapping at his keyboard.

Beth padded across to the wall and began examining the images. Some were photographs — black and white, colour, digital, pre-digital. Others were paintings, some small and intimate, others more grand, formal. All held pictures of Nick with other people; arms around each other, laughing, playing golf, in bars, abseiling... perhaps a thousand images were carefully positioned along two walls.

Beth leaned in to take a closer look. All but perhaps forty of the images showed two men enjoying life. Sometimes they were alone, but mostly they were with a group of other people. In almost all of them, their joy, their friendship, was evident.

Feeling Nick come up behind her, she pointed at the man in the images beside Nick.

His hair was light, skin dark, eyes a dazzling lagoon blue. The shape of his face gave away nothing of ethnicity. With characteristics she could attribute to Native Americans, Asians, Africans, White Europeans, even Aboriginals, the man's face was truly universal in appearance. The definition of mixed-race... of beauty.

"That's Him, isn't it?" she asked.

"Yes. It is," Nick said softly.

Beth breathed deeply, feeling the effect of His presence even through the two-dimensional images. "He is..." Beth turned to look at Nick, who smiled knowingly at her lack of an accurate description of Him.

"He is God," Nick said.

Beth merely nodded. Turning her attention back to His face, Beth placed a hand gently across her own heart and felt it race as she took in His countenance.

"Are you still friends?" she asked, voice a whisper.

"Of course," Nick replied. "Best friends."

"How? How can that be, with what you know, with how He is?" Beth gestured at the office pods outside. "How can you love Him when you oppose Him with such conviction.

Nick smiled. He was clearly making allowances for the limits of her imagination, of her understanding.

"The easy answer is *because He is God*, the Creator. A more truthful answer is to remind you that the reason I fight so hard to send souls to Him is not simply out of concern for humans, whom I believe are out of nature, but also from a desire to magnify my Creator's glory: His Kingdom."

Beth blinked hard and shook her head as though to dispel a fug.

"Come and sit and I'll continue my story, as I promised. Perhaps you'll gain more insight, but when we're done, we will get to the real reason why I brought you here."

Beth suppressed a surge of anger. "Don't do that again," she said flatly.

Nick's eyebrows shot up in surprise.

"Do what?"

"Each time we get intimate in our discussion, as you show a vulnerability or goodness in yourself, you seem to feel the need to slap me down, to remind me who you are. The first mention of my Uncle Harry frightened me enough."

Nick still looked surprised. "Very well. Let me say this though: you *are* here for a specific purpose. I did not come randomly to your bar. In your time with me, you will face a difficult decision that may very well change everything about your life, but I will not harm you in any way."

Nick scanned her eyes.

"Is that acceptable for now?" he asked.

Beth gave a single, curt nod. "Yes. Let's get on with it. You were going to tell me about the prophets. How the three of them came to Earth, and why."

Nick reclined into his office chair and waited for Beth to be seated. Producing a bottle of Grey Goose from his desk, along with an ice bucket and two glasses, Nick prepared drinks for them as he spoke.

"I suppose that it'd be best to relay events in the order they happened, according to your measure of time.

"Moses' story has been reported fairly accurately in your religious texts, however he was not a Hebrew. Moses, just as Ramses, his brother, was a son of Pharaoh. Born into royalty and truly extreme wealth, Moses was a much greater man, much more an empath than the Bible gives him credit for."

"He wasn't a son of slaves? He didn't deliver the Hebrews from slavery?" Beth asked.

"Oh, he did," Nick replied. "That's true, but he did not do so out of a sense of shared kinship with the Hebrews. He was not one of them. He was simply, wonderfully, a very compassionate man who could not tolerate that his dynasty built empires with the bones and blood of slaves as its stones and mortar."

Nick leaned across his desk, resting his elbows on the surface and steepling his hands. He was taking in Beth's reaction; giving her time to process.

"That makes him even more courageous and more compassionate than the Bible portrays."

"Yes," Nick said. "He was tortured by what he saw each day. He did disappear from the royal court, just as the Bible states. By his own volition he dressed as a slave, joined the legions of men, women and children treading straw into mud, moving impossibly large stones with the aid of only ropes, pulleys, rollers and their own muscle and blood and dying under the taskmasters' whips. Moses lived as a slave for six very long, painful months. He learned first-hand the daily humiliation, physical torture and utter despair felt by a nation of people and perpetuated by his family.

"When six months passed, he went home to disclose to his family all that he'd experienced and beg for the release of the slaves. Moses showed them his feet with bones broken, healed then broken once again and rehealed by the daily treading of mud for making brick. He showed them the deep calluses burned into his leathery hands from the ropes with which he'd dragged huge stones through the sand. Moses disrobed and showed his parents and his brother the deep gashes on his torso from the slave-masters' whips. His wounds were infected and rancid. He was feverish, dying. He pleaded with his family to see, to really *see* what their kingdom had done to him, as it was doing to millions of Hebrews.

"Pharaoh, his father, wept at his son's wounds and his bravery. He ordered his doctors to tend to Moses' injuries. Ramses, younger brother of Moses, was unmoved.   When they had made Moses comfortable, stripped his body of infected flesh and dressed his wounds, Pharaoh left his eldest son to recover with his mother at his side.

"Pharaoh walked the marble ramparts and temples of his palace. He watched the slaves at work. He saw for the first time the brutality of his kingdom. From his vantage point he watched a boy of perhaps ten years fall into the sand. Blood ran from his hands, turning the sand black. A slave-master stood over the boy, whip-arm raised.

"Pharaoh grimaced as the leather met skin, tearing a ribbon of pain and disfigurement into the flesh. He felt the boy's pain as though he'd watched his own son brutalised. The connection between Moses' wounds and this boy's was now real in his mind. Now that it had been made, he saw the slaves in their thousands, really saw them for the first time, the way Moses had. He saw them in a way he had not in his fifty years previously. Not as slaves, not as cattle, not as workers or fodder, but as people — as real to Pharaoh in their agony as his own son had been.

"Pharaoh felt the salt-sting of tears trailing rivulets through the ubiquitous sand blown onto his face by the night breeze.

"A movement behind startled him, breaking the spell. Ramses stood there. Bare-chested in kilt, sandals and expensive golden gantlets, his prince's lock the only hair on his shaved head. Ramses, always the least affable of his sons, glared at Pharaoh, rage blazing from painted eyes.

"'Father, you cannot have taken his mad words to heart.' It was not a question.

"Pharaoh turned from his youngest son, wiping the tears from his eyes with the back of his hand. He spoke in a whisper.

"'Come, Ramses. Look upon those below.'

"Ramses came to his father's side. His fists clenched and released at his sides as he listened to Pharaoh speak.

"'Look at the boy bleeding in the dirt. Observe the old man, barely a muscle left on his frame, bent over by endless hours treading mud bricks. The woman over there, providing food for our soldiers — see how they thank her.'

"Ramses watched one of the men before whom she'd laid a plate of meat down punch the elderly woman in the abdomen, perhaps in displeasure at his meal.

"'They are just slaves, Father.'

"Pharaoh did not take his eyes away from the Hebrews.

"'They are people. Just as we are... and we have wronged them... for generations.' He put his face in his hands and resumed weeping.

"Ramses closed his eyes in disgust. He'd sought this man's approval for years, this god king — every Pharaoh was a god — who now cried like an infant over the mewling of the animals below. Pharaoh had basked Moses in the warmth of his love, his approval and admiration whilst Ramses, the second son, had been hidden in the shade cast by Moses bathing in their father's light. Ramses had felt his pride, his sense of self-worth, diminish with every moment he was in his father's presence. That the Pharaoh, his own father, had thought so little of him had destroyed Ramses in his youth and hardened him as an adult.

"Before he knew he'd moved Ramses found his hands around Pharaoh's throat, his knee pressing onto his father's chest, pinning him to the marble floor. Powered by every rebuke, each barbed comment, by his father's casual disregard of him, Ramses' fingers tightened with the strength of a man in his prime and the fury of an abandoned child.

"Held in Ramses' powerful grip, Pharaoh was an infant. Cartilage bent and snapped. Airways constricted. Still, Ramses tightened his grip. He spat into his father's eyes as they rolled back up into his head. Feeling the resistance from beneath sag, Ramses released the vice on his father's throat, placed one hand at the rear of the old man's head, the other under his chin and twisted hard, wrecking several vertebrae.

"Rising to his feet with power, anger, relief surging through his muscles and making his heart race, Ramses slowly came back to the moment.

"Part of him expected panic to rise, but it did not. Coldly, his eyes moved over the broken body of Pharaoh, his face and back resting on the marble floor. No-one could see them atop the plinth, but that would change soon.

"Ramses swished around, his kilt flaring with the speed of his passing. Entering the main chamber his father slept in, he found the person he'd hoped would be there. The servant, a Hebrew, was arranging petals into the wash basin in Pharaoh's room. Ramses took four powerful strides towards the lad. Grabbing him from behind, he smashed the boy's face against the cold marble basin several times until grey matter joined red on the surface. Releasing the boy, Ramses summoned all of his emotion, forcing a scream.

"'The Pharaoh! The Pharaoh! A slave has killed our great father.'

"Accompanied by their mother who was held by two palace guards, Moses joined the crowd of family and servants gathered around the body of Pharaoh. For three hours the brothers sat and stood, looking at the body of their father. As each of the people left one at a time, to make preparations, to seek the boy's family and punish them also, to cry alone in their chambers, the brothers keep their vigil. Moses sat, unsteady, shaking, sweating with fever and crying. He did not bother to disguise his grief. Ramses was a standing statue. Face of marble, he looked down at both Pharaoh and his brother. One phrase repeated in his mind: *You are both weak.* Moses died from infection before the sun rose on a new day. A day that saw Ramses crowned Pharaoh."

As Nick paused his narration, Beth shook herself from the story, rubbing her temples as though to aid in her processing comprehension.

"Moses died?" she asked.

"Yes. He came to Sheol in agonising spiritual pain. I had never encountered a soul so determined, so pure in purpose. He passed through Sheol into Heaven within an hour of his entry. He also pleaded with me to come with him, to stand by his side and beg God to help his people."

Nick smiled at a memory he chose not to share with Beth, but she saw the pain dim his eyes momentarily.

"Obviously, He agreed?" Beth said.

"After a fashion," Nick replied. "Moses convinced God that the Hebrews could become His people.

That they believed with all their hearts in the glory of the one God and, if delivered from slavery, would worship only Him for generations."

Beth's eyebrows knitted into a frown. Nick made a little gesture with his hand, imploring patience.

"I knew that God did not care for the worship of humans, since *they are of nature,* and fully expected Him to humiliate Moses, refuse him, send him back to Sheol for his insolence. God did none of these things: He simply agreed to Moses' request."

"Why?"

"Why do you think, Beth?"

"I honestly don't know, Nick," she replied with a shrug. "For His own amusement?"

Nick nodded once. "Yes. He wanted to see what would happen if He proved His existence to a group of humans. I suspect that despite the curiosity, He knew exactly what would occur. After all, it wasn't the first time He'd meddled with humans. Abraham, Noah... so many others."

"He's a child burning ants with a lens," Beth spat the words.

Nick's eyes widened in surprise at what, her insolence? Her insight?

He recovered quickly, "That's one way to look at it, Beth, but it's not quite so simple. He always has a plan."

Nick leaned back into his chair.

"It suits Him to have humans worship Him, to instigate and keep them arguing over doctrine, validity, heresy. Hardly any of those who have embraced Judaism, Christianity, Islam or any of the other religions ever reach heaven. Not after millennia in Sheol. His validation of their religions is His greatest weapon for keeping them from attaining Heaven. They come to Sheol in legions and their anger, their bitterness at His betrayal, keep them here."

"He used Moses," Beth said flatly.

"Yes," Nick said, "but Moses gave Him a little more than He counted on." Humour danced in Nick's eyes. "Moses returned to the material world, to Earth, in his own body free from disease or scarring. He returned not to Egypt but to Midian where, on Mount Horeb, God did the burning bush thing, giving Moses a symbol of His power to convey to the Egyptians and the Hebrews. Moses eventually returned to Egypt, and demands, refusals, plagues and deaths occurred. Seas parted, an army died and a nation was delivered from slavery." Nick grinned across the table at Beth. "Your Bible got most of those events, correct... more or less."

"So he went to Mount Sinai? He received The Ten Commandments?" Beth was caught in the narrative, once again the theology student in rapture at the truths being disclosed.

"Not exactly," Nick said. "God gave Moses One Commandment for his people." Nick nodded at her. "You know."

Beth's mouth opened in a wide O.

"No," she whispered.

Nick laughed bitterly. "Uh huh. Can you imagine that poor bastard Moses' reaction? He'd freed a whole nation of people, a whole race, promised them a land of milk and honey, God's blessing and so on, and He gives him one simple phrase to relay to the Hebrews. *Don't be a cunt.*

"Moses was utterly destroyed in spirit on that mountain. The realisation of what had happened hit him very hard. He spent many days crying, breaking his hands striking rocks, cursing Heaven. Moses spent weeks wandering the peaks, raging, planning and healing. He couldn't do it. He couldn't pass God's words to his desperate people. Not out of fear, but for simple love, Moses spent another month carving Ten Commandments into stone tablets. The poor bastard truly believed that the good, honourable words he etched into the rock would tie his people to God and keep their path true and honourable. Not for Him, but for them: that a nation might thrive."

Nick took a deep breath before continuing.

"He succeeded, partly. Moses did strengthen and deepen the connection of the Hebrews with God.

The Ten Commandments were simply the well-intentioned, honourable lies of a good man, but they did what Moses intended them to: they kept the nation focused on survival and morally stable."

"Was God angry?" Beth asked.

"He was fucking livid, Beth," Nick laughed loudly. "Moses hasn't ever got over the dressing down he got when he finally returned to Heaven. The lad's still petrified whenever God is nearby, but fuck, it was worth it."

Nick's smile died.

"God didn't really care what the Hebrews believed. Moses had set in motion what He had intended: the Hebrews worshipped God and were moving in a direction that took them further from accessing Heaven. A whole nation of people who considered themselves *God's people... chosen...* duped. He laughed his bollocks off over that. Happy as a pig in shite, He was, but He was pissed that Moses had attempted to provide more moral guidance to His people than God wished them to have.

"He would repeat this many times over the centuries. Found, stoke or guide religions with the aid of prophets, normally good men like Moses or Muhammed, many centuries later, who'd attained entry to Heaven and begged for His help for their people.

"Of course, there was also Jesus. He brought an entirely unprecedented storm in his wake."

22

Jay and Mo

FIVE MINUTES AFTER THE BRIDGE'S structure was altered, news crews in San Francisco and in Scotland were joining people on foot, crossing their respective bridge at the midway point. Emerging into a different bridge, in a different country, continent and time-zone, some laughed and danced.

Others embraced each other, weeping openly. Many fell to their knees and prayed.

In Scotland the impossible strip of California sunshine remained, a steady stream of people now travelling on foot and bike and car across the tear in reality. In San Francisco a strip of night sky, chilled and brightly lit with a full, buoyant moon and prickled with stars, tore the daytime. Scots were running and dancing, praying and celebrating.

A little group of students carried a beer-filled cooler out into the Californian heat.

"Taps aff," one of them yelled, handing a beer to a bewildered local heading the other direction... towards Scotland.

An athletic-looking woman in shorts and vest-top, partway through her evening run, stood over the midway point where the two bridges and countries met. One leg with goose pimples up in response to the cold in Scotland, the other leg resting in San Francisco. She laughed loudly as she straddled continents.

News presenters, transmitting live to their networks, walked back and forth between night and day, Europe and America. All stoic professionalism was gone, their faces filled with wonder as they demonstrated the impossible for the viewers at home.

Slumped on the floor of the little Zodiac, resting his head on Mo's knees, Jay took a final look up at the torn sky and restructured bridge. As the dinghy bobbed along, towards Leith, Jay grinned, knowing that this time... this time he'd done it right.

Let's see them explain that.

∞∞∞

As the early hours passed, Jay slept and Mo scanned the news channels, first from Miriam's jet, and later from a large flat-screen in a spacious apartment inside Kensington Palace. Jay didn't know who Miriam worked with, but she was obviously seriously connected.

Upon arrival he'd wandered the rooms and halls, amongst sleeping orphans and homeless families transported to Britain at the Old Trafford Event and rehomed, temporarily at least, by the Queen. The scale of Jay's actions staggered even Mo, who thought that he knew exactly how things would play out on Earth.

Part of him had begun to wonder if perhaps his friend might have a chance of success after all. Walking the rows of sleeping people, Mo decided that his original assessment had been correct: humans simply did not have the capacity to conquer their nature. Sure, a portion managed to attain Heaven, but only after instruction. God was demanding that every soul on Earth be fit for Heaven by Friday.

Looking around at the poor and the hungry, the forgotten and the abused, Mo's heart hardened once again.

After five hours of watching the global reaction to the Bridge Miracle, Mo was suffering deep internal conflict once again.

Physicists and structural engineers from the most prestigious universities across America and Scotland, as well as Europe, Africa and Asia, had begun to congregate at the bridges.

Scientists criss-crossed them, measuring temperature, humidity, air pollution, relative position of stars in the sky, GPS co-ordinates — the list of tests seemed as infinite as Heaven itself.

Astronomers gasped as they examined the skies. The slash of night over San Francisco had become a vent through which a beautifully bright and cold Scottish morning shone. Over the Firth of Forth a slice of night broke the daytime sky.

In both countries, where the Forth and the Golden Gate Bridges were fused together, a deep scar ran the length of the joined sections.

Engineers and metallurgists had been taking extensive samples throughout the night/evening from the metals for analysis, carbon dating, structural inspection and a comparison of the oxidation processes of the bridges' respective cables.

Early results showed that the bridges appeared to have been separated, transported thousands of miles and fused together, flawlessly, in a nano-second. The components, the wires and cables, rivets and beams of each half of each bridge precisely matched its partner — now situated half a world away — forming a stable structure with a portion of another bridge.

The pope had been conducting a single, long vigil and Mass since Jay's departure the day before, counselling the millions gathered in Rome and through the TV airways on the requirements for their souls to enter Heaven.

Religious leaders from across the globe gave sermons to and held vigils with impossible numbers of people who had begun to take Jay's words as literal gospel.

Some preached that Jay, in his assertion that God did not love His creations, was a blasphemer, perhaps Satan himself, and that he was readying the souls of those who followed him for Hell. Many recycled the same useless dogma and doctrine their religion had remained faithful to for centuries, their faith in tradition and God unshaken.

Overwhelmingly, as the news and data and scientific bafflement trickled through, people began to consider and then believe Jay's words. They flocked to nearby churches and chapels belonging to those religions who'd asserted their belief in Jay's message. Many churches had to conduct Mass outside due to the number of people who'd begun streaming to their doors. The ministers, priests, pastors, shamans and rabbis, themselves newly convinced of the need to prepare their flocks' souls, struggled to convey the message. They needed Jay.

Some played Jay's words from The Event, or the Bridge Miracle, or his first appearance on Lorraine Kelly's show on screens inside and outside their churches. Football stadiums had begun to invite the worshippers in tens of thousands into their stands to watch Jay on their big screens.

The Hyde Park Mass, later that day, was being broadcast to many stadiums, churches, clubs and homes across the world. People seemed desperate to listen to his instructions, to strive for Heaven.

Bloggers wrote long articles on evolution, God's obvious and callous absence, Jay's miracles and the physics behind them.

Inevitably, the United States military had stationed themselves on the American side of the portal between countries, and were now restricting access in either direction. The words *potential terrorist attack* were being bandied around.

Mo clicked the TV's sound off. Rubbing at tired eyes, he replayed the most positive images in his mind's eye, trying once again to believe in his friend; that he really might pull it off.

Mo forced a loud, exasperated whistle through his teeth,

"Fuck it," he said, scooping his phone up from the arm of his chair. "It's me," he said flatly into it.

Mo winced as the person on the other side of the call shared some colourful obscenities.

"Yeah, very good, but it don't change a thing. I'm not telling you his exit strategy, just stick to the plan. Agitate, instigate. That's it."

Mo jabbed the disconnect button. Tossing his phone onto the chair opposite, he rose from his chair. Catching his reflection, or rather Chris Pillans' reflection, he threw a disgusted look at himself before setting off down the people-strewn corridors to rouse Jay.

23

Nick and Beth

"Jesus?" Beth said.

Nick Grinned. "Yeah... Jesus," Nick said. "You do want to hear his story, don't you?"

Beth's eyebrows rose. "Well, yeah... of course. It's just that..."

"You're worried that I'll shatter one too many of the truths you've clung to throughout your life," Nick said flatly.

Beth shrugged. "Maybe. I don't know that I ever really believed in Jesus."

"Yes, you did," Nick interrupted. "You still do, Beth, you've just grown accustomed to accepting that no-on cares enough to save you. You've been that way," Nick noticed the horror on Beth's face, "since Uncle Harry," he said kindly this time, no taunting.

Having steeled herself to admonish Nick once more, she took a second or two to compose herself. When her face relaxed once again, Nick reached across to touch her hand.

"We can get to *that* right now if you wish, Bethany. I can show you why you're here, why... what *he* did matters as much to me as it does to you."

"Not possible," Beth spat out before she meant to.

Shrinking back into her chair, she glared at Nick.

"He can't possibly matter to you the way he did to me," she said.

Nick chose not to press the point. "Okay, Bethany. The choice remains: Harry or Jesus?"

Beth did not have to think.

"I'd like to hear about Jesus... if that's okay?"

Nick merely nodded his agreement.

"It was probably around one thousand BC, your time," Nick said. "Best guess. As I said, time is a little screwy, meaningless really, in the immaterial plane."

Beth nodded, keen for Nick to continue.

"Stewart... God, had been so angry, so critical, vindictive and separate, so very different from the loving, forgiving, inclusive Creator He'd been for so long by that point that many of us doubted our own memories of who and what He'd been before I had accused Him and become His *Adversary*. More than a few of us had given up all hope that He would ever be the benign Father once again. And then Jesus came.

"Gabriel had come to me in Sheol. *God is creating a new Angel,* he'd said. The last of His Angels had been gifted sentience millions, probably more like billions, of years previously. I, as His First Angel, had seen the process unfold many times. Despite this, it had been so long since God had created one of us my heart swelled with the hope that perhaps God had found His loving nature once again. If He had not, perhaps the act of Creation may reignite that flame.

"I cast off the trappings of Sheol. Taking my Angelic form, I screamed like a comet into Heaven. What I found was not a sibling Angel being created, but God Himself being ripped apart."

Beth's mouth gaped.

"Not literally, it only seemed that way. As I came into His presence, I saw His limitless Light, the power that comprised Him, being torn. Not in half, but a fragment of His being was being ripped from Him.

"This was not how Angels were created. I worried that some outside force was attacking Him, though what I thought that could have been I cannot imagine. Nothing existed then or now in all of Creation, material or immaterial, without His having brought it into being. Anyway, I rushed to Him, only to be struck by His hand. I scuttled back, away from Him, eyes fixed to what was emerging.

"A rip had appeared in His being. His face was set in pain, and this was unprecedented: God did not experience pain or loss or even the sting of challenge. God merely decreed and it was so... but this, this was costing Him dearly. I recall thinking that all the universe might end.

"A tendril stretched from Him and terminated in a bulb-shaped, dense pocket of energy that swirled and ebbed. God roared in triumph as the offshoot began to take shape.

"This had not occurred in His making of His Angels, or in creating matter, or sentient life, or forging planets, or indeed the universe in its entirety. He had simply *willed* those entities and things into existence at no cost or diminishment to Himself. None that His Angels could identify, at any rate.

"Now, with the creation of this thing, He was reduced. That's the only way I can describe it: reduced.

"Not by much — His power was and is infinite — but a fragment had left Him, given by Him willingly to this new entity, unique in all of Creation."

"Jesus, "Beth said in awe.

"Jesus, His own son," Nick said smiling. "The Angels crowded around, instantly recognising Jesus for what he was. They fell at his feet, began praying to him, but, already fully the being he would always be, he bid them to rise. 'Do not worship me,' he told them. 'Worship my Father as you always have. I wish merely to learn from you, His Angels.'

"By God, they... we loved the kid for that," Nick said. "God was pleased also. He instructed His Angels to show Jesus the universe his Father had created. Before my siblings had the chance to spirit the fledgling Jesus from Heaven, to show him the wonders of His father's universe, the soul of a man came forward. A broken man, who'd been in Heaven for around one millennium... Moses."

Beth smiled bitterly.

Nick returned her smile, nodding.

"Yes. Moses put himself forward as Jesus' guide. He requested that, as a former human, he might be permitted to introduce Jesus to God's *finest creations* on Earth.

"Any hope I'd had that Jesus' birth would soften God vanished at that moment. God had not forgiven Moses for his attempts to elevate human souls so many Earth years before. If anything, time, as well as Moses' friendship with me, had increased God's anger at Moses.

"God screamed at him, 'Why in the name of fuck wold I entrust my son to a fuck-up shit-stain, such as yersel'? Moses, the fuckin' man wi' the plan. The cunt that cannae follow one simple bastardin' rule? Get yersel' tae fuck, afore I fuckin' end ye.'

"Jesus stepped forward, shielding Moses. 'Thank you for your guidance, but I believe that I can choose for myself, Father.'

"All of Heaven stood frozen, each and every Angel, human soul, God Himself. Jesus merely smiled warmly and sincerely, awaiting God's response.

"'Aye, good. Off ye go then, son. But if that wee cunt gives ye any shite about human souls and Heaven, get him chased.'

"Jesus gave God a courteous bow, before guiding Moses to the exit."

A hint of a smile played on Beth's lips. "I like him already," she said.

Nick returned the smile. "Everyone loves that kid. Even Stewart. He's the best of all of us," Nick said sincerely. "So Jesus — most of us call him Jay — and Moses built on that moment, and become firm friends. Best of friends, brothers really. Over the next few hundred years, they immersed themselves in the wonders of God's universe. Planets and life-forms scattered many light-years from Earth. Cosmic phenomena, even the odd fishing trip. Always, they returned to Earth. Always, they questioned why the humans weren't admitted to Heaven.

"During that time, as you might expect, Jay, Moses and I became friends, united by the shared belief that humans deserved their shot at Heaven and that we three might be able to convince God to establish a fairer system for admittance, and to replace my hellish school in Sheol.

"Eventually, God gave in, mostly because of his soft spot for Jay, and agreed that the kid could go to Earth, be a rallying symbol for them. God decreed that His single rule still held.

"Don't be a cunt.

"Fulfil that, and they might get into Heaven. Jay, being Jay, didn't argue the subtleties of what exactly classified being a cunt in God's world. Kid figured that so long as he succeeded in teaching humans to be good people, his father would have little room to classify them as *cunts* and deny them Heaven.

"So down he went. Born of a virgin. Messiah of prophecy. Sacrificed for humanity's sins." Nick's eyes filled with bitterness. "All that pish."

"I don't follow, Nick," Beth said. "Why did he allow himself to be executed at all?"

Nick rubbed at his eyes before answering.

Partly because he had come to realise what a shit his Father was, but mostly because he believed that his sacrifice would cause a cataclysmic change on Earth."

Nick leaned back into his chair.

"Obviously, Jay's time here on Earth made a big impact, just not the one he had planned for.

"He gave the humans the best of himself. Lessons in acceptance, tolerance, love for one another, you know the stories, Bethany. The New Testament isn't too misleading regarding Jay's basic message. He also tried to teach them, as best he could based on God's vague requirement that they not be cunts, how they might enter Heaven.

"Very early on in his short service, Jay became aware that he couldn't eradicate the human fear of the Divine or their predisposition to self-sabotage. He decided to use it.

"Jay allowed dissention to spread throughout the region he'd been travelling. He didn't attempt to explain his outlook to the priests or rabbis or the Roman governors when he could have. He allowed those in power to plan and execute plots to humiliate and eliminate him. What they did not suspect was that Jay wanted to be the sacrifice. He felt that by indulging the basic human need for sacrifice, he might better enable them to attain Heaven."

Beth wore a cynical expression.

"Why not just do miracle after miracle. Show them so that they could not dispute who and what he was? Why die for them? There were so many other ways he could have convinced them of who he was and what he wished for their souls."

Nick nodded. "It was a different time. More superstitious, yes, but also more dangerous in many ways. If Jay succeeded in convincing one town of people of his identity and their need to prepare their souls for Heaven in a manner totally at odds with their beliefs, he'd have to start again a few miles down the road. Inevitably, as he travelled his followers' belief in him and his message would waver during his absence. Doubts and dissention would arise. Eventually aggression and anger at having being *duped*.

"Jay understood the times and the people he was immersed in and was one of. He always does. That's his gift. Empathy."

Nick looked a little wistful.

"You love him," she said.

Nick shrugged. "Of course, everybody does. All of Heaven. Loving Jay is probably the only thing most Angels in Heaven agree on anymore. Anyway," Nick said, making a dismissive gesture with his hand, "Jay knew that the people of the time and the region, be they Roman or pagan or Jewish, being descended from Moses' people were limited in their understanding of God and Heaven.

"He knew that they could not conceive of a God who did not demand goodness from them, or cared nothing for their earthly lives. Jay understood also that *they* could not comprehend a Divine Creator without attaching an element of sacrifice to their beliefs or rituals.

"Humans had created these rituals based on sacrifice instinctively from the earliest origins of man, millions of years before Moses or Jay ever touched Earth, Bethany. Because of their suffering, the hardships they faced in life, they accepted and believed in their souls that sacrifice was and must be part of nature and of the Divine. That is the way God created their world."

"Part of nature," Beth repeated.

"Exactly," Nick said. "That was always the flaw. God made death and suffering and disease and loss everyday things for all living organisms, but humans alone had evolved a soul that enabled them to transcend the natural world. To almost become one of His Angels. That this did not occur upon their death was known to man from very early times. Shamans and spiritual leaders, priests and witchdoctors, communing with the lost souls in Sheol long before I came to rule that terrible region — these leaders knew that Heaven did not exist, or was at least inaccessible. Because of this revelation, humans developed religious practices which attached an element of sacrifice and exclusion to their religions and their methods of worship. How could they not, based on the pain He visited on them in life and in the afterlife?

"There were two main consequences.

"The first was the concept of sacrifice to ingratiate themselves with whichever Divine being they worshipped. Sometimes animal, sometimes human sacrifice. In the mind of the worshipper, they are repaying God for the sacrifice He made for them during their Creation or thanking Him for the gifts they received in life. This persists strongly in many parts of the world.

"The other practice to emerge was one of the representation of the dying god. Sacrificing effigies of their God or gods or humans believed to be possessed or blessed by the Creator. This practice arose from humans' basic mistake in believing that

God must have sacrificed a significant part of Himself to create the universe. How else did change or birth or Creation occur? That was what they'd learned from living under His cruel laws of nature."

Nick paused for a moment to allow Beth to process his words. She was a theology student and was more able than most to give context to his revelations, but she was only human, after all, and needed time to allow her understanding to adjust.

After a few moments of silence, Bethany motioned to him that he could continue.

"Jay understood this mind-set perfectly and gave them their dying god on the wood they so needed to validate their belief, their need to feel as though they'd paid somehow for perceived sins — or that Jay had paid for them in this case. He became the symbol of goodness and self-sacrifice, sending an ever-growing torrent of souls straight from Earth to Heaven. At least for a while."

Nick smiled sadly.

"Humans being humans inevitably twisted his message, used him as a symbol to victimise, to marginalise, to cleanse whole nations of *infidels* or convert them. The death and persecution that has stemmed from Christianity is almost unfathomable to even me, Bethany. They took this good, pure entity, brutalised him, sacrificed him to their superstitions then used his death as justification for every fucking horrible act you can imagine for two thousand years."

Beth nodded along.

"God fucking loved that, I can tell you. Christianity, collectively, was the largest single blow to my progress in millennia. No other religion — not Islam, Hindu, paganism, fucking voodoo, or any other — comes close to impeding the elevation of the human soul so effectively."

They sat in silence for several long moments, Beth sorting through the complex feelings and reactions she was experiencing, Nick merely watching her.

Eventually, Beth asked, "Why me, Nick. Why am I here?"

Nick leaned forward, placing his elbows on the desk and steepling his fingers. He peered over them at her.

"This will be emotionally painful, Bethany. I can return you now and clear your memory. You can go back to life with a gap in your memory of where you've been to account for..." Nick checked his watch, "looks like a few days, Earth time. Or we can continue? We can get to the reason for your presence in Sheol?"

Beth did not have to think about her response.

"I'm ready," she said.

An instant later, he'd taken her in his Angelic arms and once again they were *somewhere* else.

24

Jay and Mo

WITH BERLIN BELOW, JAY STRETCHED HIS LONG LEGS out in front of him, enjoying the pop and tension in his joints. Despite the unrelenting pace of the last few days, combined with his exertion at the Forth Road Bridge, Jay felt awake, refreshed, purposeful and truly alive. His heart was filled with hope, thanks in part to the reaction he'd been receiving during his earlier Masses in London and Paris, but mostly because he was truly beginning to believe that he and Mo might succeed in convincing every human of his words, if not outright saving their souls.

Jay could feel that change in the humans. They wanted to believe — it had been the same in Nazareth and Jerusalem two thousand years before. The trick was in getting them to ignore the natural suspicion they felt, and reducing the influence of their innate urge for self-sabotage.

Many times in the last few days, Jay had reflected on how much easier his mission might be without the pervasive twenty-first century cynicism, which hadn't been the default for most people on his previous mission in the Middle-East.

Having said that, technology was of huge assistance in this modern world. Without their broadband, TV, radio, smartphones and tablets, Jay would have reached only those who could be in his physical presence. Sure, the miracles helped spread the word and bring people to the point where they could at least consider the Divine, but for the state of mind and soul that God was demanding of them, the technology of these times was his only realistic hope of spreading his voice, image, presence and words far and wide.

Glancing over at Mo, who lay sleeping in a reclined chair, Jay took in his friend's appearance. Even wearing Chris Pillans' face and body, even fast asleep, Jay could see his friend's true presence beneath the man he wore.

Worry creased his brow, even as he snored. Jay smiled sadly. He regretted the anxiety and the stress he was causing Mo, but there was simply no other way for him to do what he had to do without placing himself right into the midst of the humans. Despite Mo's protests, Jay had to be among them, not standing on a platform or a stage, high above, lecturing them on how to be humble and forgiving.

At the Hyde Park Mass, a feeling of understanding and acceptance had permeated the crowd. Families, men and women and children, listened to him speak for thirty minutes, instructing them on how they could save their eternal souls. The crowd had been spellbound, completely silent. Jay had spotted a few *Buddy Christ* t-shirts, as well as banners and posters with his face as it had been in Palestine, Photoshopped next to Garry Crawford's face with *Jesus 2.0* emblazoned across it.

The crowd, which had numbered close to half a million people, many more spilling out onto and along Park Lane beyond, had showed no sign of malevolence despite its size. Not until, as it had in Edinburgh, the mood took a sudden shift, resulting in the crowd surging towards Speaker's Corner, once again flattening the barriers and security; once again causing Jay and Mo to flee to a waiting helicopter whilst men and women put themselves in harm's way to protect them. Jay regretted the necessity of this deeply, but it *was* necessary: he had to lead from amongst them.

Mo begged him afterwards to reconsider an elevated, more controlled venue or custom-built platform for the next Mass. Jay refused and had spoken for an hour to hundreds of thousands gathered at the base of the Eiffel Tower and its parks. This time, when the crowd came forward, a single shot rang out. Jay had turned his head frantically left and right as he ran towards the waiting chopper, trying desperately to discover the victim. Dougie, Miriam, Mo, Helen, along with his team of security, each of them alive, unharmed and shepherding him away from the growing chaos.

Jay had screamed at his team to let him reach injured people who'd fallen or been crushed. Dougie and Mo had grabbed and dragged him from the scene. Face pressed to the glass of the helicopter doors, Jay had watched anger and fear and malice take the receding crowd below.

Miriam stepped from the cockpit into the jet's main cabin, pulling Jay from his reflections.

"He could sleep anywhere, that one," she said, nodding over at Mo.

"He's had a lot on his mind," Jay said. "We all have."

Miriam took the seat opposite Jay, leaning onto the little table between them.

"What happened today, Jay?" Miriam asked. "The crowds seemed so engaged... so peaceful. And then..."

Jay nodded. "All it takes is a handful of people pushing, yelling, spreading hate and fear," Jay sighed. "A single flame is able begin a reaction that can destroy even the mightiest of cities, Miriam."

Miriam smiled sadly, giving a quick darting glance up to the left as a strong memory presented itself to her.

"You sound like Mr Saluzar," she said. Her voice was tinged with melancholy, but she was clearly comforted at the familiarity.

"I suppose that would make sense," Jay said.

Miriam's eyes narrowed. "How do you know each other? How did you know I worked for him, almost the instant we met?"

Jay shrugged. "I think it best that... Mr Saluzar tell you himself."

Miriam looked hurt.

"It isn't my secret to tell you, Miriam," Jay said kindly.

Long accustomed to the peculiarities of Mr Saluzar, as well as his kindness, she was used to tucking curiosity away in the faith that Saluzar would disclose when he wished to or when she needed him to.

"Okay," Miriam said, "that's fair, I suppose." Miriam chewed at her bottom lip for a moment. "He will be okay, won't he? When I last saw him, he looked moments from death, Jay."

Jay smiled broadly. "I promise, Miriam. Your mentor will be just fine."

"Thank you," she said. "I'll be flying back to London, after the Berlin Mass. I promised Mr Saluzar I'd be there when he, hopefully, recovers."

Jay looked at her quizzically.

"Four days, he said."

A lopsided smile growing, Jay replied," Of course, four days..."

The jet swooped around in a semi-circle, beginning its descent into Berlin's Tegel Airport. Miriam checked her watch.

Ninety minutes until Jay would speak in the Olympiastadion.

Less open, more contained and with pre-planned secure entrances and exits, Miriam hoped that crowd control would be easier in the structure. Sooner or later Jay was going to get killed if they carried on in the same manner they had so far.

Miriam's cheek twitched as something occurred to her. Reaching across the table, she placed a hand lightly on his chest.

"You can be hurt, but can you die, Jay?"

"Yes," he said, simply. "I could heal this," he placed his hand over Miriam's, "but like I said, some wounds need to be shown."

Miriam nodded that she understood. "But if you die?"

"I don't have time to die," Jay laughed. He was trying to divert her.

"If you do?" Miriam pressed.

Jay sighed. "I'll heal myself. Reanimate Garry Crawford and get straight back to work."

"God will allow you to?"

Jay shrugged.

"Of course. We have seven days to do what we can. No strings."

Miriam's eyes were wide, but she relaxed somewhat, reassured.

"So you're not in any real danger from humans at the Masses? Why is Mo so concerned about your safety? He must know what you can and can't do?"

Jay smiled silently for a moment as he considered what to tell her.

"Aye… Mo isn't worried about people hurting me," he said.

"Who? What then?"

Jay shrugged, attempting to convey nonchalance.

"He expects someone else to interfere."

Miriam started into his eyes, momentarily confused.

"You just said God wouldn't…"

"Not God," he interrupted. "At least, not directly."

Miriam's eyes flashed fear.

"Satan?" she asked.

Jay laughed loudly.

"Fuck, no," he roared. "He'd be the last one to stand in our way. No, not Satan." Jay chuckled, clearly tickled by the thought.

Miriam looked more than a little annoyed.

"Sorry," Jay said. "It's kind of hard to explain."

"Try," Miriam said flatly.

"There are beings who could send me back to Heaven against my will. There are even beings who could destroy me utterly — body and Heavenly presence. That is what Mo is worried about."

Miriam considered for a moment.

"If one of these... beings kills you, you'll die?"

"No, Miriam, I'll be completely eradicated from existence and then God will do the same to the universe."

∞∞∞

"Ignore pain — old pain, real pain, imagined pain. Let old wounds, emotional, mental and physical, heal and wear them proudly as symbols of a life you lived and loved.

"Seek that place in your hearts, the simple, pure, uncomplicated, unspoiled part of you we all possessed as children. The part that knows good from bad, the part that doesn't care who made you, or what your purpose is. The part of you that simply loves the moment you're in. I promise you that you can find that part then....

"Fuck these lives lived through a lens. These manufactured moments of fleeting comfort and joy you capture with a camera-phone held at arm's length and plaster on Facebook or Twitter, Instagram or fuckin' Snapchat.

"Reconnect with that child you were who ran because it was fun. Who felt loved, who danced in circles, spinning for the joy of life, or the love of rain on your skin, or to make yourself laugh.

"Disconnect yourself from the material, and from the need for approval from online friends, parents, or from God. Just be who and what you are in that single moment. Love what and where and who you are completely. Don't bemoan the perceived missing objects or people or feeling.

"Revel in being you because you are the only soul in all of Creation that is exactly what and where and who you are.

"Live. Live without fear or guilt or greed or expectations. Without the need for approval or validation from anyone. Do this and you will rush to Heaven in an unstoppable tsunami."

Jay turned in a slow circle, scanning the faces of those gathered around him on all sides. From his raised platform, his knees level with their faces, their hands touching him as he passed, Jay moved along the length of the plinth, slightly above, through the crowd to the round central part of the platform.

Smiling, he told them simply,

"Do these things and perhaps we can save each other."

The crowd sang, prayed and danced. They embraced and kissed each other. They called to Jay in gratitude.

Mo stepped forward, emerging from the rear of the stage where it disappeared into an exit tunnel used by soccer players and athletes. This was the exact point at which things had turned to shit in London and in Paris.

His intense eyes scanned faces and elevated parts of the stadium and recessed, shadowy spots. He saw nothing. Felt none of the spark of malice he'd experienced previously, and saw no threat.

Mo watched as Jay went down into a crouch, bringing his face close to a woman's in the front row... a kiss.

That was when the single shot rang out. The woman's brain matter blossomed from the back and side of her head as the bullet tore her brain and skull apart, splashing the matter onto Jay and the stage.

Jay roared in rage, catching the limp woman as she fell into his arms.

Placing his hands at either side of her ruined head, Jay closed his eyes, searching for the portion of his Father's power that would enable him to return the poor woman.

A long painful scream tore its way from his throat.

Jay's eyes searched for Mo's, connecting in a second.

He can't heal her, Mo realised. *Her soul is dead.*

Even at a distance, Mo could see that Jay's eyes were filled with tears and fury.

Along with five of the security team, Mo sprinted at Jay. As he tore towards his friend, Dougie stepped out into his path, poleaxing him with one beefy arm across the upper-chest.

"Let security handle it," Dougie said. "We have to keep you safe also, Mo."

Mo rolled from his back onto his chest just in time to see Jay disappear into the middle of a swarm of worshippers who had clambered up onto the stage to form a three-deep circle around him.

"Those are your people?" Mo asked.

Hauling him up onto his feet, Dougie grunted, "Of course. Now move."

A final look back at Jay confirmed for him that Dougie's people had his friend safe. He was being barrelled along the stage, uninjured, straining against his protectors once again, trying to help the injured woman.

Mo felt a pit open up in his heart as the realisation hit him hard.

Fucking Azrael.

25

Nick and Beth

Beth felt her feet against the solid floor and sank to her knees, dizzy with the sudden displacement.

She was alone.

In the dark.

In Hell.

A dim bulb shone in the centre of the ceiling. Rather than allowing Beth to relax, the presence of the light served merely to increase her fear. The weak light made the shadows more threatening, but illuminated enough of the room for Beth to recognise where and when she was instantly.

Red carpet; deep and sticky on bare feet.

A coal fire, which flared into life as soon as she noticed the hearth, its orange flames flickering, pulling and pausing the shadows around the room. The extra light exposed a dark red, wingback chair in which a fat, ginger tomcat licked at itself, pausing for a moment to throw her a disgusted look.

Beth's heart lurched violently in her chest as she scrambled backwards, crablike, towards the door, which she already knew would be locked. She clawed at the handle, shaking the door in its frame.

The cold little lightbulb in the centre of the ceiling began to shine more intensely, as though someone had increased the electricity in the room along with the fear.

Still facing the door, Beth closed her eyes tightly, refusing to accept where she was.

I'm in the bar. Or in Nick's office. It's just a glimpse. Not real. A glimpse.

Slowly her heart began to reduce its frantic rhythm. Listening closely, the only sounds she heard were those of the crackling fire and the cat's rough tongue rasping over some part of its body.

Beth slowed her breathing. Letting go of the door handle she steeled herself.

Just a test of some sort. No harm. He said no harm will come to me.

Beth nodded once in affirmation before turning around to come face to face with Uncle Harry.

Bloated, red, wobbling face and cheeks, sweat running in rivulets from his bald head down his face, Harry licked at the salt as it tickled the corner of his cracked lips. Beth's terror escalated as he leered at her, his nose almost touching hers. He leaned in and smelled at her bare neck.

"Hello Bethany. Come to play with Uncle Harry?"

As Harry's fat hands grasped at her, one around her throat and the other clawing at her thigh, moving to her crotch, Beth began to scream.

She found the strength in herself that she never had when Harry was alive. Bringing her right hand over and around his arms, she made talons of her fingers. Pushing three of her fingers into the top of his eye socket, her thumb underneath, she felt a sickening peeling sensation as her nails tore through cornea in their passing. Applying more force, she slid the nails and fingertips deeper before tightening the claws once more. In one smooth movement she pulled the eye from Uncle Harry's head.

Harry did not scream; his face creased into a wide, joyful smile. His reaction sent a wave of plain terror through her.

"I'm proud of you, Bethany." His voice was playful.

Watching this man, her father's brother, the beast, watching him beam at her with not just lust in his expression but also admiration, pride, was more than Beth could process.

Something precious inside her, a fragile thing hanging by a tendril of hope since childhood, untouched by his actions, finally snapped free of its moorings.

Something broke inside Bethany and a cold, logical calm slid over her.

Harry was reaching for her again, gently this time. His lips were moving, but she couldn't hear the words. Her ears were filled with a rushing sound. Her eyes obscured by a sepia-red shade that had formed over the room.

Beth's hand reached to her left, finding the stem of a standing lamp she remembered from childhood. It lit as she acknowledged its presence, throwing a stark light onto Harry's face which deepened the set of his eyes and highlighted the rapist's lust there.

Bethany turned the lamp horizontal. The oversized red velvet shade dangled and danced merrily, throwing shadows onto the wall to dance along with it.

Beth shoved her knee up violently, whilst crashing the stand onto it, snapping the lamp stand into two jagged halves.

"Whatcha gonna do wiv that, girly?" Harry snarled, stepping towards her.

Beth dipped her chin, widened her stance, and glared up at him. "Come find out, fat-boy," she said flatly.

Harry began a laugh but did not have time to finish it. Beth speared his remaining eye with the jagged end of the shade-bearing half of the lamp. This time he did scream. To Beth's ears his cries were more beautiful than a symphony, more comforting than any lullaby could ever be.

She stalked towards him. Coming down to a crouch beside him, she took a light grip on the wooden shaft, a few inches above the place where his slick hands slipped and slithered trying to grip and pull. Beth closed her hand around it and pushed downwards, shoving the wooden shaft deeper into the socket. As Harry's song grew wilder, more intense, Beth closed her eyes to concentrate more fully, stopping the shaft only as it scraped against something.

Releasing the pressure, she sat back onto her haunches. Head cocked to the side, she absorbed the music of Harry's pain. Watching herself dispassionately, as though from afar, Beth considered that she may have lost her mind, then gave a mental shrug.

Fuck it.

Snatching up the remainder of the lamp stand, she twirled it around, like a little majorette, bringing the heavy weighted end nearer her face.

A sardonic smile tugged at the corners of her mouth.

Swinging down in a high, long arc, Beth brought the metal base down, sledge-hammer-like, crushing Harry's genitals.

His screams reached new peaks, stimulating Beth's adrenal glands to treat her to a surge. Riding the crest of adrenaline, she systematically broke a series of bones in his arms, legs, chest, jaw and pelvis, working her way through the list of bones she could still identify from high school science class. Teeth fell in a hail of amalgam-tainted shrapnel.

She did not rush.

After twenty minutes, and a beautiful reprise of Harry's first chorus, Bethany stepped back to admire the puddle of gristle, white protrusions and pulp she'd created. The lamp slid from her bloodied hands. A thought occurred to Beth and she walked calmly to the blazing fireplace. With tongs she raked through the red hot coals, searching for a piece just hot enough, correctly sized.

Selecting an oblong, glowing chunk Beth held it tightly in the tongs at arm's length. Placing it close to Harry's left cheek, she watched, fascinated, as the skin blistered and burst under the heat. A gurgling sound came from what had formerly been Harry's mouth.

Beth ignored the garbled slurs and wet sounds, focusing instead on placing the hot coal gently above the centre of Uncle Harry's forehead.

"If I were more skilled I'd have made this last for hours. As it is, you got off lightly." Beth's voice completely lacked emotion. "Fuck you, Uncle Harry."

Dropping the coal onto the skin beneath, Beth brought her face to his. As the coal made its way inevitably through skin, bone, blood vessels, brain matter and nerve tissue, Beth committed the sizzling sound, pork smell and his dying song to memory so that she could revisit them in the years to come.

Intense light flooded the room. Shielding her eyes, Beth slowly allowed the light to filter through her fingertips, allowing her eyes to adjust.

Peering through half-closed lids, Beth saw Nick standing alongside her. Face impassive he took in the room. The stark light showed the grotesque scene more vividly. Harry's shabby, seventies décor, splashed liberally with his blood and tissues, instantly changed from the warm, comforting charnel house she'd controlled moments before to a theatre of horrors. The scales had fallen from her eyes with the light. Beth, on her knees, shook in terror at what she'd done.

"Why are you crying for him?" Nick asked.

Between sobs, Beth replied, "I'm… not… crying for him."

"Ah," Nick said. "So you are shocked, devastated by the look of you, by what you've done to him."

Snot and tears and horror on her face, Beth stammered, "Yes. I'm a monster."

"Don't you think that he deserved to suffer? That he needed to pay for what he did to you?"

Beth was shuddering and crying uncontrollably, like an infant who'd lost all control, having long forgotten what they began to cry for. She was starting to lose herself to madness.

Nick slapped her hard across the face, stunning her into silence.

"Don't you think he should be punished?" he asked, his voice growing in intensity.

Beth's eyes filled with anger as the torturer she'd been minutes before resurfaced.

"Yes," she roared at Nick. Rising to her feet she shoved against his chest with both hands. "He deserves worse than this. I just wanted to be like every other eight year old. Birthday parties, pretty dresses and cake. On my birthday I didn't get a fucking Barbie," Beth kicked at Harry's body, "all I got was his rancid hairy cock."

Beth's eyes blazed with intense hatred.

"He held me down, he made me do things to him and to his friends for years. He only stopped when I hit puberty."

Beth kicked him again.

"If I could I'd do all of this all over again."

Nick nodded calmly.

"I can bring him back if you'd like. I can restore him, and you can torture and kill him over and over again for eternity."

Beth's eyes grew wide with desire.

She smiled as she scanned Harry's body, her mind flipping through so many wonderful methods she might employ to eke out every last shred of pain from the rapist at her feet.

Slowly her eyes misted, softened and took on a hint of her usual intelligence.

"No. I won't be like him. Let him suffer for as long as he deserves. Let someone do it who needs it more than me, and who can bear it."

Nick's face was passive but his eyes danced with joy.

"Get me away from here," she said.

With one last look at Uncle Harry's corpse, Bethany fell into Nick's waiting arms. This time anticipating the rush of movement rather than fearing it.

∞∞∞

Back in Nick's office once again, Beth pressed her face to Nick's chest, absorbing strength from him.

"Why?" she asked.

"I had to know if you were ready," Nick said softly, stroking her hair.

Looking up at him, Beth asked, "For what?"

"I've been watching you for a long time, Bethany. Despite your life, your determination and intelligence, your compassion and good heart have turned you into the ideal candidate for me."

Nick pushed her back gently.

"I want you to come work with me, Bethany. Be my assistant, help me get these souls into Heaven."

Before Beth could answer, Meg barged through the open door into Nick's office. "Sir, we've been trying to reach you," she gasped.

Nick gave Beth a questioning look. *You okay?*

After a nod in the affirmative, he let her go. Turning to Meg he said, "I've been on Level Thirty, with Bethany."

Meg gave a curt nod. No communication on Level Thirty.

"What's the problem, Meg?" Nick asked.

Handing her boss a tablet, Meg said, "We know how Crawford and Pillans came to be here, sir."

Nick flicked at the screen, scanning through a series of images and text detailing, Garry Crawford's and Chris Pillans' exploits on Earth over the past few days.

Nick recognised the presence of Jay and Mo behind the bodies they wore with a single glance. As he absorbed the details of their movements and actions, Nick's face broke into a broad smile.

They're doing it. They're making the humans believe.

The smile vanished as Nick read one of Jay's sermons.

"We have seven days. On the seventh day, this Friday, God will obliterate every... On the seventh day, God will end everything. Every cell of life, every spark of energy, every atom of matter in the universe. Unless you can show Him that you are worthy of His Heaven."

Nick's head swam.

Stewart, what have you done?

Cursing the time difference between the physical world and his own, Nick checked his tablet.

"Shit." It was Wednesday on Earth. Jay and Mo had been there since Saturday. *Two days left. That translates to maybe ten minutes in our time.*

Nick blinked hard a few times, his eyes darting between Meg, Beth and the walls that held so many pictures of himself and Stewart.

Enveloping Beth once again in his arms, Nick altered his form, his true Angelic-self emerging a split second before he tore the fabric of reality once again, sending himself and Bethany directly to Heaven to confront God for the last time.

26

Jay and Mo

SWEEPING INTO THE VIP LOUNGE in the airport, Jay barked at Dougie, "I could've fuckin' helped her, your guys didn't give me a chance." Jay jabbed a finger into Dougie's chest.

Dougie's eyes wavered, but he stood his ground.

"Your safety was under threat. I did my job."

Jay shoved Dougie hard enough to make the big cop stagger back a few steps.

"Fuck yer job and fuck my safety. That woman is dead because of your decision. I could've brought her back."

Dougie's face creased. A moment ago, he'd been so certain that he'd done the right thing. His conviction faltered as he processed the fact that the Son of God was the man currently furious at him.

Miriam stood close by, assessing the men, trying to determine if she should intervene or let the argument run its course.

Mo stepped between them, one hand on each of their chests, pushing them apart.

"No you couldn't have, Jay. You tried and you failed."

Jay's eyes narrowed. "I just fucked up, I could've…"

"No," Mo interrupted. "You could not have helped that woman." Mo's eyes filled with sadness. "Her soul was gone, destroyed in an instant."

Jay's eyes widened as the realisation struck him. Anger surged through his entire body, making his muscles twitch. He glared at Mo accusingly.

Mo simply nodded. "It was Azrael… and it was my fault."

Jay swept around. Taking a few angry paces, deliberately putting some distance between himself and Mo, he shouted, "What the fuck have you done, Mo?"

Miriam placed a hand on Jay's upper arm, trying to comfort, perhaps calm him.

Covering his face with both hands, Mo rubbed at his eyelids, as though clearing his vision for the first time since they'd arrived.

"I was worried about you. I couldn't just watch them," Mo pointed at Dougie and Miriam, as though they represented all humankind, "I couldn't let them torture you again."

Jay feigned understanding

"Oh, that's all right then, pal. You were worried about me." Sarcasm laced his tone. "So you thought to yourself, *I'll partner up with one of only three beings in the universe who could actually remove Jay from existence… that'll do the trick.*"

Jay threw his arms up, exasperated.

"What the fuck, Mo?" he yelled, eyes searching Mo's face.

Tears began to track along Mo's cheeks. His hands in front of him, he pleaded,

"It wasn't like that, Jay. She was already here, on Earth, preparing, sabotaging. She was planning to massacre millions when I contacted her under... under His orders. Az was supposed to make sure the humans believed that God's wrath was on them as punishment for listening to a false Messiah... You. God sent her to Earth moments after we arrived."

Jay's face hardened.

"So you teamed up, traded me for a few hundred thousand humans, when all of Creation hangs by a baw-hair?"

"NO!" Mo blurted. "I gave Az our itinerary and a sense of what you'd speak about, your timing. She was supposed to seed the crowds with a few agitators. Turn them against you. Maybe kill a few humans. Dilute the impact of the message."

Miriam interrupted. "You, and this Az? You were responsible for the crowds turning like they did? How could you do that, Mo? All those people who got hurt, who died."

"Your responsibility, Mo," Jay said, flatly.

"I thought it was a small price to pay to keep them from really believing you."

"Because you don't believe in me, that I can succeed?" Jay asked.

"Because I don't believe in *them*," Mo spat. "God is right, Jay, they don't deserve Heaven, they never did.

You, me, even Nick, we're fucking kidding ourselves. We gave our lives, thousands of years of torturous effort for them for fucking nothing. These fucking apes will tear you apart, string you up and shit on your goodness, just like they did last time."

"At least it would be my choice," Jay roared. "And theirs."

Jay's eyes bore into Mo, as though trying to figure out who he was.

"My survival doesn't matter. Any pain or torture or brutality I endure is insignificant. If we… if I don't show these people the path, the only path to Heaven, everything is finished. Every planet, every galaxy: a universe full of sentient life and wonders… gone."

Jay's face softened for a moment as he tried to see some empathy in Mo's face. Finding Mo clinging stoically to the virtue of his chosen path, Jay resumed.

"You know this, and you still chose to sabotage me, your best friend? You would choose the end of everything in the material universe over elevating humans? How did you come to despise life so much, Moses?"

Finally, Mo's face broke into grief once again.

"I don't despise life, Jay. I thought I could dampen Azrael's impact. I…" Mo searched for more justifications, before lowering his head. "I just wanted to help my friend. You know I'd never hurt you," Mo said, wincing at his own pathetic words.

Jay sagged. Processing Mo's betrayal, he tried to see events from Mo's perspective. Mo cared deeply about him, he always had. He'd defended and protected Jay many times from God's disapproval. Mo had loved him from the moment he'd been created, seeing in Jay a kindred spirit, one who would fight eternally for the rights of human souls.

Something had broken in Mo upon Jay's crucifixion two millennia previously. Jay could see that now. Watching Jay brutalised, and knowing that his suffering in Jerusalem had accomplished nothing, had sown the seed of fear that had led Mo to this point. That paralysing fear had made him so stunted and blinded by his fears for Jay that he'd willingly traded his life for that of a universe.

Instantly, Jay forgave his friend.

Standing straight, once more, Jay walked towards Mo, taking him in a strong embrace.

"You did what you thought you should out of love for me, I get it."

Mo sagged against him. "Yes," he cried.

Jay released him. Pushing him out to arm's length, Jay spoke softly, without anger or rebuke, just plain forgiveness.

"You should have loved life more than you love me. You're done here. Go home, Mo."

Falling to his knees, then onto the carpet, curling into a foetal position, Mo wept unashamedly as he watched the team and his best friend leave the lounge to board the little jet, bound for Rio.

Miriam alone stayed behind. Eyes closed, burning with tears, Mo felt her kneel beside him. Her fingers stroked his hair.

"Come on," she said gently. "Let's get you cleaned up."

Thursday

Interlude

Saluzar and Miriam

"We'll see you next time, sir."

Mr L smiled warmly at the assistant who'd been keeping him company these past few hours during the countdown to his return.

"Thank you, Meg. You've been very kind," he said.

Meg nodded once, smiling as his form began to fade.

"You're welcome, sir. See you next time."

∞∞∞

Miriam pushed her noodle salad around on the plate disinterestedly. Every few minutes she'd half-heartedly chew on a piece of pepper or some tofu, eyes glued on the hidden panel on the south wall of the boardroom, behind which she'd left Mr Saluzar dying in an oxygen tent surrounded by a bank of machines four days previously.

Miriam shook her head as though to dispel the disbelief.

Four days.

So much had happened in that time. So much still to happen: tomorrow this might all end. Tomorrow God may eradicate the entire universe.

Only one person stood in His way. A very kind, very alone man, who'd lost his oldest friend and on whom the media was now turning, the trust of people he was trying to save along with it. The death of the woman in Berlin and Jay's inability to resuscitate her had shaken many people's faith in their new Messiah. As they entered the final forty-eight hours left to them, humans seemed to have begun the process of casting aside the one man who might save their race.

The enormity of it all pressed in on her emotionally, threatening to render her useless.

Miriam heard a creak. Her eyes moved quickly to the hidden panel. Nothing, just someone passing by the door outside. Perhaps Mo.

He seemed a hollowed-out shell of a man. Neutered by the realisation of what he had done, he'd followed her back to London meekly, lost in his own thoughts. Mo hadn't spoken a word to anyone since Berlin the night before. Miriam had left him in the lobby whilst she waited hopefully for Mr Saluzar, coffee ignored and cooling on the table in front of her.

Miriam checked the time on her phone. Jay would touch down in Rio and begin his tour of Brazil, Argentina and Chile, before heading up to North America where Miriam planned to catch up to them first thing on Friday morning. If the end was indeed coming tomorrow, she needed to be with him when it came. Hopefully Mr Saluzar could be with them too.

Thinking of the men together made her mind drift off, imagining the circumstances in which her enigmatic, benevolent mentor had met and befriended Jay.

Lost in her daydream, Miriam did not hear the bare feet padding across the carpet towards her. A hand on her shoulder startled her, making her leap from the chair she'd been slouched in, sending her noodles across the carpet.

Turning she looked up into the face of her mentor. Smiling uncharacteristically at her, beaming actually. A rejuvenated-looking Saluzar — dressed in the same clothes he'd been in when she'd locked him away four days previously — raised his eyebrows, the eyes underneath emanating good humour.

"Not hungry, Miriam, my dear?" he asked, playfully.

Miriam rushed at him. Burying her face into his chest, she felt the new strength in her mentor's body as her arms went around him, pulling him tight to her.

"Thank God," she said.

Saluzar returned her embrace. "Not God," he said, gently. "Thank Jay."

∞∞∞

Miriam had been explaining for over an hour, with the aid of news articles and YouTube clips from the London, Paris and Berlin Masses, as well as footage from the Old Trafford Event and the Bridge Miracle on the Forth. Mr Saluzar interrupted occasionally, to clarify the odd fact or simply to state his amazement, but for the most he part merely allowed Miriam to speak.

Now dressed in comfortable denims and black long-sleeve-T, Mr Saluzar stared in wonder at the images. He took on the appearance of a child on Christmas morning. To Miriam, he looked as though he'd been born again. It wasn't just the unusually informal clothing he'd dressed in; something else had altered significantly. The vitality he'd lost in degrees over the last decade or so had returned. His eyes were quick once more, his face alive and animated when recently it had greyed and lined with age and mileage.

Miriam could swear he'd been at a health retreat for a year, he looked so much happier, more youthful: so much more alive. How could a man who'd suffered a massive heart attack, been on the verge of death, have recovered so fully in four short days?

Saluzar giggled to himself, a trait she thought him no longer capable of. Laughter hadn't figured in his world for many years.

"What?" she asked.

Saluzar shrugged and made an offhand gesture at the screens.

"Just amazed at him. Even here in this modern world, nothing fazes him. He seems to know instinctively what to do, how to use the mood of the times, hook into the public sub-consciousness. He connects with people, even in this age, so cynical and self-absorbed, but he touches a part of them they didn't know existed... Amazing."

Miriam looked at Mr Saluzar for a long moment in silence. Finally he became aware of her and drew his eyes from the tablet screen he'd been scanning. Saluzar gave a little jerk of his chin.

"What is it, Miriam?" he asked.

Miriam chewed at her bottom lip, deciding what and how to ask.

"How do you know him? Jay."

Mr Saluzar raised his eyebrows. "He didn't tell you?"

"No. Jay said that your story wasn't his to tell," Miriam replied.

Saluzar's face broke into a wide grin. He nodded knowingly. "Yes, of course he would." Saluzar placed a hand on each of Miriam's cheeks. "Better to show you, I think, my dear," he said.

Rising, Saluzar beckoned for Miriam to come with him through to the room he'd lain in for four days. Following along behind her mentor, Miriam marvelled at how much lighter, how much more vital his step was.

Emerging into the little medical room, Miriam took note of the equipment. All lay as before although a little grubbier, and smells of chemical detergents, perhaps bodily waste, clawed underneath.

Saluzar, at the rear of the room, smiled at her.

"Through here," he said, pushing against the wall, which opened inwards with a pneumatic hiss.

Disappearing through the opening, Miriam heard him padding into the room and a switch being used before stark, very bright light flooded through the open door.

"C'mon, Miriam," Saluzar said playfully.

Miriam could not believe the difference in him. Saluzar looked and behaved twenty years younger than the day he'd collapsed.

Miriam smiled at the change in him once again and followed him into the next room.

Mr Saluzar stood at the centre of a fairly large chamber. With stark white walls and brown oak floor, glass cases, deep and tall travel chests, crates everywhere and walls filled with painted and photographic images, the room struck her as an odd cross between a stuffy museum and an overly-modern loft apartment or office.

At the south wall a window reached up from the floor, across the ceiling and terminated at the top of the north wall, which held the door she'd entered by. The brilliant light in the room was provided by the combined light from this unusual window and several huge halogen lights, two on each wall.

Mr Saluzar stood facing a wall adorned with art. He waved her over.

"Come, my dear. Look here," he said pointing at a recent photo of himself. Again, she marvelled at how much older he'd looked only days before.

Saluzar made a sweeping motion along the wall.

"Please, follow them along to the other corner," he said.

Miriam's brow furrowed as she peered at each of the images hanging against the white wall. They were arranged in rows, taking up a six-foot section top to bottom and forty feet along the wall. As she moved along, moving her eyes up and down the images,

Miriam became aware that she was looking back through Saluzar's lifetime.

After a few paces, she stopped to look more closely at a photograph of her mentor, his arm around Martin Luther King. Miriam's eyes widened in recognition. She looked back at Saluzar, raising her brow.

"Is that…"

"Yes, Dr King," he confirmed without pride. Merely a fact. "Look more closely at *my* face, Miriam," he said gently.

Miriam moved a little closer, taking in Saluzar's face. "Mr Saluzar, this can't be you. This picture must be…" She double-checked the maths and the history in her head. "This must be almost fifty years old."

"That is correct, my dear. A beautiful morning. Dr King and I raised significant funds for social housing that year."

Miriam rubbed at her eyes, as though clearing them might expose a new angle, one in which the man standing beside her did not so closely, so agelessly, resemble the man smiling in a fifty-year-old photograph.

Saluzar coughed, snapping her attention back.

"Please," he motioned further along the wall.

Miriam glanced along, very aware suddenly that it was a long wall, with perhaps a thousand images.

"Do proceed, my dear," Saluzar said.

Miriam smiled nervously, but did as asked. As she side-stepped along the wall, images of the same man throughout many years appeared before her. Mr Saluzar at an archaeological dig in Israel. Mr Saluzar with Queen Victoria, surrounded by the poor, who were smiling gratefully at them. Mr Saluzar on horseback, his back to a clock on the ground that was about to be lifted into a newly-built tower, where two men stood having their own photo taken. One old, grey-haired and enthusiastic, the other a teenager, modern-looking haircut, face full of good humour. Mr Saluzar, dressed in eighteenth-century garb, pointing off into the distance in a beautifully rendered oil painting.

Miriam crouched down low and, holding her chest, she gasped. "I can't... I can't breathe," she panted.

Mr Saluzar came to her side. With strong hands, he helped her turn to sit with her back against the wall, whose adornments she could no longer bear to look upon.

"It's okay, Miriam. It's a mild panic attack, just focus on deep breaths, in and out." Mr Saluzar helped her compose herself for several minutes.

Finally, face flushed and sweaty, Miriam said, "I'm so sorry, Mr Saluzar... It's just so..."

Saluzar took her hand gently in his. "I know, my dear. Actually, you've taken it very well. I've experienced some much more extreme reactions in the past." Saluzar laughed kindly at a memory he chose not to share.

Miriam closed her eyes, nodding her thanks. When she opened them again, Miriam looked at the man who had guided her almost her entire life. A man she knew so very well and not at all, it seemed.

"Mr Saluzar, how can you be... Who are you?" she asked.

Saluzar's brow knitted at the centre. Holding the back of his hand against Miriam's brow, he asked, "Are you feeling stable enough to stand?"

Miriam nodded. Holding an arm out for Mr Saluzar to take, she once again marvelled at his new strength as he helped her, wobbly, to her feet.

Guiding her to a nearby case with a large, old, leatherbound book atop it, Saluzar let her go, keeping his hands hovering a few centimetres from her arm for a few seconds. Once certain she wasn't going to topple, Saluzar placed a hand lightly on top of the book.

It wasn't bound like a modern book, rather its pages were laced together in beautifully constructed loops and stitches that must have been painstaking work for its maker.

Saluzar felt along the side. Finding the exact page with his fingernail, he used both hands to open the book. Beckoning Miriam over, he stood aside slightly to allow her to inspect the pages

Miriam placed her right hand gently on the surface. Adorned with beautifully painted words and pictures in reds and browns and golds, the images were at once familiar to her. It was a scene from the Bible.

Specifically it showed images of Jesus of Nazareth, long dark hair and beard, simple carpenter's robes, walking along a narrow sand path through rocky terrain.

She touched his face. "Jay," she said, recognising his eyes. "The person who painted this must have met him," she said.

Saluzar nodded. "Yes. The artist-writer lived at the time of Christ and spent many weeks travelling with him. He spent decades constructing this tome. Turn the page," he said.

Miriam found herself almost as reluctant to turn away from the image of Jay as she was desperate to discover Saluzar's secret.

Finally she did turn the page.

The scene depicted on the next double spread was unmistakable to anyone with even the most superficial knowledge of Bible stories. Feeling the images with her fingers, Miriam sensed a connection to each of them. She scanned along the words and images.

Jesus in Bethany.

Martha telling Jesus that he is too late.

Jesus weeping.

The stone to a tomb being removed.

Jesus, arms raised, standing at the open tomb.

A man, wrapped in grave-cloths, walking into the light.

The grave-cloths removed and the resurrected man reunited with his sister.

Miriam noticed something splash onto the page of the ancient book. Gently Saluzar came alongside her, dabbing at her tear with a cotton handkerchief. He followed Miriam's finger which gently stroked at the face of the resurrected man.

The face of Lazarus.

His face.

Miriam's eyes were red and steaming tears freely when she finally looked up at him.

"You?"

Saluzar simply nodded.

"Two thousand years, Miriam. I die, I go… elsewhere. Four days later I return; rejuvenated, stronger and more vigorous once more. Sometimes I die of old age. Sometimes I am killed by other means. Always I return four days later."

Miriam watched as her mentor placed a finger gently onto the image of Jesus in the book before them.

"His gift to me."

Miriam laughed, a little manically.

"A fucking anagram. Saluzar… Lazarus."

She slapped her own forehead.

Mr Saluzar, Lazarus, laughed. "Don't be too hard on yourself, Miriam. I've had a very long time to learn to blend in, to *die* and create new identities or pass my wealth onto *ancestors*."

Miriam laughed again, sounding more lost, more on the brink than ever. "Oh, you must have met Moses. He's waiting in reception," she said, like everything was normal in the world and she was his assistant once again. Miriam held a hand up courteously, indicating the door beyond which Moses sat, slumped in a deep depression, before she collapsed in a heap to the oak floor.

Lazarus smiled kindly before using his newly-returned physical strength to lift her gently into his arms. As he carried his Miriam through to the main boardroom, Lazarus' chest swelled with pride at the courage she had shown during his absence and his revelations.

27

Nick and Beth

Beth fell at Nick's feet as their momentum stopped. Nick, brilliantly ethereal, stunning in his Angelic form, his natural appearance, hauled her roughly to her feet.

Finding herself in another office environment, Beth glared up at him.

"What the fuck, Nick?"

He was already leaving the office, striding angrily into an open area, not unlike the space he worked out of in Sheol. Hundreds of pairs of eyes turned to follow him as he tore into the central area.

"Stay nearby," he said to Beth. "Where is He?" Nick yelled at nobody in particular.

After a beat, during which no answer came, Nick roared loudly, "Where the fuck is He?"

A woman, business-like, approached Nick.

"Sir," she said nervously, "He is in the viewing room."

"Course He fucking is," Nick spat.

Beth followed after him, two strides at double the pace to each of his.

Crashing through a set of frosted glass doors, Nick continued shouting.

"What the fuck are you thinking?" he demanded.

Bethany slipped quietly into the room, moving around Nick to see its occupant. Nick placed an arm out in front of her. Shoving gently, he guided her off to the side of the room. His face was creased in anger, glaring at the back of a man's head.

Sitting on a large sofa, His back to the door, a wall of screens showing events on Earth in front of Him, He had one arm spread across the rear of the couch, the other holding a whiskey to his lips. He gave a throaty, humourless laugh.

"Nicholas, always a pleasure, my boy."

Without turning, Stewart held a single finger up in warning. His voice lost its faux-joviality.

"Watch the fucking tone though," He said maliciously.

Bethany watched Nick's shoulders tense. He cracked his neck to the side before proceeding.

"Who's the cow?" Stewart asked. "Another one of yer hoors?"

Nick composed himself. Softening his voice he buried his anger and fear.

"This is Bethany, she's the candidate for my assistant's role."

Stewart whistled through his teeth. "Good choice, damaged goods, moral compass good and fixed like you like them... tidy erse on her, as well," Stewart said.

Nick stepped forward.

"My Lord, please stop what you are doing on Earth," he said.

Stewart made a gesture with his hands. The screens paused.

Standing, He fished a cigarette from a little table in front of him, lighting it as He walked around the couch to stand a few paces from Nick.

"Why? Those cunts have had their chance. So have you, Nick, and those two wankers down there," Stewart gestured at a frozen image of Jay and Mo on his screens.

Nick changed tack. "Why now?" He asked. "After all these years, the opportunities you've given me to elevate them? Jay and Mo, both of them, allowed by you to make their own attempts. Why now? What's changed?"

Stewart laughed loudly. "Fuck all, I'm just bored with the experiment. Time tae start a-fuckin-gain," Stewart said.

Nick's anger began to rise once again.

"They're not an experiment," Nick said, stepping closer to Stewart.

Stewart blew a plume of smoke into Nick's face.

"Of course they are. The whole bastard universe is an experiment, a big fucking sand-pit to explore and manipulate and observe." Stewart leaned into Nick's space. "Haven't you learned anything in all these years? Am I alone in understanding nature?" Stewart's eyes danced with cold, mocking humour.

Nick's anger threatened to take his reason at the exact moment he needed it more than ever.

Swallowing hard, Nick replayed Creation as he'd witnessed it and as he'd relayed it to Beth.

God alone.

Alone.

God had been good and kind and honourable. Then came Nick and then the rest of His angels.

Then matter, cells, life and death.

All of it replayed in Nick's mind's eye.

God alone.

Something pulled at Nick's awareness. Like remembering something but not quite well enough to relay it to someone else.

Forcing his eternal memory to analyse, to pull the lost moments to life, he cast in front of himself a mental image of God shortly after Nick's creation.

God had been babbling. Delighted to create a companion after so long alone... Billions of years alone, without a single clue as to what He was or where or how He Himself had been created.

In those first few moments of Nick's existence, God had been recovering from eons of madness — the madness of eternal isolation.

Nick's creation had brought Him to a semblance of lucidity, of sanity.

He'd babbled for hours. The first words Nick had ever heard were those of a semi-sane deity professing His joy at ending His isolation. Long-forgotten words came back to Nick.

You will save me. I'll make more. I'll discover how I came to be. I need you.

Nick fell to his knees as the memories resurfaced.

"You did it all — made the universe, uncountable trillions of worlds and beings — just to discover what you are?"

Nick wept for Creation.

Stewart took a long pull on his cigarette before answering.

"Wouldn't you? I was alone for so very long, or was it moments? In nothingness, it's impossible to tell, Nicholas. I had no parent, no language... no light, save my own. No awareness of anything other than my own self, because that is all that existed: just my own presence. I sat in silence for millennia. I screamed, alone, unheard, for a billion, billion years. I wished to stop existing more times than there are worlds in the universe. I planned universes in my mind's eye and destroyed them. I learned to make my Kingdom and to make others. You, then my Angels, but none like me.

Everything else outside Heaven was an experiment to see if the evolution of humans would culminate in another like myself."

Stewart glared contemptuously at Beth.

"Imagine my disappointment in those hairless apes. Aye, they evolved a soul that palely resembled an Angelic form, but the experiment and my interest in it ended there. It's finished, Nick."

Nick wept freely now. "But they can still be so much more, so can all of the other lifeforms throughout the universe. Your Creations are wonderful. Why can't you see it? Please, my Lord, spare them."

"Na," Stewart said without hesitation. "Fuck 'em."

Eyes wide in horror, Nick rose to his feet.

"What about Jay? Your son?"

Before Stewart could answer, the frosted glass doors exploded inwards.

Beth cowered at the side of the room as shards of glass flew in all directions.

Nick peered through the doors, and gasped as he saw the man entering.

28

Jay

CROUCHED, ARSE HALF ON A WALL at the base of Christ the Redeemer on the peak of Corcovado Mountain, Jay looked out over Rio de Janeiro. Lost in his own grief, his eyes did not see the city and neighbourhoods below. He never imagined that he could feel so alone. Not even held by iron pins to a wooden cross had he felt so completely abandoned. Then, he'd known that Heaven awaited him, that Earth would continue and that humans might be enriched by his time amongst them. Even the knowledge that his Father would be waiting for him had strengthened his resolve to see the execution through to the last. Jay had also had Moses in Heaven fighting his cause. Moses had been there for Jay since the moment of his creation: an immovable force for goodness, a confidant, a fearless ally and, simply, a friend.

And now Mo was gone.

Jay was falling into the deepest loneliness he'd experienced in his existence.

Mo's choices had hurt him more than he had expected. Jay knew his friend well enough that he did not doubt the sincerity or the altruistic motives of his allying with Azrael. He did not doubt Mo's good heart, but what had carved his own heart was Mo's seeming acceptance that losing all of the material universe was somehow a price worth paying to ensure Jay's safety.

Jay sighed heavily and turned to look up at the statue behind him. Arms wide, welcoming the world, Christ the Redeemer possessed all the peace, confidence and purpose he himself felt none of at that moment.

Jay touched the pedestal of the statue, like a human would. For the first time he understood the human desire, the need, to make physical contact with an icon or statue. That hope that a portion of what one saw in the object might empower one, that some strength would heal a wounded spirit.

Feeling only soapstone, Jay pulled his hand back, shoving it deep into the pockets of his denims.

Bringing the sprawling city below into focus, Jay breathed deeply, filling his lungs with the smells of the mountain and his being with Heaven's Light. Allowing himself to connect with the material world and Heaven's immateriality simultaneously, with closed eyes he examined the intricacies of the people, the city and the mood below.

Excitement. Determination. Joy. Fear.

All the emotions and feelings he'd come to expect from a crowd of people anticipating his presence. As with all of the other cities he'd visited so far, there was no sense of pressing danger. Yes, there were elements of hate, people protesting his message, and him, but nothing immediately threatening.

Jay funnelled a larger portion of Heaven, at the same time diminishing his sense of the physical world around him, to the point where he was unaware of the stone and sand beneath his feet or the pedestal he leaned on.

With all of his ethereal senses he scanned the city for signs of Azrael.

Mo had told him that he had helped Azrael plan where and how her agents — human mercenaries who cared nothing for who paid them or why — would be most effective in riling and inciting the crowd. Hundreds of them, some dressed in Muslim attire, some posing as Christian fundamentalists or Jews, had seeded the crowd, sought out *like-minded* people and fanned the embers of outrage until fires broke out, joined and became unstoppable swells of violence.

Jay doubted Azrael was present in the city below. She was too experienced to allow Jay the opportunity to sense her, and he would do so if she were nearby. Azrael was the Angel of Death, after all. She'd annihilated millions, razed whole cities, flooded the whole fucking world and all at God's behest. Azrael left rather a large wake in the immaterial world, as well as the physical one.

Satisfied that no obvious threats lay below, Jay pulled himself back into the flesh, limiting himself once again to the physical plane.

"We should get going, Jay," Dougie said.

The cop was standing next to him, having arrived whilst Jay's attention was elsewhere.

Jay nodded. "Thanks, Dougie," he said without looking at him.

Jay felt Dougie's mood shift from all-business to concern.

Dougie planked his backside against the soapstone next to Jay's.

"Did I ever tell you about Tommy Two-Dicks?" he asked.

Despite his morose mood, Jay let out a snort of laughter. "I think I'd remember if you had, Dougie," he said, nudging him.

Dougie shrugged. Looking off into the distance, he folded his arms, relaxing against the pedestal at the foot of Christ the Redeemer.

"I was in the army, as a kid, y'know, before I became a copper."

Jay nodded. Sometimes people did this — told him their story. It was natural for humans, especially when they accepted who and what he was. That Heaven was real and Hell was too. It made eternity loom large for them

He'd had the experience many times back in the Middle-East. It was how he'd met most of the apostles.

The compulsion wasn't unlike what people felt sometimes when talking to a priest or other preacher. They liked to unburden themselves, especially when the end was coming.

With millions waiting for Jay below, and God only knew how many across the airways and internet, Dougie could've picked a better moment, but Hell, he'd earned the right to say whatever he chose to Jay, whenever he chose.

"Aye. I knew that, Dougie. What's on your mind?"

Dougie pointed out at the city below.

"People. That's what being a soldier is about. At least, it was for me. Sure there are orders, Queen and country and all that, but in the end it's about people."

Dougie glanced at Jay, acknowledging his nod of agreement.

"When you're a kid and you enlist, in your head it's about good people holding back or fighting against bad people. You have all the permission, the justification you need to put a bullet in someone, or build a wall, or knock one down. Good guys, bad guys, simple." Dougie held his hands out, palms up. "You get a bit older and the black and white simplicity of youth becomes greyer — a million shades of fuckin' grey. The motives become murkier and the justifications more elaborate. Good and bad guys are replaced in your mind by awareness of political and corporate agendas that were always there but you were too naïve or uneducated or selfish to notice.

"So you begin to feel the weight of being someone's tool. You accept that people higher than you on the pay-scale make the decisions and you execute them. It can still be simple, if you want it to be."

Dougie cast a glance again at Jay, who was nodding along.

"You get married, you start a family and you keep believing that what you do is good. Meaningful. That your superiors are privy to intel you aren't. That you're making a difference, being the good guy. Bringing your beliefs and standards to people who are oppressed. That the country you're invading really needs you there, whether they want you and your superior culture or not."

Dougie kicked at a rock, sending it flying out into the blackening sky.

"That the father with a rock in his hand, standing outside the shell of a home you just bombed into the dust, boy cowering behind him, is the enemy and not exactly what you would be if your roles were reversed. That your country did this cruel, heinous act for reasons of virtue you don't comprehend, but desperately strain to accept on faith... That it was about people... and not oil."

Dougie gave a long sigh. Jay placed a hand on his shoulder. "You are good man, Dougie."

The big cop realised Jay thought that he was confessing or offloading and smiled. "This ain't about me Jay," he said. "It's about Tommy Two-Dicks, remember?"

Jay smiled at his own assumption. He should have known better than to underestimate Dougie. He motioned for Dougie to continue.

"So Tommy Two-Dicks." Noticing Jay grinning, Dougie offered a half-hearted smile of his own, acknowledging the ridiculous nickname. "He didn't have two dicks, just behaved like a dog with two. Y'know? Happy as fuck all the time. First to volunteer for every job. Never complained, saw an opportunity for laughter in every task."

Jay smiled in acknowledgment.

"Yeah," Dougie continued. "Annoying cunt, so he was, but he was *my* best friend. Had been since the day we met."

Dougie took a moment, replaying a memory he didn't care to share with Jay.

"Anyway, my unit were making an arrest. Two middle-aged locals in Helmand. Chubby little guys, all jokes and waving hands when we arrived. Suspected of leaving IEDs along military routes. Pick up and detain. Simple.

"Four of us arrived in our transport and these two guys are standing at the roadside makeshift grill which is burning away, cooking fuck knows what, chugging cold water from bottles fished from an ice-filled cooler at their feet.

"We follow protocol. Park a hundred metres away, approach in formation, assess the environment, all the usual crap. There's no-one else around, just these two guys having themselves a barbecue at the roadside. Nearest building is a bombed-to-fuck little house two hundred metres away.

"They're dressed in fucking trousers and Man Utd tops; no weapons visible. Waving us over, one of them holding a slab of meat up with a long fork.

"'Welcome, Americans...' he's shouting. Probably the only English he knows.

"I recall one of the guys grumbling about being taken for a fuckin' Yank.

"So we're on alert, but there's on alert and on alert. We're fairly confident that these guys are a couple of clowns. The only real potential danger is the ice-cooler, but bombs and watery ice don't generally go too well, which means that as *alert* as we are, we're also smelling the charred meat.

"Dooley, big guy, team leader, growls at me out the corner of his mouth, 'Let's get these pricks cable-tied and get some refreshments.'

"I remember shrugging.

"It goes unsaid: follow protocol. Secure the men and the area. It doesn't need to be said because no-one, aside from the barbecue-boys, is even close to relaxed."

Dougie whistled through his teeth, nodding. Acknowledging Jay's knowing glance.

 "Yeah, everyone except Tommy Two-Dicks."

Dougie kicked another stone across the dirt.

"Fuck knows whether Tommy's brain has baked in the afternoon sun, or if he just fuckin' loves steak, but he breaks formation, stows his rifle and runs half-pace straight towards these guys.

"Fuckin' smallest one — little rectangular glasses propped at the end of his nose, looks like a school teacher — he fucking grins at Two-Dicks, waving the meat at him.

"Dooley yells at him, 'Corporal McTavish, fall in!'

Tommy laughs, he actually fuckin' laughs, and approaches the steak-waving motherfucker, waving us over, *c'mon, guys.*

"Dooley and I and the third guy — can't remember his fuckin' name — we fan out, try to cover both these happy barbecuing cunts without getting Two-Dicks in our line of fire.

 "Straight away, we clock how badly Tommy has fucked up. The two guys are fuckin' pros.

"They shift positions, eyes on us the whole time, faces still smiling for Tommy's benefit, but they've positioned themselves fuckin' perfectly, placing

Tommy in our line of fire. The older guy reaches down to the cooler, pulls off a three-inch-thick upturned lid, exposing the deep container beneath. Free from water and ice, it holds a fucking IED the size of an iPhone. The old cunt kicks the cooler over, leans in to touch it and falls to his knees. Steak-Waver starts laughing, but quickly falls to his knees, joining his mate in prayer.

"Tommy finally spots the set-up. He skids to a stop, maybe a metre away. We're perhaps ten metres behind.

"Dooley does what all good leaders do and puts himself in harm's way for his men. At a sprint he tears through the sand towards Two-Dicks. We didn't have a clue how long the charge was set for. Tommy was already in range and now Dooley had joined the hot zone. What the fuck Dooley was thinking, I don't know, he just acted on instinct.

"Tommy does this comedy double-take, back and forward for perhaps two seconds and gets this weird look, like he's suddenly figured out what's wrong with the world and accepted a burden of some sort. The happy, tail-wagging Labrador expression he's worn his entire life vanishes and he runs at the IED.

"It's laying face-down on the sand, thirty centimetres away from each of the barbecue-boys, almost exactly between them. They've made their peace and are clearly happy to take two coalition soldiers with them.

"Two-Dicks had other ideas.

"He threw himself into the sprint of his life, leaping onto the IED. Folding his body around it, Tommy held there for a second before being spread over thirty metres by the blast.

"In his head, I think the over-eager bastard thought he was gonna Captain America the shit out of the situation. Take the blast. Protect Dooley, bad guys' death wish foiled."

Jay's eyes filled with sadness.

Dougie continued.

"The barbecue guys were killed instantly. One had his skull incinerated by the blast, the other had his chest opened. Dooley, who had got within five metres of the blast, lost most of his right arm, his face, his eyes and his left leg."

"It's a horrible story, Dougie. I'm really sorry you had to go through that," Jay said.

"Yeah, well, like I said, I ain't telling it for my benefit."

Jay scrunched his eyes in confusion.

"Tommy Two-Dicks was a good bloke: heart of gold, found good in everyone, joy in everything. Couldn't see people unhappy, loved life, loved his mates. Fucked up and put 'em in harm's way."

Jay rubbed at the back of his head.

"I'm not angry with Mo, Dougie. I understand what he did. I'm all about peace and love and forgiveness... remember?"

"Dougie nodded. Yeah, Jay, I know, but that ain't what I'm getting at. I told you, it's about people. All of it is. Friends especially."

Dougie lifted his backside from the stone. Moving around in front of Jay, he took his shoulders and gave him a gentle shake.

"Tommy tried to please his friends, and then protect them. He made a cunt of it. That's what people do. He died. Mo's still here. He won't fuck up again. You have a chance to finish this thing together, with your best friend. Have you any idea what some people would give for that?"

Jay looked down at his feet.

Several long seconds passed whilst he chewed the inside of his cheek and thought hard about Dougie's words.

Finally he looked into the big cop's eyes.

"Thank you for trusting me with your story," he said. He meant it. It was always a privilege when people... friends shared themselves with you. Especially when they were trying to save you from pain they had suffered.

"But it's different for us. Mo and I. We have eternity. When this is over, we return to... our existence. We'll be exactly as we were before. Unchanging."

Dougie straightened his posture. A tic of annoyance pulled at his cheek.

"Forgive me, Jay, but if you believe that, you're a fucking fool."

Jay smiled at him. A smile that held thousands of years of knowledge, of confidence, of certainty that Dougie could not comprehend. An unintentionally condescending smile that said *you're a mortal. You can't understand.*

Dougie spotted it immediately and turned away briefly before whirling back around. He wasn't angry, just determined.

"People are people, Jay, and friends are friends. You're wrong about this. Everything's changed between you and Mo, but you do have a chance to repair it, before it ends. If you can't do that... why should any of these people believe you can save them?"

Dougie didn't wait for an answer. Treading off downhill into the night, he waved, beckoning Jay to follow after.

"Either way, boss," Dougie said over his shoulder, "let's get going. There are people waiting for you to give them all the answers."

Interlude

Mo

"You were supposed to sow dissent in the crowd, not start firing at them," Mo hissed into the phone.

He glanced across the private lounge to where Miriam and Lazarus made their final preparations for their flight to New York City, where they planned to rejoin Jay for his final Masses. By the time their flight arrived, it would be early Friday morning. Mo and Jay figured that they had until midnight before God instructed Azrael to begin Earth's destruction.

By all accounts the South American Masses had gone without incident. Despite the growing backlash in the Western media, it seemed that South America, along with Africa, most of Asia and Eastern Europe, had recognised Jay and his message for what they were. Salvation.

Mo was unsurprised, but relieved that the South American Masses had proceeded smoothly. So far as Mo knew, Azrael hadn't had any intention of attending them or seeding the crowds with her agents.

"Who said I was firing on the crowd?" Azrael asked flatly.

Mo grimaced in response to her reply.

"You took a fuckin' shot at him. Are you so desperate to unleash chaos that you'll try to murder God's own son?" Mo asked, incredulous.

Azrael's reply turned Mo's blood to ice in his borrowed veins.

Disconnecting Az, Mo shoved his phone deep into his pocket. His eyes, busy with anger and outrage, darted slightly left and right as he processed and planned.

Mo darted towards Miriam and Lazarus.

"I'm not coming with you guys, I have something I need to do," he said.

Lazarus smiled sympathetically. "He will forgive you, Moses. Most likely he already has," Lazarus said kindly.

Mo shook his head. "It ain't that, Laz. There's something else."

Lazarus cocked an eyebrow. Miriam, who'd been chatting to their pilot, stepped forward to take Mo's hand. "What's happened, Mo?" she asked.

"Azrael. I have to intercept her."

"That's one of the reasons we're going to Jay now," Miriam said.

"No," Mo blurted. "I can't let Azrael anywhere near Jay again. I know where she'll be in the lead-up to the final Mass in Boston. It has to be me," he said, eyes lowered in shame.

Lazarus held Mo's cheek gently. "Mo, you're talking about Azrael. The Angel of Death. God's own assassin. What exactly is it you hope to accomplish against her?"

Mo let go of Miriam's hand. Taking a step away from Lazarus, he scooped up his rucksack from the tiled floor.

"Can you arrange transport for me, Laz?"

"Where to?" Lazarus asked.

Mo smiled sadly, but did not answer.

"Fair enough," Lazarus replied. Handing Mo a company credit card, Lazarus held it in Mo's palm for a few seconds.

"This will get you wherever, however, you wish to travel. Funds are unlimited, borders and visas taken care of. Think of it as a company perk," Lazarus said.

"You're sure?" Miriam asked Mo.

Mo nodded before leaving without another word, Azrael's final words stabbing his heart.

Who do you think authorised the hit?

∞∞∞

Mo stood at the foot of the little staircase leading up to the jet Miriam had arranged for him. Azrael's words kept playing on a loop inside his head.

Who do you think authorised the hit?

Frozen by indecision, Mo sat on the lowest stair. Looking to the sky he asked himself again how he could stop Azrael. The answer was plain: he couldn't.

As the simple truth washed over him, melting the paralysing fears, Mo grinned broadly as he realised exactly how he might help Jay.

Mo took off at a sprint, laughing as he tore across the tarmac, out to the nearest runway. Some yellow-jackets had spotted him and had started after him, their hi-viz waistcoats flapping loudly in their wake. Mo flipped a middle finger at them. Continuing his run out onto the smallest runway, Mo heard the yellow jackets shouting after him.

"Look where you're going."

"Stop!"

Mo knew exactly where he was headed. Pouring on the speed, he ran straight at a little Cessna 162 Skycatcher. Moments later Chris Pillans' body, once worth so many millions in the Premiership, now lay sprayed, tossed and chopped across the tarmac and over the propeller and window of the light aircraft.

Friday

29

Nick and Beth

STEWART LIFTED HIS EYES TO SEE MO striding into the room. His face was contorted with anger. All fear of God had vanished from him.

Pointing at Stewart accusingly, he bellowed, "That bastard has sent Azrael to kill his own fucking son."

"What?" asked Nick.

"It's true, Nick," Mo said. His eyes were filled with anger and pain.

Turning from Mo to face Stewart, Nick shook his head, unable to accept Mo's words.

The weight of his own recently-resurfaced memories and Mo's accusation were destroying the last slender threads of faith he had that the God he'd so loved, and still did, might re-emerge, casting aside the bitter, angry, petty persona of the last few million years.

Nick looked desperately at the angry, vindictive, spiteful and pitiless face of his Creator, searching for a minute shade of the pure love and joy He had once possessed for all of life.

Stewart glowered at His creations, his once blue, empathetic eyes bottomless in their malice.

Nick and Mo fell to their knees. Cowed under the power of His presence, they battled, each with their own fear, trying to summon the courage needed to oppose Him.

Bethany was less than an insect, completely beneath His notice.

Nick forced himself to look into the eyes of his Creator. "Please, Lord, not Jay. He is the best of us."

Stewart laughed horribly once again. "Of course he is," he said. "Jay is exactly what I created him to be.

Pure, good, flawless in his love for all of Creation." Stewart sneered as he lowered himself into a crouch between Mo and Nick.

With a gesture, he lifted them to their feet, suspending them in the air. Another gesture filled the screens on the wall they faced with Jay's face. He was on Earth, outside St Patrick's Cathedral in New York, frozen in a moment.

"Like all I willed into reality, he was created for a purpose." Stewart went silent, waiting for one of them to reach the answer.

"You wanted another like you?" Nick asked.

"Fuck sake, Nick. You are blinded by your love of life. C'mon, you're better than that. Try again," He commanded.

Nick searched his memory and his heart. No answer came.

Mo found some courage.

"You love him. Whatever you made him for, you love him now."

Stewart placed a nicotine-stained index finger one centimetre from Mo's forehead.

"Yes, I do love Jay. Of all my Creations, he is the one I will miss the most."

Stewart pressed the tip of his finger to Mo's forehead, light as a butterfly kissing a flower. Mo's immaterial form exploded in a cloud of light. Each particle that had once been the man of Egypt called Moses, the Deliverer, ceased to be and was absorbed into Stewart.

Nick cried out in despair.

"Bastard. You bastard!"

Stewart side-stepped to his right, closing the gap between Himself and Nick until they were face to face.

Nick spat into the face of God, a blob of light, which simply disappeared into God.

"Why did you ever create Jay?" he asked, head dropping to the floor.

Stewart's expression changed from one of mocking cruelty, like a kid pulling the wings from an insect, to an expression of genuine amusement.

He had a short internal conversation, deciding something, before speaking.

"I discovered how I came to be. One like me existed before I did. She was exactly as I am. She created universes filled with life, with love, with empathy, but with no death. For trillions of trillions of years Her universe thrived. She was known by Her creations. All of them. They knew Her as God. Spoke to Her. Worshipped and loved Her as She did them.

"Her time came. Our kind, mine and Hers," Stewart's eyes glazed slightly as He relayed the story of Her.

"And when it came She filled with all the energy of her universes. Every lifeform, every star, every planet, every organism, cell and atom ceased to be, its energy returning to Her in one violent tsunami. The energy was uncontainable but She knew that. She knew this thing would happen before it occurred. Her predecessor had taught Her this. That all She created would cease to be, and return to Her, ending Her life. Ending all life."

A single tear trickled down Stewart's face.

"Her universes were filled with love and co-operation and acceptance. Each of Her creations knew for certain that She existed and that She had given them their existence out of love. When Her end came, the energy exploded outwards, as it had with the one who existed before Her. As it had before, during Her birth, the energy had contracted into a more concentrated, contained form. The Cycle of Divine Life began again. With my birth."

Nick spoke weakly. "You coward."

Stewart nodded, his face showing amusement.

"Exactly," he said, "exactly right, Nicholas. I spent millions of years experimenting with life, trying to determine how I came to exist. Why I alone was such an entity. A fragment of energy came to me some years ago. She, like all of our ancestors, had seeded me with it that I might learn our origins when I came to the age when I must soon expire."

Stewart's leer returned, his accent thickening into Scots once more.

"It was a bit ay a fuckin' shock, I'll tell ye that for fuck all, son."

He made a dismissive gesture with his hand.

"Anyway, I figured out that I could stop myself fae restarting the cycle. So I gave away a wee bit ay myself. Boom. Jesus is created. A little reservoir of my own essence, just enough to let me control what's coming."

Stewart jabbed a thumb over his shoulder at Jay's face on the screens behind him.

"He's a great cunt, I'll gie him that. Love that wee cunt tae fuck, so I dae, Nick. But I don't love him enough to end my existence for him."

Nick's eye's narrowed.

"You're going to destroy everything in your own controlled way; re-absorb every scrap of energy you filled the universe with, but a little at a time. Jay's your insurance policy. You absorb almost everything, he prevents you filling with enough energy to end your existence, and you start again and kill him when you don't need him anymore."

Stewart's eyes widened. He looked impressed.

"Fuckin' bingo, lad. Check you out, ya cunt." He gave Nick a gentle slap to the cheek. "Az is waiting for my signal. As soon as I start the process, Jay's life will be measured in seconds."

The screen behind Nick flowed back into life once again. Jay stood at the entrance to St Patrick's doing what he always did — speaking, teaching, saving souls. Azrael stood nearby, in human form, waiting.

A shade of genuine sadness passed over Stewart's face.

"I'll miss ye, Nicholas. If it means anything tae ye, the very first being I create next time around will be a version of you... but less of a self-righteous wank."

Stewart lifted his index finger, hovering it above Nick's forehead.

"Cheerio, Nick."

30

Jay

Chris Pillans commits suicide on Heathrow runway.
Police suspect guilt over his part in worldwide con.

Violence erupts once again at gathering in Boston.
Fifty crushed in riot.

Pope stands by Jay. Calls him "Humanity's only hope".

Mayor of New York promises heavy police presence in New York City.

"You should ignore that shit, Jay," Dougie said, placing a finger to his earpiece to listen into the surveillance feed.

Jay flicked off the news feed he'd been reading. Dougie was right: the traditional media had turned against him in a drastic manner. Social media still championed his cause, but there was a growing feel of the tide shifting there also. Despite the heartache of reading the news, Jay still needed to keep himself informed. If his words were to affect the people, he needed to understand them first.

Mo's suicide hadn't really surprised Jay. He probably felt that he could do more to help from Heaven than he could on Earth. What Mo thought that could be, Jay couldn't guess. A wave of deep sadness passed over Jay as it dawned on him that Mo really wouldn't be there with him, now, at the end.

Jay nodded his thanks to Dougie, who was chatting into a microphone in his cuff.

Pacing around the cathedral, Jay tried to calm his thoughts, accept the gentle lapping feel of Heaven's power, and allow it to bring him the words he needed. Reaching into the immaterial realm, Jay jerked violently.

Something was… different about the flow. Jay closed his eyes, trying to determine what felt so unusual about the essence of Heaven he'd been filled with for his entire existence.

The current of power had definitely changed, become more forceful. Where once it had been a calm trickle, it was growing into a rapidly flowing river. Where once he'd dipped his consciousness into its waters, so like a relaxing spa, its strength had increased such that it required that he held it back.

The change was entirely unprecedented. Jay focused himself on holding his portion of Heaven's power in check.

Lost in his task, he did not notice a man and woman enter the church. He didn't hear the joyful laughter from the man, nor his steps echoing around the cathedral as the man approached him.

A hand on Jay's shoulder startled him from his task and caused him to jump back.

When he opened his eyes, all stress and fear vanished.

"Laz," he said, tears already making tracks along his cheeks.

The old friends embraced for several long moments before Jay broke off. Taking Lazarus' cheeks in his hands, he said, "Laz, I'm so glad you are here."

Dougie interrupted them with a cough.

"Boss, it's ten minutes until," he shifted his feet uncomfortably, "until full-time, y'know?"

Jay nodded. Taking Lazarus by the arm, he made his way to the doors.

"Let's go see in the end together, then."

31

As it is in Heaven...

AZRAEL SHIFTED A FOOT TO HER LEFT, no little task in a densely-packed crowd, but the smell of the human who had been directly in front of her had been threatening to make her own human body empty its stomach. Thumbing a piece of extra-strength gum from the packet, she popped it into her mouth to join the three previous pieces she was working on, hoping that the strong menthol waves emanating would suppress the smells around her and her own gag reflex.

The doors of St Patrick's opened, causing a surge forward. Her rage growing, Azrael allowed herself to be moved with the crowd, telling herself, *soon. You can kill every being on this pathetic world. Patience.*

A smallish man crushed against her right shoulder, looked up at her apologetically, fear shadowing the smile he offered.

"Uh, sorry, lady," he said, eyes glued to hers. Trapped against each other by the weight of thousands around them, he was close enough to sense her *otherness*.

They always did with Azrael, especially if her eyes met theirs. Something in them prickled the primitive part of their subconscious. Something in them recognised her as the predator she was.

Azrael could smell him. A mix of dog hair, beef burrito and cheap cologne. He was trying to find an egress, his mouth still smiling apologetically, his eyes panic-stricken.

Azrael waited until the crowd pulsed forward once again, noting that Jay and Lazarus had come out of the open doors. As the wave of momentum carried her and her new friend forward, Azrael lifted her right foot only to bring it down onto his lower legs. Beneath her foot, the bones may as well have been chalk. The man screamed in agony, falling to the tarmac as Azrael crushed his bones, calf and shin muscles, blood vessels and turned them to an irreparable paste, walking calmly on with her next step, with the crowd, leaving him to his pain.

Azrael's hand moved to her waist. Finding the heavy outline of her pistol, a surge of reassurance and satisfaction pulsed through her. The gun, a Ruger SR40, was unlike any weapon in the material universe. Made by God's own hand, the pistol's bullets were soul-takers. It killed whatever it hit, destroyed the immaterial soul, and held an infinite supply of bullets. This was a gun to kill any entity in the material or immaterial realm and had been gifted to her by God as an alternative to her ancient sword.

Just thinking of her sword made Azrael smile. So many triumphs, so many deaths. So much joy. The blade was a part of her and she missed it badly. Currently it hung on the wall of one of God's own private rooms in Heaven.

Azrael intended to retrieve it when the planet-wide killing began.

Scanning the faces around her which so resembled those of their ape ancestors, Azrael smiled. *Soon. Patience.*

∞∞∞

Jay looked out at the sea of faces out along 5th Avenue. This would be the last sermon he would give. Then the end was upon them. They perhaps seven minutes before God sent Azrael to annihilate the humans. He wasn't kidding himself, Jay knew that his mission to save them had failed: he'd known before he and Mo came to Earth that it would fail. Succeeding wasn't the point, Mo hadn't understood that. It only mattered that they tried, that they had done what they could do.

Looking at the faces before him, Jay smiled kindly back at the eyes that begged him to save them, the fear-filled faces, wondering if they had seen their last sunrise, eaten their last meal. The families huddled together, holding each other, just needing to be there. The angry faces, shouting "*Blasphemer.*" The media, mocking, crucifying him in an entirely metaphorical manner this time. He had to admit, it was better than the last time.

The difference this time was that it truly was over, for him and for them. For every being, cell and atom in the universe to ever exist. This was it.

Jay felt Lazarus take his hand and smiled. He'd done what he had set out to do. His goal had always been realistic: save as many souls as they could. Be better than God.

Kill that bastard Azrael and force God to do His own dirty work. If He wanted the universe destroyed, He'd have to fucking do it Himself.

Jay had sensed Azrael in the crowd long before he'd left the Cathedral. He could see her now, standing just that little bit taller than most. Moving with a fraction too much Angelic mannerism. She'd only ever spent time amongst humans to flood or slaughter or eradicate. She'd never bothered to learn to hide her true self effectively.

To Jay, she appeared as a shark amongst an ocean of krill.

Holding his hands up in a beckoning *c'mon then* gesture, he glared at the Angel of Death standing four metres from him.

Azrael merely smiled. Nodding at him with faux-respect, she mouthed, *All in good time... my Lord.*

∞∞∞

"Cheerio, Nick."

Stewart smiled warmly at his best friend as He closed the centimetres between His fingertip and Nick's head.

Pain seared through him.

Pain.

Stewart had never felt pain before. He looked at Nick's face and saw his friend's eyes as startled as His own must surely be. His face splashed with the essence, the life-force of God Himself, Nick's mouth worked but no words came.

Stewart looked at His feet, finding his lower arm lying there between Him and Nick.

"Fuck you." The words came from a cold place, one which Beth had visited very recently when she'd turned her rapist uncle into a puddle of gristle.

"Fuck you that you're so pathetic and pitiless."

Stewart blinked dumbly several times, trying to focus His eyes on Bethany. Standing with Azrael's ancient sword, God's own essence staining its blade, Bethany's entire body shook with anger and fear. Her hands, though, they were steady and primed to deliver another blow.

Stewart looked down at his severed arm and back at Bethany. A bewildered smile grew into a sarcastic one.

"What the fuck are you gonnae dae tae me, hen?" he asked.

Beth's eyes filled with hate.

"I will not let you kill him," she said, nodding down at Nick who'd fallen to his knees.

Stewart laughed. Picking up the arm, he placed it back against the stump left behind. Instantly it reattached in a barely noticeable burst of light.

Stewart rubbed at his chin, before pointing a finger of his newly-reattached hand at Bethany.

"Put that fuckin' thing down ya silly wee cow," he said. "before I start tae get angry wi' ye."

Bethany raised the tip of the sword, bringing it closer to and level with Stewart's chest.

"Fine," Stewart said, exasperated. He made a gesture with his hand. "Azrael. Kill him, kill all of them," Stewart said as Bethany pushed three feet of Angelic, holy steel made by God Himself through the Creator's chest.

Pulling the sword out and up, Bethany cleaved Him from sternum through and out of his skull.

Nick cried out in agony and was joined by every soul in Heaven.

∞∞∞

Transforming into her full Angelic self, Azrael pulled her pistol smoothly as her human clothes, shredded by her Angelic form, slipped in rags from her body.

Humans all around began screaming as her immovable, powerful Angelic body tore and crushed them as she moved through the crowd toward Jay. Jay saw her movement, but did not try to move. He merely stood, arms at his side, accepting his fate.

Free again, happy for the first time in millennia, Azrael smiled, aimed at Jay's face and pulled the trigger.

∞∞∞

Jay stared into Azrael's eyes. He'd miscalculated, badly. Jay had wanted to attack Azrael before she'd made her move. He thought that she'd wait until the last moment. Obviously he'd been wrong and was about to forfeit his eternal existence because of his stupidity.

As he waited for Azrael to pull the trigger, Jay felt someone shoulder him to the ground as the sound of the shot rang out.

"Laz," Jay yelled, scrambling along the concrete to drag his friend to him. Lazarus, hole in his chest, pulled Jay's head towards himself.

"Get that bitch," he said.

A moment later, Lazarus died, a true death this time, at long last. His essence scattered to Heaven, never to return.

Miriam screamed from inside the Cathedral. Jay whipped his head around and watched as Dougie dragged her inside, throwing Jay a look.

Don't, the big cop's eyes pleaded. He could see the rage in Jay's eyes.

Jay roared Azrael's name. From the ground, unable to will his legs to lift him, he searched between the feet of the running humans and saw Azrael's Angelic form crushing, killing, striding calmly to where he crouched

Jay rose to his feet and locked eyes with the Angel of Death. Azrael was lifting her pistol in both hands, ready to take aim at him once again.

Filling himself with Heaven's Light, he streamed comet-like towards Azrael, knocking her gun from her huge hands as he impacted against her. Azrael, strong as she was, was rocked hard by his attack, but this was a seasoned warrior against a well-meaning hippie. Picking him up by his throat, she crushed two vertebrae before biting into his cheek, tearing a lump of flesh from it.

Azrael spat it back into Jay's face, disgusted by the taste.

"Now you die," she snarled at him.

Violently, Jay was thrown ten feet away, his skull cracking against the sidewalk as he landed. A paralysing energy flooded him, threatening to rob him of consciousness.

With every ounce of his considerable will, Jay forced his eyes to remain open and focus on Azrael. She had also been thrown, though in the opposite direction from him, as if an explosion had separated them. Whilst Jay was feeling the effects, Azrael was already on her feet, glowering at him. It would have been impressive if it hadn't been so fucking terrifying

As Jay tried to rise, she stalked wearily towards his position. Obviously she thought that he had been the source of the jolt they'd both felt.

As he considered this, how he might use her uncharacteristic wariness against her, another jolt hit them, bringing Azrael to her knees this time. Jay fared much worse.

His human body — Garry Crawford's body — exploded, fragments spreading out over a twenty-foot radius. Jay's true form, his immaterial self, remained and began pulsing with power he could not hold back and could not contain.

Fuck, he thought. *What now?*

There could only be one reason: God had begun Armageddon.

Jay looked across 5th Avenue. Azrael was back on her feet and had begun killing humans. Tearing her way through them effortlessly, she cried out in ecstasy, completely invigorated that her time had finally come.

∞∞∞

Still reeling from the jolt he and every entity of Heaven had felt when Bethany had injured Stewart, Nick stared up at his Creator. Cleaved into two parts from waist to head, Stewart remained on His feet. The centre of Him was already pulling the disparate parts back together, like a zip. His face, sliced neatly in two, scowled at Bethany. Nick watched as God repaired his immaterial self and realised that He'd begun the rebirth process.

Heaven's Light was pulling towards and into Him. He was a black hole, sucking all of existence into His own form.

This is it, Nick thought.

Everything ends here and now.

This is truly the end.

Stewart, whole again, sneered at Bethany and at Nick as all of Heaven broke down into its component parts, flowing back to the source.

Him.

Stewart laughed loudly, revelling in the rush of power — power of such intensity, power on a level He had not known since His own birth.

Nick's eyes adjusted to the spectacle he was witness to. One second before he began to lose his own form and mind to the irresistible vacuum named Stewart, the pulling ebbed. Not much, but enough for Nick to cling to consciousness for a few more moments.

Peering at Stewart, Nick's Angelic eyes noted that Stewart suddenly did not look quite so victorious. Nick cast a glance to Bethany. Passed out on the floor at his side, the courageous mortal had shamed him with her bravery.

Nick struggled up onto one knee and then onto his feet. He felt that every ounce of gravity in the universe was trying to pin him to the floor. He rose anyway.

Squinting closer at Stewart, Nick felt the pull of the black hole He'd become dampen once more. A thin smoky-opaque tendril forming on Stewart's body wound off into the ether.

Stewart looked frightened.

Nick's lips curled into a smile.

"Looks like your insurance policy has his own ideas about your rebirth, Stewart," Nick said, before collapsing face-first once more to the floor.

∞∞∞

Jay watched as Azrael tore through the crowd. Angelic hands and feet scythed, stabbed and hammered at their frail bodies. A path of broken, torn and crushed bodies marked her progress. Less than three seconds had passed and she had killed hundreds. Her face was a twisted thing, conveying only dark joy at her task. With her surge of bloodlust spent for the time being, Azrael licked the blood from her lips and fixed her eyes back on Jay.

Her gun, back in her hand, slowly raised and her smile widened.

Bodiless, Jay allowed Heaven's power to infuse him. Casting a glance at Lazarus, at Miriam, Dougie, and all around at the humans, dead and alive, Jay opened himself up to Heaven's rushing power.

The instant Jay allowed the power to flow, he realised that something irreversible had occurred.

The increase in intensity of Heaven's flow to him had grown in potency once gain. Now a thousand-fold, his access to Heaven brought such a surge of force and knowledge, Jay felt that he would either explode or go insane.

How can one being contain this? he thought.

Everything around him slowed to a stop. Jay abandoned all attempt to limit Heaven's unstoppable flow into him. Allowing himself to be filled, overfilled and broken into a billion fragments, only to be reformed by the devastating power that was now his. Jay had never before accessed so much power. Never shared so much of God's consciousness and seemingly limitless energy.

Jay found his consciousness expanding. He was on Earth in his own form, but he was also in Heaven, looking down at Nick and a woman named Bethany through his Father's eyes.

Jay gasped as he felt a wave of pure malice emanating through God and himself. Every thought, deed, plot, plan, action, intention God had experienced, ever, was now accessible to Jay. As he watched Nick on his knees, weeping, Jay felt tears track down his own face back on Earth. The realisation of what He had planned, of why He had created Jay, both crushed and fortified Jay's soul.

Hate was born in Jay at that moment, but it did not truly belong to him: the hate he felt was being poured into the shared essence of Heaven by the part of Jay that was Stewart.

Jay rejected the intensely dark maliciousness immediately, allowing it to fuel his draw on the source.

Pulling with everything he was, Jay began to take the power into himself. The scales tipped. Jay held the greater portion, not by much, but enough that once it started, the process was irreversible.

As he reached the tipping point, the event horizon at which Heaven's power was channelling unstoppably into him in its entirety, Jay merged himself with the universe, viewing all of Heaven and Hell, and the entire physical universe at one time.

This is what God sees... saw, he corrected himself.

How can he see this, know this... how can He be this and feel such isolation, such bitterness?

∞∞∞

Face pressed firmly to the floor, Nick looked at the face of God and found hope, compassion, empathy and love residing there as it had so many thousands of years previously.

For a moment, Nick's soul sang with joy, sure that Stewart had realised His own faults upon opening Himself to heaven so fully.

As Nick's eyes adjusted, the truth became clear. He could not distinguish between Jay's face and that of Stewart. They were one — fully one being. One moment the face was Stewart's, the next, Jay's. At times a mixture existed.

A battle was raging and Jay was winning. Nick's heart sang once more as the weight pressing him lifted. Beth's hand reached for and gripped his own. Side by side, they watched a new God being born, both wishing with all their souls that their new master would not be Stewart.

∞∞∞

Jay broke apart, the components of his immaterial form dispersing and diffusing amongst the atoms of the material universe and the very substance of Heaven.

Suffusing each particle and atom, both in the physical and immaterial realms, with his love, compassion, desire to understand and survive, Jay spread every fragment of himself amongst the universe and amongst Heaven's beings.

Filling his spirit with pure understanding and love, Jay pulled all of Heaven's power — his power now — through his being, sharing the glory of Heaven with every Angel, every human soul in Heaven and in Sheol and on Earth. Every sentient creature in the universe felt the touch of Jay's power as he pulled every last scrap of it from his Father's being. In Heaven, Nick watched Stewart grow weak and small as Jay took everything from Him.

On Earth, humans stopped and stared at nothing, lost in the touch of Heaven they experienced, the fears and hopes, loves, trials, desires, victories and losses of every being in the universe. They comprehended their own significance and their utter insignificance.

They shared each other's pain and joy. They understood each other.

Rapists wept, their souls in agony as the fear and humiliation and mental strength and courage of their victims became a part of their own psyche. Falling to their knees, leaping to their deaths, blowing their brains over the wall, the men who'd been rapists felt everything their victims had experienced and removed themselves from life, destroyed by the terror they had visited on others.

Their victims knew the sharp, dark desires that had driven their attackers and wept in pity for them, understanding for the first time how random their attacks had been. Free for the first time from the guilt they'd carried. They did not forgive their rapists, they merely understood.

Men in cells, on death row, in death squads and terrorist cells, wept for their victims, for their children, even for themselves as the impact of their actions surged through them, damaging their emotions and their psyche as they had done to their victims.

On expensive yachts, in corridors of power, in mansions and castles and on remote islands, those of wealth curled into foetal balls and wept at how very much they'd clawed to themselves whilst children died alone in sewer pipes; whilst people were sold into slavery across Europe. Whilst billions starved to death as they accumulated the things of metal and paper and rock they'd prized over human life.

The British Prime Minister threw himself from Westminster Bridge, the names of children and the poor he'd never cared to know on his lips as surely as their suffering scarred his soul. A long line of politicians waiting their turn snaked along towards and passed the House of Commons.

Pimps begged forgiveness at the feet of their girls. Men and women, many more men than women, cursed their deeds and their inaction and greed, and dedicated themselves to atoning, if they could.

Every being on Earth for one brief moment became a single entity, fully aware of each other and infused by the pure, unconditional love of Jay. Fully one family of beings for the first time in human history, they basked in the glory of Heaven's power. They knew that they were not alone and simply loved each other.

Black, Caucasian, African, European, Asian, all races, all ages, every ethnicity and religion. Unified. One.

∞∞∞

Jay, present in all eras, in all places throughout the universe, in every cell of every being, an unmistakable ray of light in each and every soul in Heaven, Hell and on Earth, finally, reluctantly, contracted his power, pulling it into Himself.

Condensing it, He took eternities, or perhaps moments — for Him they were one and the same — to learn how to contain, survive and then utilise Heaven's power. His power now.

On Earth, humans had flocked back to the part of Him that remained on their world. At His feet they prayed.

Jay looked over the sea of people into Azrael's fear-filled eyes. She still had her gun held on him. With a thought Jay turned her gun to dust. Azrael dropped the weapon, but the effect continued along up fingers, up her arm and across her torso. She nodded acceptance, waiting arms wide as her body and spirit were erased from existence.

Jay smiled and the people Azrael had dismembered and brutalised returned to life, whole, intact, sound of body and spirit.

Tears fell, salting the ground of every land.

People danced and cheered in euphoric celebration that they were saved.

Jay lifted His chin and the world went silent.

"Know this, my people. You *are* God's people now. My people. Be good, show love for others, concern and goodwill and you will ascend to my Heaven upon your mortal death.

"Use what you have learned of each other this day to build bridges, literal and metaphorical. Do not worship me but honour me instead, by living your lives as good men and women who care for their brothers and sisters. Leave no-one to go hungry or sick if they can be helped. Abandon these values that brought you so close to annihilation. Value each other instead.

"We will be together once again, in Heaven."

Jay vanished from the world.

People continued to cheer and dance, celebrating their new awakening, celebrating their survival and salvation.

Many, the vast majority of them men, continued to end their lives, driven to suicide by the experience of having suffered that which they brought to others. Billions chose to die because of what they had done in life. Sheol awaited them.

When it was over, and all who wished to die were gone, almost six days had passed and two billion men had gone to Sheol. Women were now in the majority by a ratio of four to one.

The human population entered an unprecedented era in which women would hold all the key positions of power and which men, in the minority, as well as women truly understood the needs of their species as a result of the insights Jay had blessed them with during what they now called The Glimpse.

∞∞∞

Nick looked upon the benevolent face of his God.

"Jay, I..."

Jay reached down to take Nick's face in both His hands. A rush of energy and strength flooded Nick's body.

Rising to his feet, he smiled up at Jay.

No words were needed.

Nick turned to Bethany who was also now standing on shaky legs, staring into the face of their newly-birthed God.

"This is Bethany," said Nick. "She's going to be helping out in Sheol from now on?" Nick phrased it as a question, his eyes searching Beth's.

Lost in the glory of Jay's face, she merely nodded her acceptance.

Nick laughed loudly, freely and with joy for the first time in many, many years.

Around them, Heaven celebrated. Songs of love and kinship echoed.

Jay placed an arm around Nick's shoulder.

"Let's see about getting some new rules in place for you in Sheol."

Epilogue 1

Nick leaned back against the bar and took in the room. An involuntary smile formed on his lips. It was just *His* kind of place. Cheap beer, a lax policy on weed, and a live band playing for a small stage. Ordering a gin and tonic for himself and bottle of Innes and Gunn ale for Him, Nick slipped his smartphone from his pocket and reminded himself of a few key details in his notes.

Ten days at Level Two,

Four months at Level Three.

Further education programme complete.

Dedicated and enthusiastic approach demonstrated consistently by the candidates.

All phases of training complete.

Recommend promotion to Level One.

Nick didn't really need to read the notes because he had committed the candidates' details to memory. However, it comforted him to read the words, reminded him of how far he'd come. How far they'd all come.

Twenty years had passed on Earth since The Glimpse had changed humankind forever. The most fleeting of insights into each other's souls had catalysed mass suicide, yes, but the revelations and new empathy that resulted had truly changed the lives of every human on Earth. No one was hungry, not a single person on Earth. The passing of the Golden Rice Bill, as well as the arrival of a sustainable artificial meat source indiscernible from the real thing, had assisted the new world leaders, the women, to reduce and phase out animal farming.

Vast resources and energies once spent on producing grain and other crops for livestock were now utilised in producing natural, clean organic crops in such mass that nobody went without.

The development of clean sources of energy had been radically fast-tracked. The CEOs of the large corporations had all either killed themselves or committed their lives to finding new, sustainable methods of supplying non-polluting, renewable, free energy to all.

Currency was slowly being phased out in favour of a barter system based on greater need.

Socially-responsible companies grew and thrived. Cars ran on hydrogen fuel cells. Crime was almost non-existent. Rape and murder had become things that had happened in the Old World, tales that parents told their children about the time before The Glimpse.

Churches housed people. Banks were converted to communal areas for recreation or housing. Borders fell. People moved freely and were welcomed in the countries they migrated to or through.

The planet had changed also. The oceans, clean and plentiful. The cities, smog- and pollution-free. The streets of every neighbourhood, safe for children, safe for everyone.

Wars were inconceivable to these people. The thought of hurting another person was unthinkable, akin to hurting oneself.

Religion was dead. The people knew their God though He did not appear to them on Earth. They had plenty of footage to refer to, but more importantly each of them carried the tiny insight into each other He had gifted them, and they knew what He demanded of them.

Be decent to each other.

In a strange way, it was almost exactly what his predecessor had asked for: *don't be a cunt.*

Spotting Jay entering the venue, Nick held His pint up for him, waving Him over with his other hand. Jay was dressed in denims, Cons and a Kurt Cobain t-shirt. He looked relaxed and happy.

"Hey, Nick," he said, taking the beer from his friend. "How's it hanging, mate?"

Nick smiled broadly. *Heaven above, he loved this kid.*

"I'm great, Jay. Thanks."

Jay nodded His approval. "How's Beth?" He asked taking a sip from His beer. An appreciative nod followed.

"She's brilliant, settled in very smoothly. Just keeping her away from swords, y'know?"

Jay laughed warmly.

"Probably a good idea," He grinned.

Joining Nick in leaning on the bar, the friends scanned the dancefloor. Men and women of all ages danced to alternative rock, smiling, laughing, sharing anecdotes and a joint or a beer.

"This all of them, Nick?" Jay asked, nodding over at the dancefloor.

"Yeah, just under eight hundred this one."

Jay smiled his approval. "You're doing brilliantly, Nick. Sheol's numbers must be at an all-time low."

Nick nodded. "Yeah, I've actually had time for a personal life recently," Nick grinned.

"Beth? Hey, that's fuckin' awesome, Nick," Jay said.

A shade of playfulness shone in His eyes.

"Me and Mo were beginning to wonder if you'd ever show any interest."

Nick nudged him with an elbow.

"Fuck off. I've been a bit busy the last few million years."

Jay nodded, thoughts turning momentarily to His Father.

"How's Mo?" Nick asked.

Jay had recovered Mo's essence minutes after ascending to Heaven. Lazarus, unfortunately, was gone. There was no reforming those killed by Azrael's bullets, or sword.

"Still a prick," Jay smiled. "But he's our prick, y'know? We actually had a long chat last night about our time in other people's bodies. Great idea for a book."

Nick nodded. "Sounds like something that lad Bracha would write."

They sipped their drinks in silence for a few moments, each thinking of the friends they'd lost.

Nick eventually broke the moment.

"Shall we?" he asked.

Jay scanned the faces in the room. Each of them had been through the wringer in Sheol. Quickest turnaround times for souls in Sheol's existence, but still they'd had to suffer to cleanse their souls.

As the new era progressed and the peaceful nature of the people passed from generation to generation, Jay hoped that Sheol would become unnecessary; that all humans would simply ascend upon their deaths... that Nick could come home.

Jay would see that day come, and soon. He would make it so...

Stepping out into the middle of the dancefloor, Jay supped the last of His beer. Throwing a nod to the DJ, Jay waited as the venue became still, silent.

Enfolding His Heavenly presence around each present, He said simply, "My children. Let's go home."

Epilogue 2

As the last of the board members cleared the room, Miriam sighed wearily. Having assumed control of Mr Sal... Lazarus' company at his request via his last will and testament, Miriam had been involved in an astonishing array of projects. Irrigation in Ethiopia, drug research in Argentina, food redistribution, golden rice, and research into parasite eradication. The list was endless and endlessly satisfying.

Lazarus himself could not have imagined the reach his company had acquired and the good it had done in the two years since his death.

Volunteer numbers were at an all-time high, resources were an embarrassment of riches, and for the first time in the history of the company the board were actually contemplating a reduction in project initiations. Not because of resource or supply limit, simply because the need for charity had been reduced so effectively.

Their most recent projections forecast an end to world hunger and the eradication of poverty within twenty-five years.

The newly-renamed Lazarus Foundation would dedicate almost the entirety of its vast resources into founding schools and hospitals. The rest would be used for reproductive research.

Leaning heavily back into her chair, Miriam looked out at London beneath her.

Blowing a kiss she sent her love to her predecessor.

Epilogue 3

Catching sight of himself in a nearby mirror, he scanned his eyes over the face he wore and threw himself a wink.

Life was good. Garry had woken up in a new body, aged twenty-one, lean and fit, his whole life in front of him.

Strolling through to his garage, Garry patted the bonnet of his Lamborghini Murcielago as he passed. After a moment's pause, he lifted the keys for the '67 Shelby GT 500.

Eleanor.

Spinning the keys around his index finger, Garry whistled to himself as he took his seat in the gorgeous vintage car. So many millions in the bank, bassist in the biggest rock-band in the world, supermodels queuing for a ride.

Garry didn't grudge himself a bit of it.

Having said that, these days, in this new, post-Glimpse world, it wasn't wise to be too much of a wank about the fame and the money.

Garry offset the tremendous luck he held by volunteering at the local citizens centre every day he was off-tour.

Serving meals, teaching life-skills, donating cash, he was keeping his nose clean. No fucking way was Gaz going back to Sheol next time around.

Garry had had a brief conversation with Chris that morning about exactly that. Pillans had returned to his former life as a Premiership footballer, his brief time as Moses seemingly having been erased from human memory.

Chris had also dedicated his fame and a large portion of his income to aiding those less fortunate. They'd met several times in the years since returning from Sheol. Finding each other a stark reminder of the tortures they had faced in Hell, they'd agreed to see each other regularly, to keep each other honest.

Parking the car, Garry strolled along to the Lazarus Centre, shaking hands with a few familiar people as he passed.

No doubt about it, Garry felt good about this new face, name and life he'd been given. As Garry passed the main hall inside the centre, a familiar, deep voice reached his ears. Garry's arse cheeks clenched tightly in response. Slowing his pace, Garry peeked around the wall, confirming that it was just the TV.

Relaxing, he continued past the television into the office. On the screen, Michael Clark Duncan in his role as John Coffey told the wardens his troubles.

The End

Also by Mark Wilson:

Bobby's Boy (Lanarkshire Strays)

Naebody's Hero (Lanarkshire Strays)

Head Boy (Lanarkshire Strays)

Paddy's Daddy

The Man Who Sold His Son (Lanarkshire Strays)

Lanarkshire Strays: Collected Edition

dEaDINBURGH: Vantage (Din Eidyn Corpus 1)

dEaDINBURGH: Alliances (Din Eidyn Corpus 2)

dEaDINBURGH: Origins (Din Eidyn Corpus 3)

dEaDINBURGH: Collected Edition

Parental Advisory: A Transgressive Double A-Side
with Ryan Bracha's *The Switched*

These titles are available on kindle and paperback
from Amazon, US and UK as well as other formats at
Paddy's Daddy Publishing.

Author's Note

Thank you for reading my book. Please consider visiting your retailer and leaving a review.

You May Also Enjoy:

The Switched

by Ryan Bracha

What would you do if you were no longer you?"

It's as crass and tactless and coarse as anything I've read, and I loved every minute of it." - **Grant Nicol, author of The Mistake.**

"A flowing, unforgettable masterpiece..." - **Craig Furchtenicht, author of Dimebag Bandits and Behind the 8 ball.**

"The perfect blend of creative flair with technical skill from a writer who is at the peak of his powers... so far." - **Mark Wilson, author of the dEaDINBURGH series.**

"A real mindfuck..." - *Liam Sweeny, pulpfire.com "One of the most vibrant writers the UK has seen in years... My favourite read since Trainspotting..."* - **Phil Jones, The End Fanzine.**

One summer morning, totally unconnected people wake up as somebody else. They have their names, their lives, and their problems. Nobody knows how or why it's happened, and nobody knows if or when they'll ever get their own lives back. They must quickly learn to accept, adapt to, and in some cases embrace their new personas, if they are to survive in a world where the people known as The Switched will do anything to get their old bodies back from others who will desperately do anything to protect their true identity, and hide deep behind their new face.

Against the backdrop of a nationwide search for popular television presenter Francesca O'Reilly, whose very public breakdown and disappearance sparks chaos on social media, it quickly becomes apparent that the switching phenomenon is far more widespread than anybody could have known, and The Switched become the most famous people in the country.

Take a trip into the darkest corners of the darkest minds in this supernatural thriller, the blackest work yet by Ryan Bracha, the best-selling author of Strangers Are Just Friends You Haven't Killed Yet and the Dead Man Trilogy.

Available now on Amazon, UK and Amazon, US

26658656R00262

Printed in Great Britain
by Amazon